# Mars Adrift

## The Halo Trilogy
Book Three

Kathleen McFall

Clark Hays

ISBN: 978-1-7345197-6-1
Copyright © 2022 Kathleen McFall and Clark Hays
All rights reserved.
Library of Congress Control Number: 2021923159
Series cover design: Ian Koviak at *The*BookDesigners
Pumpjack Press
Portland, Oregon
https://www.pumpjackpress.com

# 1

*Stardust University, Neuro-Lecture Interface 75.32, Earth*

History is dead.

The past exists only as an imperfect composite, an understanding of individual minds. Collective agreement about what happened in the past, even what is meant by the past, is impossible.

It is the most frequent comment from her brightest students, especially at the start of the popular module on recent history. *Aren't you conflating agreement on the facts of the past with agreement on their interpretation?*

Chancellor Lauren Valentine needs her students to think more deeply on the question of history.

But this is no easy task, especially now.

Given the sheer magnitude of available data—billions of exabytes—for every single event and action occurring over the last century, no matter the significance, from election theft to an individual anniversary to a worldwide revolution, how can anyone come to an agreement on any story about the past? What set of facts is deemed more valuable than another? Who decides?

When every living person is both documentarian and subject, when each minute and each second are captured from a million perspectives—saved, shared, archived and forever accessible—what does it even mean to be a historian?

This is the urgent question facing the discipline of history. And it is not merely an academic question. Because there is one truth about the past that few dispute—when humans disagree on historical events, conflict follows. Usually violent conflict. Sometimes conflict resulting in millions of deaths.

Knowing all this, and after a decades-long career as a historian, Lauren Valentine has begun to wonder if the very concept of objectivity is a trick the human mind plays on itself.

Maybe Crucial was right.

Maybe history is a work in progress and we are always creating and recreating the story of ourselves, a story that has no chronological boundaries, no past or future. Only flux.

In which case, why try to capture history at all? A useless endeavor. Crucial said that many times too, usually with that annoying smile that made it hard to gauge if he was serious or joking.

But then Valentine looks at the screen filled with bright, expectant faces—most of them avatars—and as a swarm of salutations light up her feed she feels the surge of confidence she always does in the early days of new modules. These brilliant young people, selected from across the universe, will find new ways to answer her questions. Valentine's role now is only as a guide and mentor, to introduce the rules they must follow and the structures they must work within to understand history and tame its messy implications.

"Welcome to our second session of Recent History-Building," she says. "Let's pick up where we left off, in the year 2188. As we all know, the events of that year had a significant impact on both Mars and Earth. We will use these events as source material throughout this module to illustrate how to build a revised historical narrative."

In response, a chorus of "Greetings, Chancellor Valentine" filters through her auditory channel.

She calls up a clip weaving together highlights from their last session, a blend of voices and text and video, all linked by neural-pleasing pops of light and sound.

"Our task is to develop a plan for identifying the important bits of information, to separate the verifiable facts from the purposefully confusing, misleading and poorly understood, and"—she pauses to take sip of her filbertccino—"put it together again in a new way that helps us grow as well as honor and rectify past mistakes of interpretation, and then move forward with strength and clarity."

Because, she thinks, the only meaningful outcome of the discipline of history—of organizing the past into stories—is to understand what the future needs of us.

She pauses, taking a read of their temporal lobe activity. It's spiking, indicating comprehension of their collective purpose. "Now, let's pick up where we left off last time and talk about ..."

A node lights up. Someone has a question.

"Yes, Quintzen?"

"Chancellor Valentine, I'm honored to be part of this project, as we all are, but I'm struggling to truly feel the lesson. Would you be willing to personalize it for us, since, you know, you were there?"

She smiles. Quintzen is 19 years old. He has only known peace.

"I'm not opposed," she says. "But I must warn you, those were challenging times. Terraforming was not as advanced as today and humans lived under domes, which were all badly damaged. There was widespread suffering and many deaths."

She decides impulsively, and uncharacteristically, to introduce a new variable into today's lesson. The ENC. Using it goes off-script, but why not? Her time teaching students is ending. Why not make as big an impact as possible?

She shares the revised plan with the class and the collective surprise, followed by appreciation, registers on the screen.

"An ENC?" Quintzen asks.

"Yes," she says. "I can share the experience with just Quintzen, or if enough of you are interested, I can connect the entire class. Participation is voluntary, of course."

There is a surge of activity as 98.2 percent of the nodes light up purple in favor of joining the activity.

"Very well. Let me prepare."

Only eleven people among the two planets and all the outposts have the expertise and authorization to use ENC technology. The process is so powerful, the associations formed so strong, that strict guidelines govern its use. The fact that Valentine is one of those people explains, in part, the huge interest in her classes.

The ENC, or experiential neural correlate, technology synthesizes cognitive models of emotional and biologic reactions to reinforce the learning process.

Valentine focuses on her memories of the attack, isolates the neural pathways and copies the data into an ENC pulse. Then she submits it to the council, which reviews and authorizes the transfer in under a millisecond.

"Remember, participation is not mandatory," she says. "But for those of you who do, you will experience what it was truly like on Mars in Jezero during those terrible days."

The first light sparks, followed quickly by others, until

the neuro-hall assumes the familiar look of a night sky, blanketed by a constellation of bright stars. Within minutes, the ENC assembly is complete.

"Ready? Here we go. Our session begins with the invasion of Mars."

Such a strange thing, Valentine thinks, to live through history long enough to teach it.

If only Crucial had been so lucky.

# 2

**About fifty years earlier, Mars**

"Mars is trying to kick me off in style," I say, looking up at meteors streaking across the night sky, their glittering tails cutting through constellations of stars.

Sanders looks at me curiously. "Please explain, Crucial."

For a newly indestructible state-of-the-art cybanism with enough cognitive processing power to run an entire planet, Sanders is not great with inference.

"The meteors. It's like a going-away light show."

Sanders is helping me guide an intoxicated and very unsteady Jynks Martine to the door of the space elevator. Jynks and I are shipping out for Earth. She's the former fiancée of my ex, Mel, and apparently, my new boss after we get back to Earth.

A few days ago, I cleared Jynks of a murder charge for allegedly killing the highest-ranking member of the Five Families, who was only pretending to be dead to draw out whoever was trying to get a family promotion by taking advantage of the Martian brain-wasting disease.

It's complicated. Well, not all of it. I hate Mars. That's not at all complicated.

"Those are asteroids, not meteors," Sanders says. "Interestingly, the reclassification of asteroids into meteors occurs after asteroids enter the atmosphere of a planet."

I've come to the painful realization that any sentence from Sanders starting with "interestingly" rarely is.

"There are so many tonight," I say. "Kind of looks like they're headed right at us. Does that seem right to you? I mean, shouldn't at least some of them be going in other directions?"

"There certainly are an anomalous number. Further, these asteroids, soon to become meteors, are not on the current star charts. That's extremely odd." Sanders cocks his head slightly. "Even odder, the star charts are not updating as expected, despite how close these asteroids are to becoming meteors."

"Are you saying Halo is glitching?"

"That's not potential," Jynks says, then tries to shake some clarity into her head. "I mean not possible. Not potentially possible."

Jynks is three loose stabilizer fins to the solar wind. When we get to Earth, she'll probably never drink again.

"It's very curious," Sanders says. "Halo seems to be malfunctioning. Perhaps the universe does have sentience and is, as you say, providing a celebratory farewell light show for your kickoff. A plausible albeit highly improbable scenario."

"Goodbye, Marsh," Jynks slurs as her knees wobble. "Mars, I mean. It's been, it's been … something, all right, really something."

We probably shouldn't have ordered that last round of drinks. Jynks is a mess. I need to get her on board where she can sleep it off.

"This little light show better not postpone our flight," I say. "I'm ready to be back in my Earth squat."

Especially since I now have enough credits to buy the whole of Multnomah Ward, courtesy of a dying Singhroy

Able. All I had to do was watch out for her sniveling little nephew, Darlinius, which I mostly did. I hope he likes his new hand.

I'm keeping my wealth status to myself though. It's only one of the secrets, the smallest secret, I'm keeping from Halo. For an all-knowing, all-seeing AI able to run the two-planet system, it's becoming increasingly easy to hide things from it. And not just because I have digital-detection-evading nanites in my blood stream, courtesy of my sister Essential and her role in the resistance.

I look up at the night sky past the asteroids. Right now, Essential is on Deimos, the smaller of the two moons orbiting Mars, where she finally located the Halo servers. She's up there figuring out how to complete the last act of her super-secret resistance plan to introduce the empathy hack into Halo, forcing the AI to stop preferentially helping the wealthiest.

Or something like that.

My dream is that she can turn all this over to whoever is their deep cover agent, the one who actually *has* the empathy hack, and come back to Earth where she'll be safe when the whole thing falls apart. Safe with me.

You can't beat the system. Not for long anyway.

Essential is about to learn that very hard lesson. But I'll be there to soften the fall. Like always.

I watch the meteors, or the asteroids—whatever the prok they are—and they really do appear to be heading our way. I was already worried about the trip back to Earth in a clattering quantum rocket; those turd-rockets are always one irregularity away from a jump to the distant edge of the universe or right the prok into the sun.

This unexpected and strange meteor shower is only adding to my anxiety.

An intense flash shoots through the upper atmosphere,

and the light is bright enough to chase away the night shadows. Suddenly, alarms are clanging and our feeds are flooded with emergency alerts. And then an asteroid rips through the orbital platform high above us.

In an instant, the waiting Dart—the quantum loop ship that runs between Earth and Mars and my ride back home—is gone, along with everyone on it. The crew, the passengers, the operations staff on the orbital platform, all those people pulverized into human dust.

If we'd left five minutes sooner to board, Jynks and I would have been two more data points in that body count. Those extra drinks saved our lives.

The space elevator in front of us grows slack. All 600 kilometers of it is about to collapse into a pile of metallic fabric right on top of us, along with who knows how much metal and debris.

Sanders knows. He's already run the calculations. I can see it on his face.

"How long do we have?"

"Exactly forty five point three seconds."

"Beneath the Button is our best chance."

"It's your only chance." His new blast-resistant skin has made him a little cocky. I like it.

The Button is a massive disk of pure frissive palladium alloy able to capture and diffuse the energy of the falling space elevators. With a big enough impact from the tube dropping down from the orbital platform, the metal momentarily vibrates into an almost liquid state then quickly hardens again. The trick is shaking it loose. To retract it, the elevators are ringed with an oscillating lithotrip that sends out a controlled energy pulse to convince the palladium to loosen its grip.

It's our way in.

"Can you jack into the ring and get us below?" I ask.

Sanders nods, in that always-calm way that makes me a little crazy. And grateful.

Above the dome, light flares as debris heats up on its way toward the surface. Toward us.

"Leave me," Jynks says. "Dammit, leave me. I'm no good like this."

I still don't know why Jynks and Mel are on the outs, or why she's leaving Mars, or why she drank herself into this state. But I'm not letting her die out here if only so I can always hold it over her.

"I'm not leaving anyone. Especially my new boss." Luckily, I always carry a detox flush or two, for obvious reasons. I pop one and give her a spritz. "You want to drain fuel like an old fizzle rocket, you better start carrying these."

She takes the detox well. The flush makes it feel like your blood is turning to steam for ten long seconds as it expels the toxins.

Jynks is tough and doesn't flinch or say a word. She's pale but ready. Just like that.

There's a hum and the ground shakes. The shock waves in the ring liquefy the metal inside. We can see the thin arm of the elevator stretching up through the dome above us. It's starting to sag and twist and crumple, and bits of the dome edge where it passes through are chipping off in agitation as it falls inward.

A piece of molten metal crashes through the dome and the oxygen starts to whoosh out, and the Choke—the airless, freezing, deadly Choke—starts to pour in through the shattered hole.

"We have to go now!" I yell, and we jump through the sagging door of the elevator, dropping down onto the spongy floor of the tunnel below, one of the many tangled passages under Port Zunil where people and freight move.

Jynks is first. She's a pro. By the time I land behind her, she's already got a supply closet open. She tosses me two airhoodies and a thermal skin. Sanders doesn't need either.

The ground above us is shaking harder. The whole planet feels like it's shaking.

"We need to get deeper," I say.

The hall is filled with a panicked mass of Dockers, lottery workers and staff. Some are bloodied and burned. Everyone is yelling. Our feeds are chaotic.

Sanders is sharing the schematics. There's a ramp 30 meters ahead that leads down into an underused storage area for unclaimed freight.

"Down, down!" Jynks yells, guiding people to follow us. Shoving them, really.

I've got the storage door open and the lights on. It's huge and cluttered with containers of every size, all covered with a fine layer of red Martian dust. People are streaming in and then the lights flicker and everything jumps sideways. Something big just hit. A ball of flame and smoke belches down the hall.

I grab Jynks, pull her in and slam the door closed just as the concussive arrives and sends us all tumbling.

But we're alive.

Someone sprays light foam on the wall, illuminating our new home.

"That was close," Sanders says. Then he looks at me, head cocked again. Is it possible for a cybanism to be worried?

"What is it?"

"Crucial, another meteoroid just struck Holden." He pauses. "It was almost totally destroyed. All the domes have been damaged. These meteors are being directed. The inescapable conclusion is that Mars is under attack."

Shit. Mel. I don't even want to ask but I need to. My

mouth is dry. "Jezero?"

"The Grande Dome has been badly damaged."

Everything goes white and empty as I think about Mel. She'll be okay. She must be okay. I need to help her. She's all right and we can help her. I can deal with this.

Then it gets a million times worse.

"I'm getting very confusing information," Sanders says. "An asteroid is on a collision course for Deimos. Halo is flagging it as a condition critical but I'm not sure why—"

Our feeds stop. Just like that, everything stops. Our OCDs are no longer connected to each other, to anything.

Halo is gone.

And Sanders is gone. He slumps to the floor, eyes rolled back in his head, only the whites visible.

The meteors must have hit Deimos, destroying the Halo servers. Essential was on Deimos.

I am destroyed. Twice over.

3

Sometimes it takes the absence of something—something you've taken for granted for so long that it's simply become a seamless part of your life—before you appreciate it.

"What in the starry hell are we supposed to do without Halo?" Jynks asks. She's all business, her natural leadership abilities rising to the challenge now that she's mostly sober.

She doesn't know yet. About Jezero. Or Mel.

And of course, she can't know about Essential.

I feel numb, sick. I want to scream and curl up in a ball next to Sanders and slip into a dreamless sleep and never wake up.

I've done everything wrong in my life. Everything. For so long. And now the only two people I love are dead.

Probably dead. Maybe not. Maybe not dead?

With Halo down, I can't confirm. I guess that's what hope really is—a lack of good data.

If I think about the odds, Essential is most likely dead. That's a calculus I never thought I'd have to make. Dead for real this time, not just pull-out-your-own-eyeball-to-hide-from-the-system pretend dead. An asteroid smashing into a tiny moon like Deimos, there's no chance of surviving that.

But Jezero is bigger. If the strike wasn't too close, Mel might have made it. Mel and her ridiculous miniature cat. Twist. Or Twitch. Whatever.

I realize I'm crying.

Essential is probably dead, and I must make my peace with it because I can't fall into the darkness that follows, can't give up, until I know for sure about Mel.

If Essential survived, if by some miracle she boosted before the strike, and why not, she's a Larsen: smart and lucky and a survivor, she can take care of herself until I can get a ship to her.

So I need to play the odds, which makes Mel the immediate priority. She's closer and the chances are higher that she survived.

"Did you hear me, Larsen?" Jynks asks, shaking me. "It's our duty as law officers to help these people until a rescue team arrives."

I look around the cargo bay. There are maybe a hundred others stuck in here—injured, shaken, feedblind—and all in shock, trying to deal with the reality of what just happened. None of them know the real story because our feeds were too chaotic. Only Sanders could make sense of it all before Halo went down, before he went down.

Jynks looks into my eyes. "What's wrong? Don't tell me a little asteroid strike has you rattled?"

"It's not random. Sanders sorted through the data before he, you know, collapsed. It was directed. Mars is under attack. Other domes have been hit. *All* the domes have been hit."

I let that sink in.

She looks at me, a mixture of wonder and then fear spreading across her face like a sudden bloom of charcoal algae in a hydration tower. "Mel," she whispers.

"We have to get to Jezero," I say. "We need to find out. We owe her that much. Both of us owe her that, no matter what happened between you two."

Jynks nods slowly, still trying to absorb the new heart-shattering information.

Jezero is 3,500 kilometers away on a planet under attack by unknown forces able to fling asteroids like glitter gun flechettes. Halo is down, which means even if we can find an undamaged flier, we'll have to operate on manual through hostile airspace. We'll never make it.

We'll need weapons. And booze. Especially booze. Neither seems likely stuck here in the unclaimed cargo hold, which is basically a museum of items rendered useless by technological progress, which might not be progress at all when you think about it as a force for obsolescence. And when you think about how useless all the technology is now with the grid down.

"Listen up," I say to the people gathering around. "We need to leave for Jezero but we'll send help." They think we're going there to ensure the Five Families are safe. They're so used to thinking they owe their lives to the wealthy, they don't even question why their own survival comes second.

"We'll get you situated first," I continue. "Who can access the manifesto of all this old cargo?"

"I can," a young man says. He powers up a zip strip and charges a local portal that flares to life.

I scan the list. Payload.

"Light up these containers," I say.

He manipulates the screens by hand, like in the old days of poke-screens, and the lighting system in the ceiling spotlights the cases we're looking for.

One has 10,128 servings of self-heating fermented yeast balls. It's prison food and it's horrible. They stopped making them like 20 years ago but they have all the nutrients you need to survive. I point to a woman in a Docker's uniform. "You're in charge of food until we can send a rescue squad. Get that container open and make sure folks have what they need."

Next to her is a man in a similar uniform, a fresh cut on his scalp bleeding into his eye. He looks prokked off and confident. "You good?" I ask.

"I'm fine." He swipes at the blood as if it makes him angry.

"You're in charge of hydration. There are emergency water rations in the stash closets but focus on this container for now." I point at the screen.

The container has 800 pouches of Citrulux, a syrupy sweet synthetic watermelon fizz, a drink popular a while back with kids. Too much of it at once will strip the finish off a planet corer, but the pouches will help stretch water supplies.

"Anyone with medical experience?" Jynks asks.

"I operate a health cradle," a man says.

"That's more than the rest of us," she says. "You're in charge of first aid."

"I just turn it off and on and run the diagnostics."

"You're basically an expert then. There's a kit here." She points at the screen. "With one old-fashioned first-aid bot. It'll need your hands. Get set up against the wall and help whoever you can."

"We'll send more help your way as soon as we're topside," I say. "But keep this door locked until Halo comes back online and don't open it unless it's first-aid bots or Mars security forces."

"Why, what's going on?" the man asks. "It was just an asteroid strike, wasn't it?"

"This was no accident. The damage is extensive and widespread, with many domes hit. We think Mars is under attack."

There's a collective gasp, then some confusion.

"Wait, by who?" someone asks. "Who would wage war

against the Five Families?"

"We don't know."

"Probably the resistance," someone else says. "Those filthy, clabbering gouts."

Jynks shoots me a quick look. She's thinking that too. Even though they saved her from the Five Families just last week.

"Unlikely," I say. "They wouldn't risk so many innocent lives."

"I wouldn't put it past them," the new medic says. "When we get Halo back online, I hope Mars SF glitters them all to dust."

Clearly, this group is wrong. It's not the Variance attacking. Essential is number two in the resistance now and nothing happens without her. They plan to change things without firing a single rail gun slug, much less dropping asteroids on Mars.

And their plan is pretty sophisticated—introduce that mysterious empathy hack into the AI that powers Halo so it learns how to share resources more equitably. It's a good plan, but it's doomed to fail. *Was* doomed to fail. Now it's all up in a smoke. Maybe.

Our immediate problem is that whoever did do this appears to also have a good plan—destroy everything and then take over. But who could build up this capacity of directional asteroids while hiding it all from Halo? That takes money and time, a lot of time. Years.

I'll figure that out later.

I study the manifest.

There's nothing here in the way of weapons. Well, almost nothing. I light up the ceiling tile and Jynks and I make our way over to crack the seal.

"What are these?" she asks, looking at the dusty, vaguely pistol-shaped items inside.

"Our best option for weapons." I reach for one. "Correction. Our *only* option."

"Repair tools?"

"Glue guns. From back in the day when humans had to repair the domes themselves. They shoot a pellet of quick-drying polymer that's sticky at first but dries fast and is harder than titanium when it sets. The guns are accurate to about 100 meters."

I cycle a round and shoot it at a nearby wall. There's a puff and a wet splat as the epoxy hardens into a circle a meter across and a centimeter thick.

"You want us to turn back an invading space force with glue guns?"

"Yeah, I mean, until we get our hands on some actual weapons."

"What I wouldn't give for a rail gun right now," she mutters, snatching a tool and stomping off. I take two along with extra bands of pellets.

When Jynks is out of sight, I make my way to another container and pry it open. Inside are five crates of maple rum. It's synthetic, of course—they ran out of maple trees in 2078—but the rum remained popular for a few more decades. I take three bottles.

Some of the survivors help us roll Sanders, who is surprisingly heavy, onto a float dolly and I sync it to a tracker button on my belt so it will follow me. They lock the door behind us as Jynks and I slip out into the tunnels below Port Zunil, airhoodies on, glue guns raised and Sanders floating a few paces behind.

4

Port Zunil is wrecked.

The damage from the falling debris has shattered the dome—punching a hole in the crown like a kid's juice pack—and there's no breathable air left. The automated repair systems are overwhelmed. Repair bots are clanking around aimlessly, extruding fragile towers of repair sealant that fountain up into the thin atmosphere and taper off into nothing.

Twisted chunks of metal from the orbital platform are embedded in the Button. The impact was so significant that the palladium failed and sprayed out in a now-frozen wash of tortured liquid, forming frenzied, elegant waves of gleaming metal. Debris is scattered across the Choke for kilometers, some of it glowing with the heat it gained on entry into the thin atmosphere.

Fires are raging underneath the buildings, sending up columns of thick smoke swirling into the cold night. Backup electrical systems flicker, and transport vehicles are stalled or else looping around in endless circles.

I'm thinking of Jezero. If the damage is this significant here … best not to even finish that thought. I look over at Jynks. Her expression tells me she's thinking the same thing.

I can see occasional movement as people in airhoodies, trying to make sense of the chaos and their downed feeds, wander through the wreckage. No one tries to stop us or talk to us. No one even looks in our direction. The sight of two people dragging a body behind them in the shattered and smoldering port gives no one pause.

"Why do we have him again?" Jynks asks, tilting her head back toward Sanders who floats along behind me, the dolly grimly trying to keep up with our twists and turns as we navigate the damaged corridor.

"He's the most advanced mobile cognitive processor on Mars. And he's got blast-resistant skin. He's basically the smartest weapon on the planet."

"He's powered down, ballast. A probability anchor, and a weak one at that. We could move a lot faster without him bouncing around behind us. He can find us once he reboots."

I look back at Sanders. His eyes are still rolled back in his head in that weird, gross way he has, with only the whites visible. I think that means he's processing information. A lot of information. "He's a friend. And I don't want to leave him behind. I won't leave him behind."

"He's an appliance," she says, but lets it drop.

The corridor circles around the Button. Most of the ceiling is torn off and the cold is clawing at our thermal suits. The stars are blazing and there are no more deadly meteors raining down. Not yet anyway, so that's one good thing.

There's no sign of an invading force. Maybe Sanders got it wrong. Maybe the system just missed the meteors and some random space rocks wiped out the orbital platform and Deimos—knocking out Halo—right at the same time. Maybe the other domes aren't damaged.

That's a lot of maybes.

No matter. Even if Sanders was wrong and it's not the start of a new war, getting to Jezero is still the best plan.

If we can find a flier. Or a Blackwall, one of the crazy spider-legged Choke-runners. Or even a rocketbike with a sidecar for Sanders.

According to the local schematics we grabbed back in the cargo bay, the primary hangar is about 400 meters ahead. With any luck, we can boost an undamaged flier from there.

There's a section of metal blocking the way and I struggle to navigate the float dolly up and over the obstruction. Jynks keeps walking ahead. It's going to be a long trip to Jezero.

Sirens wail, emergency lights flash and the smoke thickens. Our airhoodies are filtering it out, but I can still taste a bitter, metallic tang. Rocket fuel. I have a bad feeling.

"I don't think we're going to find a flier," Jynks says. She points through a shattered window out toward the edge of the Button where the hangar used to be. It's crushed under a huge broken-off section of the quantum Dart, the ship we both should be on now headed back to Earth. Looks like the Dart, or most of it, tumbled straight down onto the hangar facility and flattened everything. And everyone. And ignited all the rocket fuel for good measure.

The heat from the burning fuel is so intense, I can see white hot tears of metal crying along the smoldering edges.

Mars never makes anything easy.

"What about drone jackets?" Jynks asks. "We could just bundle up in double thermals and fly there."

"Drone jackets? You mean the ones you summon using Halo? And then control with your feed, which runs through Halo?"

"Yes. If we can find some, we could probably override the controls. Then set them for a safe height and just let them go."

"Maybe. I mean, they have a top speed of what, 70 kilometers per hour? So yeah, that would get us to Jezero in just about …" I cock my head the way Sanders does as if calculating higher math. "Just about never. And then only if we don't end up creped on the side of some Martian mountain because we're flying blind and can't dodge things."

"You're an ass." Her voice is tinged with desperation. "We have to do something."

I'm feeling desperate too. I can't believe how quickly things have gone to shit. That seems to happen a lot around me.

That's when it hits me. Shit, for once, *is* the solution— we can take a gonzo truck.

Gonzo. Garbage and Sanitation Overland Conveyance transports, otherwise known as gonzo trucks. They're huge, ungainly monsters that haul loads of super-compacted waste clots extruded once a month by all the electrostatic biowaste closets in each dome. The clots are forced into a rough ball shape, surrounded by a thick layer of synthetic rubber, and then carried out into the Choke by gonzo trucks like giant dung beetles. When a waste barge passes by in flight, the trucks use their forks to catapult the waste balls 20 kilometers right into the open holds.

The trucks are driverless, like most everything else that keeps the planet functioning, but they have sealed sleeper cabs for crew transport in case repairs are needed, or emergency shelter. The gonzo trucks are built for the Choke, with about a hundred independently driven wheels and a suspension system that can withstand running over small buildings.

Gonzo trucks are also fast and sturdy, and they won't draw any unwelcome attention if we are under attack.

"I've got an idea," I say. "Gonzo trucks."

She looks relieved. And irritated she didn't think of it. "Fast, sturdy and easily overlooked? Perfect."

Jynks opens a wall port and manually pulls up the local schematics. There's a waste transfer point on the map. It's only a hundred meters back the way we came from and then a couple hundred more down a spur line away from the Button.

We make pretty good time. The door to the transfer point is open and inside is a battered, dusty gonzo—a huge waste ball held in place on the horns in front—and three people in Mars SF uniforms gathered around the open control panel. Turns out we weren't the only ones who thought of these waste trucks.

"That should just about do it," a woman says, lowering the control panel.

Perfect timing.

"Officer on deck," Jynks says, expecting a salute. Instead, one of them pulls out a rail gun. An old rail gun, a first-gen with an air canister bubble on the top that's been obsolete for a hundred years.

Still, despite its obsolescence, it is more than capable of blowing our heads smoothly off our necks. Well, only one head off one neck.

The gun takes forever to recharge, so it can only take out one of us.

I hope it's Jynks. I mean, nothing personal, I would like to stay alive. There are a lot of things I need to make right. She's only got the one thing. Plus, there are three unopened bottles of maple rum in my pack.

"Don't move." The man aims the gun at us, moving it slowly back and forth.

"What the fuzzy logic are you doing?" Jynks asks. "I'm your superior officer, and I order you to stand down."

"I told you these suits would work," the woman says with a smile.

"We're not Mars SF," the man says. "We have some supplies we're going to run over to Jezero and sell to the folks who need it. The uniforms will make that easier."

"Jezero was hit?" I ask.

"Cracked wide open and everybody is in a panic. We're going to do our civic duty and make a few credits helping out where we can."

"What are you selling?" I ask.

"Food, water, medical supplies. They're all packaged up nicely in the waste ball." He points at the front of the gonzo truck.

"That's illegal," Jynks says. "Black marketeering. I'm arresting you all."

"Easy there, partner," I say. "Let's not be hasty. Can't fault them for trying to make a few extra credits. The Five Families would be proud. Never waste a crisis. We just need a ride."

They laugh. "Yeah, like we're going to climb into a gonzo truck with actual security forces. Do we look stupid?"

"I mean, yeah, but just in the normal way. We can pay."

"Halo is down so no transfers," the woman says, "And we don't take IOUs."

"How about a trade?"

"Is what you have worth our trouble?" the man asks.

"Just be calm." I slowly take out a bottle of maple rum and set it down on the ledge next to me. "I've got this."

He eyes the bottle. "That's an interesting start. But not enough. What else you got?"

"How about this?" I pull out the glue gun and fire one dead center. The pellet hits the rail gun and expands into a clear disk that gums his arm to his chest, the barrel pointing up to his chin.

"What the shit?" the woman asks. "You *glued* him?"

Jynks now has her gun out and aimed at the other two while the leader curses and struggles against the hardening sealant.

I reclaim my bottle of maple rum. "Change of plans. Looks like we're going to take the truck and the supplies and leave you behind. You can help your friend get that sealant off before it permanently hardens. But first, you're going to help me get that cybanism in the cab."

When they finally get him wedged into the cab—Sanders seems heavier each time we move him—Jynks and I climb in, fire up the gonzo and hit the exit door hatch. We watch them in the rear feed, bent over their friend and struggling to peel off the epoxy, as we rumble out into the Choke.

# 5

Now that we've cleared the far perimeter of Port Zunil, the fresh impact craters and smoldering metal debris have thinned, so there's no longer any need for active piloting. The adrenaline is leveling out as I slip the mechanical beast onto auto-psy mode. I stand and stretch, looking out at the godsforsaken Choke. The only noise is the hum of the gonzo engine.

The. Only. Thing.

From time to time and for short periods, the nanites have given me a taste of almost silence, a headspace without the constant noise and streams and shouting and avatainment of Halo. There are jammers—a few minutes with that tech gives you a little window of peace, but you need to talk fast, hurried. I got a deeper sense of quiet down in the sunbelt with the blizards and Valentine not so long ago. There, Halo was blocked the whole time we were underground, drinking ant-gin. It was heavenly, but didn't last long. For obvious reasons.

Other than that, I've never had my brain or my thoughts entirely to myself since the day I was born. No one has. They clamp the OCD in each infant before it even leaves the med-booth. From that day forward, you're constantly connected. Constantly broadcasting. Constantly receiving.

Now that we're in the Choke and there's no immediate

meteor attack to react to, no people to organize and save, no Sanders to protect, no transport to secure, no exploded craters to steer around, I am suddenly aware—and mildly disoriented—by the unfamiliarity of silence, suddenly aware of being alone with my thoughts.

Well, mostly alone. Jynks is here, battling the same demons of silence.

While I don't mind this silent world, and I'm no fan of Halo, we're flying blind. Actually, driving blind. More accurately, bouncing slowly, painfully across the Choke, blind. We need access to data to make it through, to figure out what the prok is going on.

Hopefully, we'll get Halo back by the time we hit Jezero. If the servers were destroyed, there must be a backup for the AI powering the system. The Five Families would never make their precious Halo that vulnerable.

But if the Grande Dome at Jezero was hit hard, the problem is worse than an absence of data. All the climate and atmospheric controls would be gone, with nothing to keep the Choke from just rolling right on in.

If that's the case, it's hard to imagine the chaos there, the suffering of the previously pampered class of wealthy Five Families elite. Well, it's easy to imagine, and more than a little pleasant to imagine in the case of some of those elite asses, but hard to process. Plus, if they're suffering, the lottery workers, administrators and non-family people will have it even worse.

Like Mel.

I shake that thought from my brain, which suddenly has room for way too many thoughts.

Jynks is studying a map spread across the console in front of her. It's an old-fashioned folding map with no 3D enhancement. That's what we're reduced to when Halo is down.

Lucky for us she seems to be pretty good at interpreting it. It's possible Jynks has a more disciplined mind than I do. We haven't said a word in several hours, not since we made it into the heart of the Choke.

I crack open a bottle of maple rum and offer her a sip. She shakes her head so I take her share. It's sweet and strong and dulls the ache of worry I'm feeling.

"How long before we get to Jezero?" I ask.

"We're in the Elysium Plains." She points at the map. "It's relatively flat here and will be for a while, so we're making decent time. But about a thousand kilometers outside of Jezero, we come up against the Aeolis Mensai Uprising. I'm looking for a crossing now."

"What's that?"

"A long narrow ridge, probably an ancient streambed the Five Families turned into a raised aqueduct. It pulls fresh water from the polar cap. Mel has rights to some of that water because—"

She stops herself. I know that feeling too well. It's when you automatically talk about someone you love as if they are still in your life, but then in the middle of the sentence you realize they're not part of your life anymore.

Or in this case, maybe not even alive.

Prok, I have got to get control of my thoughts. Which is harder to do now that there is literally nothing I can pull up on my non-existent scroll to distract myself. I can't go down this road or I'll be completely useless. Now isn't the time to wallow. Or overthink. Or think at all. Now is the time to draw on the skills perfected over a lifetime of ignoring my feelings, with or without Halo.

I need to focus on being my own source of distraction.

"What'd you say this area is called?" I ask.

"The Elysium Plains."

"Interestingly, I know something about that."

Dammit, I sound like Sanders.

"You know something?" she asks. "*You*?"

"Yeah, me. A story. My Mom was into all the old texts. Like, the super old myths."

Jynks doesn't say anything, just keeps looking at the map. I interpret her silence as interest in my tale.

"In ancient times, the people on Earth thought the Elysian Fields—"

"These are the Elysium Plains, not Elysian Fields."

"Same difference. Now, as I was saying, ancient people thought the Elysian Fields were a kind of heaven, a gauzy place, not real but not unreal, where people went after they died. I don't know how they got there, like their corpses flew or their bodies reanimated or whatever. But this place was reserved only for humans who were related to or chosen by the gods. The people who were sent there got to live all happy for eternity and do whatever they wanted most while they were alive, forever."

"Sounds like life on Mars. At least before this attack."

"Except you don't have to die to get to Mars. You just need to be part of the Five Families. Or work for them."

"What about all the other people, the ones who weren't related or chosen?" she asks.

I am strangely pleased that my story has intrigued Jynks.

"I don't know. I guess they just died. Or went off down some burning river or something."

She folds up the map. "That's not much of a story."

Okay, maybe I got that wrong. Jynks is not intrigued.

"I didn't say it was a good story."

"More like a description really, and an incomplete one at that."

We go quiet again, each of us probably thinking about the same thing—Mel—while also trying to figure out how to think and act without Halo. Or maybe that's just me projecting. How would I know what she's thinking? I can't see her scroll anymore. Or mine. I don't have one.

"Maybe I will take some of that rum," she says.

I hand it over.

The sun is setting, and the landscape is starting to reflect that weird blue glow. The gonzo keeps bouncing along. The endless waves of rough red plains lull us both into a kind of half-sleep, half-awake state. I can't stop wondering what kind of devastation we'll find when we get to Jezero. Or maybe the damage won't be that significant.

"You know, it's possible she wasn't even there," Jynks says, handing the bottle back. "Maybe she was at Baldet, or the tree farm."

Turns out I did know what she was thinking.

"I'll drink to that."

Without data, why not assume it to be true? I watch the sky through the windows. I do like the purple-blue Martian sunsets. If my life ever returns to any semblance of normal, I think I'll do some updating in my holo-desert, give it a cobalt-haze setting-sun option. I'll do that when I get back to Earth.

Hard to believe how fast the tables turned. Earth, the wrecked planet, is now safer than Mars. At least, I assume Earth is okay. I guess there's no way to know anything for sure right now. Only facts matter, as Valentine would say. Best not to torture myself with possibilities. But at the very least, you can breathe on Earth without an airhoodie.

Valentine vinged me right before the attack. Said she was sorry she couldn't come see me off personally. She was calling from Singhroy University. Of all the structures in Jezero, it seems it would be one of the safest. I'm sure she's fine. I hope she's fine.

"We should get some sleep," Jynks says. "I'll take the first shift."

I nod.

"The coordinates are plugged in. Wake me up at the base of Aeolis Mensai."

Mars has a weird sense of humor. Jynks and I are the last two people who should be partnered up. Mel's ex-lover and her ex-fiancée. But there's no one I'd rather have by my side in—whatever this is. An alien invasion? A huge cosmic joke?

Jynks pulls out a thermal bag and slips inside it underneath Sanders's cot, the only spot large enough for her long frame. Her eyes are closed, but she's not sleeping. She's thinking about the last stupid thing she said to Mel. I know it because that's what I'm thinking about too.

I drain the bottle of maple rum and reach in my stuffelbag for another one.

But just as I'm about to open the next bottle, I realize maybe I shouldn't try to dampen every unpleasant thought I have. I can hear Essential laughing. *You? Since when did you grow up?*

Easy for you to say, I reply in my head. You're not worried about your stupid brave little sister. Or Mel. Or Valentine. The thoughts keep rattling around like a flock of myco-woodpeckers trapped inside a dumpster. *Really, Crucial, it's not a bad idea. You could use a break.*

I want to tell Essential's voice in my head to mind her own business but instead, reluctantly, I put the stopper in the bottle. I'll wait to share it with Mel. She loves maple rum. Hell, she probably engineered the tree that gave up its sap to make this rum.

I slump down in my seat. My brain is exhausted from the nonstop neural activity, the worry and the now-hallucinatory Essential. She's alive. She has to be. And Mel too.

"Who are you talking to? You're muttering," Jynks says.

31

"Just thinking through the scenarios we're likely to find in Jezero."

"Yeah, I was thinking about that too."

"Are you, like, having any odd thoughts? You know, because of not having a scroll and all that silence."

"Nope," she says, rolling over.

She's a worse liar than I am.

The sun is down and the lights of the gonzo fan out across our path. We're rumbling through the pitch black night now. I keep talking to Essential and Jynks keeps pretending to be asleep.

# 6

The gonzo hits something big and lurches. A warning alarm goes off.

My head jerks up. I wipe the drool from the corner of my mouth and rub my stiff neck. Jynks is standing next to the console looking out at the ceaseless red stretch before us. Pretty sure she hit a rock on purpose to wake me up.

"I thought we were sleeping in shifts," she says.

"I thought you knew me better."

I don't know how long I've been asleep, but it's daytime now.

"What's the situation, boss?" I ask.

"Don't call me boss."

"You are my boss."

"That was before Mars was attacked."

I crack my neck and Jynks winces at the sound, so I crack my knuckles too.

"About that. Any sign of, I guess, invading aliens?"

"No. And the systems are all still down."

I look over at Sanders. Still inert. "Yeah, I kind of figured."

I feel the first snap of concern. Is Sanders ever going to wake up? Is there anyone left to reboot him if it comes to that?

The gonzo is sturdily heaving and lumbering along. I

look in front of us. The terrain is rippled, a cratered series of parallel waves and valleys, each one successively taller and wider. We're moving through a valley that's a few kilometers west of the main ridges—tall and nearly vertical, about three kilometers distant, as the drone flies.

"Where are we?" I ask.

"Running right alongside the Aeolis Mensai Uprising, the feature I told you about that's now an aqueduct."

I'm curious how it got that name—it sounds vaguely female. Normally when I'm curious about anything, I query Halo. But I had already forgotten, Halo isn't there. It's getting more unsettling by the second just exactly how programmed I am, how dependent, even though I hate Halo. Now I have a burning itch from that unsatisfied mild curiosity about Aeolis Mensai. How the prok did people function in the days when access to information was finite and physically constrained?

"Can we get across?"

"Nothing on the 2D map shows a breach," Jynks says. "And think about it. When the Five Families turned the ridge into this aqueduct, there was no reason for them to plan for anything other than crossing it by air."

"Meaning, we may be taking the long way around. How much time does that add?"

She looks down at the map and shakes her head. "I have no idea how anyone ever managed to geolocate anything with this primitive technology." She runs her finger along the surface and then checks the dials on the console. "If we have to go completely around, it will take us three more days to get to Jezero."

"And if we go over?"

"Six hours."

"Then it has to be over."

"Have at it. If you see a way through on this map that

doesn't involve defying the laws of physics, let me know."

A glint of reflected light in the distance catches my eye. Steam or maybe smoke.

"What is that?" I ask.

Jynks pulls out a mono-mag and zooms in. "Looks like something big hit the top of the aqueduct. A piece of the orbital platform maybe, or an interstellar ship. Must have happened during the attack. Could be a stray projectile." She hands me the mono-mag.

"Maybe infrastructure was a specific target. Damage to this aqueduct could affect water supply in Jezero," I say, peering through the lens.

Whatever it was, it hit the top of the ridge with enough force to punch in a new valley, with jagged red boulders piled up on the new gash like a stairway. A very unsteady, uninviting stairway. But a stairway nevertheless.

"That's our ticket to Jezero," I say. "Those blasted-out boulders and rock are footholds for the gonzo."

"It'll be a bumpy ride."

"And we'll probably be crushed in a rockslide."

"Or stranded when the gonzo high-centers and leaves us slowly running out of oxygen."

But worth it if it gets us there sooner, I think, and we can find out what happened to Mel.

"But worth it if it gets us there sooner," Jynks says.

She tilts the joystick hard left, overriding the sensor-based navigation, and steers the gonzo toward the rise, up and down over the smaller foothills and ridges until we get to the uprising's base and the fresh route across. Close up, the ascent looks even more daunting. The smallest of the blasted boulders leading up to the new notch are the size of my squat. Most are much larger, and the incline is so steep, it's only barely not vertical.

But the gonzo is a tank. The hull is impenetrable and its

conveyance tracks can move over any kind of terrain.

In theory.

"Buckle up," Jynks says.

The woman is fearless.

I check that Sanders is clipped down tight and then strap myself into the seat next to Jynks. She doesn't waste any time, just aims the gonzo straight up and hits the fuel. The force slams me back into the chair as we go from flat terrain to a near right angle in less than 20 meters. The monster trash truck lurches wildly, pulling and pushing, heaving and dipping, clutching and twisting, with each turn of the wheel belt. Dust billows out on either side and in front, as the weight of the gonzo cracks and crushes the edges of the rocks.

"It's working, we're making it up," Jynks shouts above raucous grinding and groaning, her hand steady on the controls. "Halfway there."

The rocking sensation sends me hurling back in time to a boat ride with Mom and Essential at AmaDis Water Park on Earth. The park was usually reserved for Five Families administrators, but Mom won a prize drawing so it only cost a few credits to land a reservation. It was a nice night, with a full moon and favorable winds blowing the pollution away from Multnomah Ward. Mom packed some food for us, called it a picsnack or a snickpac or something like that. Bread squares with synthnutbutter.

We ate it on the little synthetic beach by the little synthetic Lake Singhroy and waited our turn to ride the little synthetic hand-powered boat. Finally, we got to the front of the line. I remember the pride I felt turning the cranks that sent us across the water, didn't even care that my palms were blistering. It was a hot night, but it's always hot on Earth, and it felt good. Essential was dragging her fingers in the water and smiling, and Mom was humming some old tune. It was one of the few memories I have of us enjoying something that wasn't tainted with the struggle to survive. It is still so vivid, even though it was long ago, wondering for the first time if this was what happiness felt like.

It didn't last long.

Whoever was running the controls thought it would be funny to scare us, or maybe something went wrong; we never found out. By the time we got to the center of the lake, the waves picked up and the boat started pitching and rocking violently. Within minutes, everything went to trash—Essential was crying and I was panicked. I'm pretty sure we both vomited up our snickpac. Mom stayed cool, as always, and helped me crank us back to shore.

When we got out of the boat, the operator was apologetic, but there was something about his smile that made me think he was to blame. I hit him with the handle from the oar crank and knocked him out cold. The juvenile cops came to judge the footage. They decided to debt us for the damage to the oar crank and ban us from the park in perpetuity. Mom wasn't happy but she wasn't mad either.

I'm feeling like I might lose my snickpac again right this second, but the only thing in my belly is maple rum.

The gonzo lurches to the right. Jynks is smiling, both hands on the joystick. She's feeling it, the synchronicity of human and machine, like she's lost her sense of self and merged with the big truck.

"You're enjoying this!" I shout. She ignores me.

We're almost to the top of the rubble staircase. As the gonzo crests the ridge, I realize we hadn't thought about the other side.

"Uh-oh," Jynks says, braking hard.

The gonzo stops with a shudder about five centimeters

from plunging over the edge, creaking and tottering slightly forward, then balancing unsteadily, our nose hanging out over the one-kilometer drop-off. It's too steep for the gonzo to stake a grip on the terrain. We're facing certain death.

"Can you back us out?" I ask quietly, as if the loudness of my words will add enough weight to tip us over the edge.

The gonzo teeters and slips forward a couple of centimeters. I unbuckle and crab-walk to the rear. Jynks does the same. Our weight stabilizes the gonzo. For a second.

"We have to jump," I say, and she nods.

I toss Jynks an airhoodie from the supply compartment and grab one for me. I unhook Sanders from the gonzo, keeping one hand on his floating cot. I nod. She moves—slowly, smoothly—to the hatch and opens it. I pull Sanders along, getting closer to Jynks. The gonzo shudders and scoots forward another centimeter. She holds up three fingers.

Three.

Two.

One.

She jumps through the hatch, and I shove Sanders toward her. As she grabs the float-dolly edge and pulls him through, I follow, landing awkwardly and rolling over sharp rocks. I stand, stumble to get my footing, and do a quick check. A few scrapes but nothing broken. I can breathe, so the airhoodie is working. We both pull on our thermals. It's deadly cold in the Choke.

The gonzo teeters. Jynks walks the few meters back and slams the hatch closed. It's just enough. The big truck tips forward and tumbles down the cliff face, banging across the rocks, flipping again and once more, until it lands on flat ground below, and with a bounce, is right side up.

"Well, I'll be godsdamned, it landed on its feet," I say. "Like that stupid cat you and Mel had. Wasp. Wink. The synth cat."

Jynks starts the scramble down the steep cliff face. I follow, navigating the rocky scree with Sanders on his platform trailing along behind me. His inert body almost slips off twice, but I nudge it back in time. Well, nudge isn't quite the right word. Shoulder is more accurate. He is so prokking heavy, and weirdly, seems heavier than yesterday. I must be tired.

Abruptly, Jynks turns around. "Wisp," she says. "The cat's name was, is, Wisp,"

"Right, Wisp."

She's staring at me through her airhoodie with big, serious eyes. "I need to ask you something, Larsen."

"Now?"

"Yeah, now."

"Now. While we are scrambling down a busted-out valley dragging a lifeless cybanism behind us after nearly falling to our deaths?"

"It's important."

"Okay. Sure. Ask away."

"How were you able to put your sister in that Terrorium? How do you live with yourself?"

That was not anywhere near what I was expecting Jynks to ask. I thought it would be something about our mutual interest in Mel.

I know that 99.9 percent of the people on Mars and Earth believe I locked Essential in a Terrorium in Jezero. But it's really Canadis Whitsend, Jynks's old boss and my commander during the Consolidation Wars, in there. Jynks doesn't know that. Mel doesn't know that either. So, everyone thinks I'm a terrible person.

Everyone might not be wrong, but not for that reason.

"Maybe we could chat about that some other time. When we're not on an exposed cliff on a planet under attack by an unknown and probably alien force able to fling meteors around like pepper puffballs."

She's not budging. "I need to know how you did it. How did you, of all people, choose loyalty to the system over love?"

It's impossible to answer, of course, because I didn't choose loyalty over love. I would never choose loyalty to any system over love. Only someone like Jynks could ever choose that. Then it hits me like a sub lethal glitter flechette right between the eyes.

"This about you and Mel. Why you left her."

She nods. "Mel told me something. Said she couldn't troth me unless I knew. Didn't want there to be any secrets between us."

"But there's nothing Mel could—" I start to say, and then I think of that stupid cat and how it lit up when Essential found Deimos. Why did Wisp respond? Only one possibility. The cat must be a resistance communications device.

"Fireballs. Mel's in the resistance."

Jynks nods.

How the hell had I missed that? Does Essential know?

"She said she was about to do something big," Jynks says.

Everything I thought I understood about Jynks just flew out the window. "You left Mel so you wouldn't have to turn her in to the Five Families."

"No, I mean I didn't want to turn her in, but I couldn't stay with her either. So, in the end, I chose loyalty to the Five Families system, not love. I said I wanted a posting on Earth, knowing she wouldn't leave Mars."

Yeah, that's right. Sure. Sacrificing your entire career

isn't loyalty to the Five Families. That's a story she's made up to live with herself. Jynks left because of love, to protect Mel.

I can't decide whether I like her better or less because of this. But it doesn't matter because the only important part of Jynks's revelation is that Mel is in the resistance. And the big thing Mel is about to do must be related to the empathy hack. What else could it be?

"You and I are a lot alike," I say. "And we're going to have some funny things to talk about someday. But until then, just know you did what you had to do. Like me. Now let's get to the gonzo, pray to the briny salts of Neptune that it's still running, and go find Mel."

## 7

**August 32, 2238**
*Stardust University, Neuro-Lecture Interface 75.32*

As she waits for full neural connectivity, Valentine checks the geodata. Physical distance is irrelevant for this or any educational module, but she likes to know where people are located. More accurately, Valentine *needs* to know where she is in relation to them.

The security habits, or as Seneca calls them, obsessions, that formed during her years in the resistance don't fade easily. And even with Seneca's gentle teasing, Valentine won't give them up. Can't give them up. She knows this carefulness, the attention to detail, is what kept her and Seneca alive in the months after the invasion when they were stranded on Mars. It's hardwired now.

Valentine shakes her head free of the past and returns her attention to the dashboard. The geodata show a good half of the students are on-planet, spread out evenly across Earth, with a small cohort of Saurians linking in from the sunbelt. That pleases her immensely. One of Valentine's proudest achievements is that she helped broker a mutual aid agreement between the Saurians and Earth in the early days.

She flashes on a memory from years ago when she and

Crucial were in the sunbelt arguing about him calling the Saurians "blizards." He eventually came around to her way of thinking. There were other pleasant memories from that expedition. A calm before the storm.

The next largest group links in from Mars, concentrated around Jezero. A dozen more data points register with an anonymous in-orbit tag. Interplanetary Intelligence, likely. And last, four faint glows from a Venus moon. The bored and lonely children of outer-edge explorers, undoubtedly.

"Welcome back to Recent History-Building, in which our meta-focus is to learn and apply, using examples from the invasion of Mars in 2188 and its aftermath, the analytical tools needed to build contemporary historical overlays. Good to see you again."

Her dashboard lights up with greetings in dozens of languages. The neural translation is instantaneous.

"Today we'll finish up our evaluation of different categories of source material," she continues. "Let's reflect on our last session in which we deployed the penultimate learning tool, the ENC, to provide you with a first-hand experience of the invasion of Mars. The ENC allowed you to share my neuronal memories to, in turn, create your own subjective experience of this past."

She pulls up a captured freeze-frame from the last instant they were all linked into the bombardment of Jezero. The adrenaline levels of the class spike. "So, how was it?"

*Terrifying.*

*I thought I was going to die.*

*I was so scared for Seneca, I wasn't sure we would be able to protect her.*

*So alone.*

*Didn't know what to do or think without Halo.*

*Horrible smells, like an explosion of farts.*

She almost laughs out loud at that last one. Those invading ships *did* smell awful.

"First-hand experience. On the face of it, a primary source that would seem the most important material for building a consensus historical narrative. But I pose the question: Why are first-hand experiences so challenging for historians?"

The dashboard lights up with the ranked response matrix.

"Not bad," Valentine says. "Your highest-ranked response is correct. First-hand material by definition embeds a perspective, even if it's your own perspective, making it only marginally better as a source than the massive troves of secondary data Halo and its derivatives have always automatically and routinely scooped up. Who wants to summarize why?"

She selects a member of the Saurian contingent to respond. "Arsotz, please share your insights."

"The volume of secondary data tends to minimize the bias," Arsotz says. "The information can be reduced to a common baseline."

"Excellent. Now, why might that also be problematic in some cases?"

"Tyranny of the masses," he says.

He would know that first-hand, she thinks.

"Well done. Let's move on to another category of source material." Valentine flashes up an image from fifty years ago. "Who is this?"

She waits for the response matrix to resolve. They all get it right, of course. One hundred percent.

Senior Scientist Melinda Hopwire in the year 2188.

Next to Mel's picture, she adds one each of Jynks and Crucial. The class endorphins explode. In the decade that she's been leading this history module, the images of these three never fail to excite the students.

The love triangle of Jynks, Crucial and Mel has become the stuff of legend.

They were never caught on record speaking about it, leaving a wide-open hatch for avatainment creators to make things up. Which they did. And still do, again and again. Hot and steamy, most often. Mel as a dominatrix. Murder plots. Threesomes. Revenge scenarios.

The latest? The threesome was abducted on Mars by an alien race and Mel was mother to a hybrid species in a different solar system that will one day return to Earth.

After all these years, decades even, these stories still get millions of daily views. She will always marvel that despite everything else that happened on Mars during those fateful weeks, it's their love story that sticks with people.

But not with everyone. There are holdouts. Some descendants of the Five Families have formed themselves into a resistance group that adamantly rejects the heroic narrative that's enveloped Mel, Crucial and Jynks, instead believing that the dynasty of the Five Families should be restored. This small but vocal group insists the official historical narrative covering the years 2075 to 2200—what's now called the Mars Founding to Earth Recovery Period—is wrong. Falsified. They want to see it overturned. Destroyed. Replaced.

Valentine was part of the process to define that period of history. The work was thorough and she, along with the council, stands by it. The questions they wrestled with took more than two decades to resolve.

Questions such as, did the Five Families accumulate unprecedented levels of wealth, which allowed them to establish the gated community on Mars, because of their ingenuity and intelligence? Were they economic and technological geniuses? Uber-humans with superpowers?

This was the story the Five Families told, propagated by Halo across every media channel, prior to the invasion. That they alone could save humanity from itself, from challenges that were in part created by their very act of wealth accumulation and distillation.

After the invasion, historians began asking new questions. Did the original members of the Five Families have mental health issues? Whether they were geniuses or just very lucky was relegated to a secondary query, and the question of if they suffered from an excess of greed, a type of hoarding complex, was elevated. The other question the historians considered was had they perversely redefined empathy as something applicable only to their own genetic tribe? Asked another way, did they suffer from a pathological excess of tribal empathy?

After two decades of study, sifting through billions of data points, witness testimony and other forms of source material, the Universal Council of Historians came to a decision about these and related questions.

Even so, Valentine knows this officially sanctioned historical narrative is fluid, and this fluidity is what the descendants of the Five Families now seek to exploit. Because history, a series of consensus retrospective connected stories, is ever-evolving.

Given this, Valentine has recently determined—making her not quite a pariah but certainly an outlier in her discipline—that history at the grand scale, when you look closely enough, comes down to a choice about what to believe.

This means that what ends up being the most important question, the only question really, about historical accuracy or relevancy, is what motivates the choices underlying belief? These students must learn the skills to discern this motivation, along with the elements of today's lesson, the skills to understand the advantages and limits of various categories of source material.

She allows a question to come through.

"Are the stories about Melinda Hopwire that run on the avatainment channels considered source material?" a student on Mars asks.

"They are source material for a historical analysis of entertainment trends, but not of history itself," Valentine answers.

"Isn't that history too? Aren't they historical facts?"

"It is now a historical fact that you have asked me a question. A century from now, the issue will not be the veracity of that fact but the relevance of it, what is believed about why you asked the question, how many people asked the same question and so on."

Valentine looks at the time and decides to push ahead. "Your question leads us into our next topic. We've discussed the challenges of source material and now we'll be talking about how to sort it. Let's start by considering an example focused on correctly identifying key events. We know that during the first days of the invasion of Mars, Crucial Larsen learned from Jynks Martine that Melinda Hopwire was a member of the resistance."

She pushes more images of Crucial, Jynks and Mel throughout their lives into the collective student feed.

They were so young, she thinks from her current vantage, to have done what they did, to have made such sacrifices.

"After the revelation of Melinda Hopwire's role in the resistance, everything that happened subsequently was in response to this fact. In the sorting of history, this is designated as a Pivot Event. Nothing would ever be the same."

# 8

Jezero is in ruins.

The Grande Dome is broken and battered.

I feel like I'm going to be sick. And not just because of the dangerously low oxygen level in my airhoodie.

Jynks and I are standing on a low ridge overlooking the remains of the city where Mel lives. Where Valentine lives. Where tens of thousands of people live. Or lived. Part of the Grande Dome is flat-out missing and the other part is hanging in tatters, as if someone dropped a rock through a sprout-your-own microgreen saladarium. Smoke rises from a dozen chemical fires across the city, the plumes twisting in the cruel cold of the Choke.

Halo is still down, which means my OCD is forced into local mode, trying to connect to a handful of built-in apps and enhancements that are still running. I magzoom in the direction of Mel's building and then use a few familiar landmarks to get closer.

There's not much left of the building. It's ripped open, rooms exposed, scraps of cloth and plastic swirling out. I hear a ragged intake of breath from Jynks beside me. She's looking at the same thing. Their apartment is still there, but we can look right inside it now because the walls and glass are gone.

Mel could have survived. If she was lucky. Smoldering craters pockmark the ruins around it, but somehow Mel's building was spared a direct hit.

Just below it, bodies are scattered in the street and a few people are moving around, stunned, waiting for help that may never come.

None of them are Mel.

"Let's go," I say. We half run, half slide down the ridge, still dragging Sanders behind us, until we're standing at the shattered edge of the Grande Dome looking at a man looking at us through the opticals of a mounted rail gun, his finger on the trigger. He's wearing a Mars SF uniform and nervous at the sight of strangers dragging a body behind them. Even though we're in uniform, without Halo he doesn't trust his eyes. Or remove his finger from the trigger. He's learning fast.

"Is that you, Commander Martine?" he asks as we get closer.

"Affirmative," Jynks says, throwing a crisp salute. "What's your name?"

"Danton Furl."

"What's the sitrep, Furl?"

She's all business, which is good. He needs that. Maybe we all need that.

He scans the sky nervously. "Asteroids hit everywhere, all at once. Domes, orbital platforms. Halo is down. We've connected to Earth on emergency channels. Their orbital platforms were hit too, and all launch sites were leveled."

She shoots me a quick look. Mars is completely cut off. Adrift. It will be weeks, maybe months, before supply ships can make the run.

"Who's in charge?" she asks.

"No one. I mean, I don't know. You, I guess? Tarteric Hoost is dead."

"For real this time?" I ask.

He doesn't know me and can't run my credentials, but

he already doesn't like me. I don't blame him. I tend to make a bad first impression, and it never really gets better.

"It seems like it. Two other members of the Fist are missing," he says to Jynks, ignoring me. "They hadn't named your replacement yet. No one is running Mars SF. Our headquarters building took a direct hit. Not even sure who is left *to* run it."

"What about the Hive?" I ask.

"A lot of damage, but mostly operational."

"Jynks Martine officially unresigns," I say. "She's in charge again."

A shadow of relief flashes across his face. "Do you have the authority to do that?"

"Yes. I'm a special envoy of the Five Families. That status remains until I am off-planet." I don't think that's exactly true, but who's going to argue?

"Larsen, I don't want to—" Jynks starts to say, but I cut her off.

"You have to. Mars needs you."

"I'm not doing anything until I know," she says.

"Fair." I look at Furl. "See that gonzo out there? It has emergency supplies in the waste ball. Gather a crew to go out there and bring the supplies back and distribute them. And keep on trying to establish communications. Until Halo comes back online, we're working blind. Try setting up some pulse points to carry signals, open only to Mars SF, and route them through Commander Martine."

He looks at Jynks. She nods. I catch Furl by the arm as he's leaving. "And we need recharges for our airhoodies, two glitter guns and a transport that can get us to the Huygens neighborhood. Transport that can accommodate dead weight." I point at Sanders.

"Maybe you should be in charge," Jynks says when Furl is out of earshot.

"My goodwill for others is almost exhausted. This is a job for someone who gives a damn."

Sanders is still color-wheeled. I'm starting to wonder if we dragged him all this way for nothing.

Furl is back soon with our transport.

"Are you kidding me?" I ask.

It's a commandeered airstaurant, a drone-powered automatic dining conveyance. He shrugs and hands us needlers and oxygen tablets. "Best I could do."

"Beats walking, I guess," I say.

It's big enough to seat six around the serving hub, the maximum to maintain a pandemic-platinum rating, so there's room to push Sanders on board.

We launch and slowly make our way above what's left of Jezero. More bodies. So many bodies. And people moving slowly through the wreckage.

The airstaurant serves booze. Grape creams. Perfect for floating above a park with your family and getting pleasantly chatty. Skimming above a conflict zone is rattling me with memories from the Consolidation Wars. I can feel the anxiety and rage starting to grow. I need more than a grape cream.

My hand is shaking as I pull out my second bottle of maple rum and take a pull. I offer it to Jynks. She shakes her head.

"If I start, I don't think I will ever stop."

"Here's the secret. You don't have to. Ever."

We're about 20 meters up. Most of the buildings we pass are damaged and there will be no repair for days or weeks, maybe months. Maybe never. But most buildings on Mars have shelter pods, so hopefully people found refuge—and breathable air—after the attack.

Furl is doing his part. A local network is unfolding and following us. Jynks is blinking out directives and feeding information back so they can focus on helping the living. We've only traveled a few kilometers and she's already talked them through setting up a mobile health cradle in an ex-con bubble, a temporary shelter designed to withstand the extreme conditions of the Choke.

She's good at this. She should be running Mars SF. And probably the Earth SF and the Labor force. Maybe she should be running the whole godsdamned universe.

She's also flying the airstaurant, which she sets down with a thud in front of what's left of their building. Her landings could use some work.

People are walking toward us. We move past them. They can wait. They have to wait. I give one of them the codes and tell him to print out as much food as they can while we're gone.

I let Jynks go first. I owe her that. It's her place and she made the most recent mistakes with Mel. I know it isn't a contest, but most likely I've made more.

The lift isn't working so we take what's left of the emergency stairs up to their floor.

The wall facing out toward the Choke is missing and the air is unbreathable. The doors gape open, the apartment is dark, the power is down.

Jynks goes in fast, gun drawn, expecting trouble, but all she finds is heartbreak. The blast pulped most of the interior, like it was targeted. We search the place high and low, sifting through the wreckage of their lives. There's no sign of her or the cat.

That's a good thing, but Jynks hasn't put it together yet.

"I don't know what to do," she says, slumping against the doorframe, eyes dull.

"She's alive," I say.

Jynks looks at me for a long five seconds. She wants to believe me but can't. "I never took you for an optimist,

Larsen."

"I'm not. But look there." I point at the emergency ambry just inside the door. It's damaged, but empty. "The airhoodies are gone. And I didn't see any sign of the carrier she kept the stupid cat in. Itch? Slip? Wasp?"

"Wisp," Jynks says softly. "She made it out."

"She made it out. Now we just have to find her."

We head downstairs and climb back into the airstaurant, trying to plan our next move while helping distribute as much printed food as this thing can handle for the refugees to stockpile. There's a screech and flash as a billion images flood across our OCDs and millions of disjointed bytes of data bounce around. It's disorienting and painful. I squeeze my eyes shut and curse.

When I open them, Sanders is sitting up. He groans, massages his temples, then looks at me.

"Crucial, how nice to see you. It appears a great deal has happened in a short period of time. Also, an armada of unfamiliar spacecraft is headed toward Mars, seemingly with hostile intent. And I'm very hungry. I see we are in an airstaurant, which is perfect. I shall need to consume a great deal of nutrients to continue functioning."

As we take off, Sanders begins dialing up slabs of printed protein choplets and eating them as fast as he can, which is pretty fast—and pretty loud—since he's a cybanism with what appears to be super-enhanced jaw strength.

# 9

I have a friend who's a historian. Well, she's more than a friend. And more than a historian, I guess—she's a member of the resistance. Lauren Valentine. I hope she's alive.

In the short time I've known her, Valentine has taught me a lot of things. About myself. And forgiveness. And history.

Mars is ruled by the Five Families. According to Valentine, almost a century ago the corporations quit pretending that governments were useful and took over everything. After the decades-long Consolidation Wars, five families, because of their enormous wealth and complete lack of morals, managed to eliminate the competition and brokered a deal that put them in charge forever.

Those families—Tarteric, DuSpoles, Fehrven, Blevin and Singhroy—are ruled by the Fist. The Fist is made up of the most senior, that is, wealthiest, representative of each family.

Right now, only two members of the Fist are alive.

Tarteric Hoost is missing and presumed vaporized. His personal residence dome took a direct hit, clearly intentional. He was a gritty warp belt of a human being, but he knew how to keep Mars running. Someone, or something, wanted him out of the way.

Word is that Blevin Flunt was on a lev-train heading toward Holden dome during the attack. The force of the nearby impact sent the train tumbling into the bottom of a canyon in the Choke. No signs of life. That was probably accidental.

Singhroy Able had the distinction of being killed just *before* the attack. She was ambushed by her nephew's consort, an Earther, who tried to extort a small fortune from the Five Families using the stolen cure for neural tryphoprionia—the fatal Martian brain-wasting disease. It was a good plan, cruel, but it almost worked. Instead, I ended up with the small fortune Able transferred to me as she died in my arms, still worrying about her nephew. The Earther, Kyrinth, was accidentally dragged into space and the Five Families got the cure for the disease about to ravage them all into blathering idiots. Although getting the cure might not matter anymore if everyone dies from the invasion.

That leaves only Fehrven Modo and DuSpoles Koryx, and given they are nowhere to be found in the flesh, they are not yet rising to the role of last leader standing, rallying the survivors. Instead, Modo and Koryx are battered and bruised, beaming over a flickering connection telling Jynks and me to come to their location in Jezero without delay.

Things change quickly on Mars. Not that long ago the Fist held all the cards, and I was a tool good for applying blunt force and tracking down lost items. Now their fancy planet is under attack by an unknown alien force and cut off from the Earth they so disdained. All the supplies that could help them plus all their credits are useless and survival is far from guaranteed.

At least Halo is on, but only partially and with huge gaps of information. Having a feed of patchy data riddled with blank spaces, static and snow is nearly as disorienting as silence. Halo must be conserving resources as it self-repairs and is prioritizing local-only mode, which means we can only direct-connect to each other, with little computational connectivity or support behind the scenes.

But Sanders is back. That's a good outcome. The partially functioning Halo doesn't seem to have affected him. So far, he's all present. And still eating.

Even though it's a long shot, I search for Mel using the diminished Halo as I know Jynks is doing the same. There's no sign of her. Under normal circumstances, death is easy to confirm. Halo quickly returns an NBFD—no biological function detected. That's all the proof you need. If the system can't find you, your data is considered extraneous. You're dead.

I'm not getting an NBFD or anything else about Mel. I even have the nanites in my blood working overtime amplifying Halo to find her, and Essential too, but no luck. I try Valentine. Nothing.

But I'm not getting anything about Jynks either and she's standing right next to me. Halo clearly can't be trusted yet, although it's working well enough for us to be summoned to the mobile field ops version of the Hive. Three Janelles—Janes modified to be smaller and faster—crewed by some worried-looking Mars SF muscle rumble up in a cloud of heat fumes.

After what happened to the lev-train, they're reasonably worried moving vehicles might be targets. They split us up, one in each Janelle, and deploy a defensive weaving pattern to get us across town to the old Interplanetary Embassy. It's the most secure building and mostly standing. Along the way, we pass the remains of the Mars security forces headquarters. It's a crater now. A direct hit. A lot of people died including Canadis Whitsend, probably. Alone in the Terrorium.

Better her than Essential.

I call up a satellite feed and get a patchy overhead visual of the original Hive. The command center of Mars was always intentionally innocuous, buried deep underground to protect it from attack, but a pair of meteors hit it dead center and splashed up a ring of pulverized rock and twisted metal. The shockwaves alone must have pulped everyone and everything close to the surface.

The front of the mobile Hive at the embassy is crumbled, so the Janelles take us around to the back. We're escorted underground, using sputtering drone jackets to drop us down a damaged lift shaft, passing three levels of gnarled, smoking wreckage.

Modo and Koryx are in an ad hoc control center with a dozen scientists and security forces personnel gathered around. They seem happy to see Jynks. And Sanders. Jynks and Sanders are useful.

I don't sense the same excitement when they see me. Especially when I start hitting them with questions.

"What do we know?"

Modo answers. "Thirty-six synthetic asteroids struck targets across Mars and Earth at just past 1900 hours. Our sensor array didn't register their activity until the very last second. Halo was malfunctioning at the time. The asteroids targeted orbital platforms on both planets and population centers but the latter only on Mars."

He points to a number on the corner of the screen. It's in the high thousands and growing. "This is our casualty census on Mars. It's incomplete and still rising."

"What about Earth?"

"Minimal deaths by comparison," Koryx says. "As noted, the attack was aimed at the orbital platforms and all major launch sites, not civilian centers. But transport is crippled. The purpose of the attack on Earth appears to be to cut off Mars, not to damage Earth or its inhabitants."

"Do we know who is responsible?"

"Probably whoever or whatever is piloting these ships," she says, pointing at another screen and flaring it up to full size. On the screen is a representation of Mars surrounded by six blinking lights.

"Bring one in closer," I say.

The image zooms in and my mind crashes.

The ships are huge and weird looking, nothing like the sleek Darts that make the trips between Mars and Earth. These are massive, blunt tubes—rough and almost woolly looking, bristling with little pointy antennae structures— and all trailing thousands of long thin tails out of one end. The tails are hundreds of kilometers long.

I turn to Sanders. "Any insights?"

"This design is unlike anything encountered before on Earth or Mars."

"What are you saying? That these could be alien spaceships?"

"It's impossible to rule that out," he says. "It does not appear they are quantum-powered. They look—" He pauses, as if not trusting his own analysis. "The ships look like giant bacterium."

"All we know is that they were not visible to our long-range sensors until several hours ago when they simply appeared in orbit," Modo says.

"And they haven't made contact?"

Modo shakes his head. "Not a pip."

"Meaning we don't know anything about the people or things operating these ships except that they can shoot meteors, have technology we don't understand and can hide from Halo at will," Jynks says.

"That's the extent of it, except they weren't hiding from Halo," Koryx says. "They took advantage of a vulnerability in Halo's operating system. Just before the attack, someone breached the perimeter of the Halo server system hidden on Deimos. When that breach occurred, Halo went into lockdown to prepare for a full download in case there was an attack."

"And the meteor that hit Deimos was the attack," I say, thinking of Essential.

"Yes. It was coordinated."

Whoever is behind this was waiting for the resistance to find the Halo servers. In her desire to introduce empathy into the system, Essential opened the door to this attack, and whoever is piloting those germ ships dropped a load of synthetic meteors right through it.

And now both planets are at risk.

# 10

As we all stare at the screen, the bacterium-looking ships flare to life. The ends without the trailing filaments open and discharge a spinning swarm of shiny black discs—millions of them—toward the planet. There's a weird metallic whistling sound in our crackling feeds as the discs fly in unison like a flock of rat-birds toward the planet.

The blue tube-ships appear to be shitting out weapons.

"That can't be good," Jynks says.

What in the eternal tall-finger is happening now? I hate this planet, I've always hated this planet, and now I hate it even more. There is no end to the depth of my hatred. As if the terminal intrigues and Earth-crushing greed of the rich and bored aren't enough, now we've got an interstellar invader in squiggly paramecium ships crapping out clouds of what are most likely weapons.

"Sanders, are those weapons?" I ask.

"Almost certainly, Crucial. While this is unfamiliar technology, I'm able to access rudimentary information because they are using fairly outdated coding parameters. It's so old, it's possibly intended as an insult."

"What's their target?"

"Given the sheer number of discs, it would appear the target is us. Or, more precisely, all of you. Humans. I will require additional data to offer any more specifics. And I presume gathering that data might be lethal."

Mars SF is tracking the swarm on-screen. First, it splits apart gracefully, and then smaller clouds spin out in different directions, looping and swirling in an almost hypnotizing synchronized way. A large mass reaches the level of the Grande Dome's cracked top, collecting and hovering there like a toxic cloud, so dense it blocks the weak sunlight trickling into the wrecked city. The thin bottom edge of the tornado disc-cloud spins almost all the way to the ground.

The whistling stops and the silence seems worse. The discs are hanging there, slowly spinning.

"Order your people to engage the invaders," Koryx says.

"I don't think that's a good idea," I say.

"I was talking to the head of Mars security."

"I don't think it's a good idea either," Jynks says.

"It's not an idea, it's an order."

Jynks clenches her jaw. "Furl, you still out there?" she asks through her OCD.

"Affirmative."

"Take a team and move closer to the discs. Do not engage yet. We need to know what the hell we are dealing with."

They redirect their feeds so we can track progress. Furl and his small team move closer, weapons raised.

"I don't know, Commander," he says, his voice crackling on the disrupted local channel. "Never seen anything like it. No markings. No open connections."

"Could it be alien?" I ask Sanders.

"The odds favoring the existence of nonhuman life-forms are very large," Sanders says. "We simply cannot rule out anything until we have more data."

"I don't like this," I say. "Fall back, Furl."

"Belay that," Modo says. "Engage one of the discs."

"You don't have to follow their orders, Furl," I say.

But he's a soldier and used to doing what he's told.

He raises his glitter gun, aims at the closest disc and shoots a single flechette.

It ricochets, deflected by the high rate of spin.

Then there's a flash of bright green and Furl and his squad are gone down to the ankles. Like, completely gone. There's a thin layer of slime where they had been standing.

Before I can even say "What the prok?" all hells blaze up. The cloud of demon discs swirls around in a whistling maelstrom and then disperses out across Jezero. People are screaming and running for cover. The discs fan out and burrow themselves shallowly into the soil, their just visible outlines almost touching, in a ring surrounding all of Jezero.

"They have encircled this entire dome," Sanders says. "And every dome on Mars."

We've been mined. Booby-trapped. We are in real trouble here. And not only this godsforsaken planet, but Earth too.

On the western side of the dome there's an explosion followed by a flash of green. Then screams. Then silence.

"Someone tried to cross the perimeter," Sanders says. "Twelve dead."

It's a warning, showing us what they can do.

I don't think this day can get much worse.

A digital flare suddenly crashes through our feeds, the syntax odd and broken.

"Attention citizens of Mars," a human-like voice says. "Your planet is under new ownership. Resistance will be met with death and termination. Give us the location of the Halo server system or we will destroy everyone on this planet."

I stand corrected. It just got worse.

"And bring forward the scientist Melinda Hopwire, dead or alive. Or expect terrible things to happen."

The transmission ends.

Well, shitjacks. It just got so much worse.

# 11

A craft appears outside the embassy, an unfamiliar flier, a knobby sphere like a kinetic super bounce ball with a hundred stubby tufts of bristles dotting the surface.

It wasn't there, then it was. Just like that.

The voice targets our comms. "DuSpoles Koryx, Fehrven Modo and underlings assisting you: We request you join us to discuss the terms of your surrender. Immediately, upon penalty of death for failure to comply."

You always imagine meeting an advanced alien race on Mars is going to be a positive, uplifting experience. Or at least less chaotic.

Of course, if they've been watching, why wouldn't they come in flaming? We're terrible. We destroyed a planet, as well as each other.

"And leave your weapons behind," the transmission continues. "Failure to comply will result in aeroflashing."

I assume that means being exploded into green slime by the discs. But I'm not asking for clarification. I don't want to find out.

Expecting the worst, and now unarmed, we make our way to the surface. Once we're standing outside the wrecked main door, a luminous ramp descends from the hovering craft.

Two humanoid figures emerge, surrounded by soldiers.

One looks male-like, with thick strands of red hair moving independently like snakes. The other looks female-like, unusually tall with blindingly white, straight hair falling nearly to her feet. They look almost human, but not quite, with skeletally thin faces and extremely narrow, pinched, upturned noses.

They descend arm in arm, as if they're floating a meter above the ramp itself.

"I'm kind of disappointed," I say. "I was hoping for some extra appendages or jelly faces or something. They look almost like regular humans."

"They're worse than regular humans," Koryx says, her face twisted with anger.

"I feel like, later, we're going to regret not shooting one of the aliens in the face right now," I say.

"They are most definitely not aliens. They are failures we thought we were long done with," Modo says. He's equally livid. "Stand down, let's hear their terms."

A grin passes over the man's face at the obvious discomfort his arrival is causing, and that seems to cause his hair to twist spontaneously and independently with what seems some kind of interpretative dancing glee. The woman remains serene.

"Spilla Hucksworth," Koryx says, sounding like she just tasted pigeon vomit. "I should have known your wretched family was behind this."

Oh, for the love of binomial aggravation. There's a sixth family.

"How dare you," Modo says.

The woman begins talking. Her voice carries well, as if amplified, but there's no visible technology. Maybe she had her voice box worked on. It's also filling our feeds.

"I am Plesca of the Family Hucksworth. I have a message for the people of both Mars and Earth. We are in control. We have liberated you from the tyranny of the Five Families. Expect a glorious future of service as you realize your true potential."

There's a weird, oily mist in the air and I realize—suddenly, nauseatingly—that it stinks. The air is dense and putrid like decaying garbage; it's leaching into our airhoodies. The stink-mist surrounding us is like a damp toxic cloud. Prok, what kind of bioweapon is this?

I wave my hand across my face but there's no escape. Jynks is finger-pinching her nose too. If it's a virus, we're done.

I look around. A small crowd has gathered on the east rim of the blasted side of the area where the Mars SF building used to stand. Probably Earth lottery workers. Their faces contort in disgust as they pick up the smell too.

"Sanders, what is that awful smell?"

"It appears the ships of the Hucksworth family are powered by a bacterial reaction. The byproduct released in the energy conversion may be unpleasant to human olfactory senses."

"*May* be unpleasant? It smells like we were attacked by killer fart ships."

"From a very superficial exterior analysis, it appears the Hucksworths and their guards have modified their nasal systems to mitigate the impact."

That explains their weird pointy noses, like they've been permanently altered to be pinched almost shut.

"With their ship in idle mode, the odor should dissipate in two minutes and thirty-seven seconds," Sanders says. "You should experience relief very soon."

He activates the timer in my feed for a fart-ship relief countdown. "Thanks, buddy."

I try to block out the smell and focus on what Plesca is saying.

"—absolute fidelity is expected. Welcome to your future."

"And what do you want?" Koryx asks.

"Everything," Spilla says. "Everything you took from us, everything you amassed since exiling us and everything we once stood to gain. More specifically and immediately, we want the location of the Halo backup servers and we want Staff Scientist Melinda Hopwire taken into custody."

"Why on Mars would you want Melinda Hopwire?" Koryx asks. Her surprise seems genuine. Unlike mine.

"You and your peers are such bungle-holes," Spilla says. "Oblivious. She's part of the resistance, her mission is to introduce an empathy hack into the system. She cannot succeed. We want to maintain Halo with the necessary tweaks to our advantage. Tell us where Halo downloaded and turn her over, and you'll be free to join the labor force and live your potential in peace."

Modo and Koryx look shocked, eyes wide and panicked, under their airhoodies. The thought of joining the labor pool has rattled them more than the invasion of Mars, more than discovering Mel is a traitor.

"You cannot be serious," Modo says.

"Deadly."

"We don't know where the Halo download is," Koryx says. "And the damage you caused to the system means we can't locate Hopwire either. We haven't been monitoring her that closely. Why would we?"

A wind roars in from the Choke, making everything gritty and gaspy and it's hard to hear.

"What did you say?" Spilla yells.

"I said come down here," Koryx says. "So we can hear you properly."

"I will not take one step for you," Spilla says in a high-pitched voice. "Not after all you've done. You come up here."

"Absolutely not," Modo says as Koryx defiantly stomps her foot. "You're the ones who attacked our planet. The least you can do is step onto Martian soil, soaked as it is with the blood of patriots."

Funny how war turns sacrifice into something shiny and special. The soil of both planets is soaked with the blood of countless pointless deaths, but they are conveniently overlooked.

Plesca gives Spilla a little nudge, but he's not moving. They wait for the wind to die down and then continue shouting at each other. The whole thing would be comical if every human life wasn't hanging in the balance.

"We don't know where Hopwire is," Koryx says. "Or if she's even alive."

"She's alive," Spilla says. He nods to Plesca who stops droning on about sacrifice and service and how debt is a patriotic duty and throws a clear holo-marble out between us. It hovers there and projects a 3D vid-screen.

It's footage of Mel. She looks beautiful. My breath catches in my throat. Jynks freezes. The shot is from inside their undamaged apartment, before the attack, before Deimos was destroyed and before Halo shut down. The Hucksworths were watching Mel prior to the attack. How long had they been surveilling her?

I put my OCD on local-record to capture every detail.

We see Mel from behind. She's looking out the window of her apartment. From this vantage, we can't tell what she's looking at, but it's clear from her body language that she's alarmed. She turns and grabs a prepper-pac from under the console. Prepper-pacs are totally off-grid; illegal seven ways to Saturn. How did she get one? I mean, I'm glad she has one—it has survival gear, food and usually a weapon.

I glance at Jynks but her face is blank.

Mel slips on the cat carrier and drops Wisp into place, grabs a pair of airhoodies from the ambry and she's gone.

She's being watched by a family of psychopaths while synthetic meteors are about to level Mars, and she takes her cat. Of course. Door open, door closed. Gone. Poof. Just like that. A few seconds later, we see through the window exploding lights from the first wave of meteors.

The vid goes black and the marble floats back to Plesca.

"Melinda Hopwire was in a surprising rush to leave," Spilla says. "Why didn't she simply await her fate? And since then, she has found a way to disable the tracking elements of her OCD, making her unreachable until Halo is fully back online. She has complicated things and put many others at risk because of her selfishness."

Modo looks at Koryx and shrugs. They both look at me like a beetler looking at a Settling Day sheetmeat roast with all the trimmings.

"Hopwire is no concern to us. You can have her, a hundred of her," Modo shouts up to Spilla. "But we don't know where she is, or the servers."

"You don't know the new location of the servers?" Spilla asks. "I find that hard to believe."

"That information died with Tarteric Hoost."

"That old titanium cog," Spilla says. "Are you certain he's dead?"

"Your asteroid vaporized his dome, so yes, we're certain."

"Our asteroid cannons are magnificent, aren't they?" Spilla looks around at the rubble of Jezero. "Although perhaps we were a bit enthusiastic."

Thousands of people died due to their "enthusiasm" and tens of thousands are suffering. I'm tempted to put a round of flechettes right up his narrow pointy nose but the perimeter of half-buried spinning death discs make me feel especially patient and mortal.

"While we don't know where Hopwire is, we know who can find her, and by extension, the servers into which Halo downloaded, assuming she has that information," Koryx says. And then she points at me. "Crucial Larsen has proven a remarkably lucky and tenacious investigator."

That was almost a compliment.

Plesca and Spilla look at me like I've got the Martian spongy brain-wasting disease.

"The Earther and the head of Mars security next to him"—Koryx nods at Jynks—"are intimately familiar with Hopwire. They can find her. You have our word."

I don't think their word means much.

"Hey, snake for brains," I shout up to Spilla. "We're not going to bring Mel back here for you to execute."

"I don't like him," Spilla says. "Execute him and send a termination squad after Melinda Hopwire. She was last seen heading northeast."

"Hold on," I say. "You make a good case. We'll find her. Just please, you know, bestow your benevolent mercy upon her."

Spilla glares at me, and I can tell he wants to slime-explode me but also wants to resolve things quickly. He looks at Modo and Koryx.

"You have 49 and a half hours."

"And if they are unsuccessful on either score?" Koryx asks.

"Mars will be wiped clean. We'll pulse Halo and replace it with our own system, and all people living on Mars will be relocated to Earth."

"Why are you doing this?" Modo asks.

"You, of all people, know why."

The staircase draws them back into their spherical fart

ship, and with a wet burp of power it disappears, clotting the air with stink.

My eyes are watering. The stink is so bad that I may retch. "What in the name of dark matter are you two playing at?"

Modo shakes his head. "We're not playing at anything. We must honor their demands. Follow us into the embassy so we can plan the search for Hopwire accordingly."

This is the craziest situation I've ever been in, but at least Mel still has a chance and maybe the rest of us do too. Jynks, Sanders and I follow the last members of the Fist into their mobile headquarters.

# 12

As we make our way into the building, Sanders stays close. He's got something to say.

"Crucial, thank you for bringing me from Port Zunil," he finally says.

"Think nothing of it."

"Thinking nothing about anything is outside my cognitive parameters. My analysis makes clear that while I would have been disoriented upon reactivation without the context presented by your physicality, I would nevertheless have adjusted in milliseconds. Further, leaving me behind would have meant significantly less risk exposure for you and Jynks Martine. Not everyone would have carried a nonfunctional cybanism with them across a dangerous traverse of Mars under hostile circumstances."

"What are friends for?" I ask.

"Almost certainly not that. Interestingly, while the evolutionary path of friendship in humans as a strategy to enhance median reproductive success is still contested by scientists—"

I hold up my hand. "Stop. I've gotten used to you and you mostly don't annoy me. But that's as close to a friend as I've got. Although I am a little worried about your sudden appetite."

"It is puzzling. Even at this moment, I am significantly nutritionally depleted. It appears that the disconnection from Halo has affected my processing requirements."

"We'll find something inside."

Modo and Koryx don't speak as they lead us deep into the embassy. Not sure why there's an embassy on Mars. Wishful thinking, I suppose, about what discoveries might be made, what new alien species encountered.

Inside the damaged building, the various ports and screens crackle and fizz out sparks as we make our way to the sublevels.

"We need to plot your route," Koryx says as we arrive at the mostly attached door of what is likely a shielded safe room. "We can access maps in the consult alcove here."

She leads us into a smaller room and then waits for Jynks to push the damaged door closed behind us. I don't see any maps or functioning screens.

"If you think we're going to track down Mel for that sharp-nosed son of a beetle mold—"

Modo shakes his head to silence me and activates a jammer. Turns out, they just want a little privacy.

"We won't have long," Koryx says. "We must assume the Hucksworths are monitoring everything, and they will not tolerate a lengthy disconnect."

"I haven't seen the Hucksworth name in years," Jynks says. "I thought their lineage was closed and rebranded in the Consolidation Wars."

"It was," Koryx says. "Or so we thought. Their living brick technology was the last surviving competitor of the Fehrven's myco-cement product, but the Fehrvens were better marketers."

"That's a nice way of saying more brutal," I say.

"We won, they lost," Modo says. "We thought they had all been assimilated into the labor pool. Apparently, they were more resourceful than anticipated."

Here we go again. Every human at the mercy of these

greedy assholes' egos. It never changes, their games never stop. Greed is like a dark form of emotional gravity, always pulling the worst behaviors out of people.

Some people. Not everyone. But most. Yes, most. I feel the weight of that truth pushing down on my shoulders, a sense of despair so heavy my chest tightens. When will all this end?

"We need you to find the location of the Halo backup servers before they do," Modo says. "We cannot let the servers fall into enemy hands."

"Sorry, they're your enemies, not mine," I say. "I'm looking for Mel."

"You can do both," Koryx says. "You know they'll kill Hopwire if given the chance. We won't. If we can protect the integrity of Halo, get it back online, we can fight the Hucksworths. But if they access the system first, or pulse it, they will be in control of everything."

"Would that be so bad?"

"Have you looked around Mars recently?" Modo asks. "They will level this planet, and all of us, including Hopwire. And I can't imagine they would go easier on your precious Earth."

He makes a good point. Better the devil you know.

Better yet, no devils at all. But that's not a choice, not yet at least.

What worries me is that the evidence is overwhelmingly piling up that the Hucksworths managed to infiltrate the resistance, or worse, started it. That's how they launched their invasion right after Essential identified the location of the Halo servers, and why they destroyed Deimos when Halo went into lockdown.

It makes me heartsick to think all her work and passion for change have been destroyed by the machinations of these wealthy jerks. But Essential couldn't have known they were playing her and the rest of her merry team of naïve do-gooders all along.

I feel the blanket of apathy settling over and numbing me. The smart play is to not care. But I need to fight it this time, not fall deeper into that comfortable safety.

The shimmering polyps who killed Essential want to kill Mel before she taints the whole system with empathy, just so they can take possession of Halo and tilt every scrap of resource toward them. All while Mars burns and people suffer because of their ruthless devotion to the gods of avarice.

Just another perfect, heart-breaking day on a planet named for the god of war. The Five Families really should have colonized Pluto, named for the god of the underworld and—so I was told—greed. I'm guessing the minus 200-degree temperatures there are a bit off-putting though, even for those richer than gods.

"Obviously, Hopwire will try to find the backup servers," Koryx says. "You find her, stop her and tell us where Halo is now residing, and she walks away unharmed. We can reinitialize Halo into active mode operating on our behalf."

They think I'm stupid. They don't give a plugged ghostcoin about the fate of Mars or Earth. Or Mel. They need something to bargain with. It's almost impossible to believe that they lost track of Halo with the death of Tarteric Hoost. It was idiotic he was the only one who knew where Halo would auto-download when it got blistered on Deimos. But because of that mistake, they're left with one play, a long-shot. Retain possession of the most valuable asset on Mars, or destroy it so they can be of value to the invaders in other ways.

I don't care about any of it. But I want to find Mel before they do.

"Fine, I'm in. Can we take Sanders with us? He has certain skills that may be useful."

"Yes. Of course. There are no official records confirming he's a cybanism, so the Hucksworths won't know. But be careful what you say. If they find out, he'll be decommissioned, or wiped and reprogrammed."

"I would not care for that," Sanders says.

"Especially if you were integrated into their fart power, like those damn ships," I say.

"Do not let the Hucksworths take possession of Halo, wherever it has downloaded," Modo says. "Destroy the servers if you must. Secured or destroyed, nothing in between."

Like don't let them be infected with empathy, I think, but keep that to myself.

There's a ruckus outside and above, lots of shouting and clumping. Sounds like someone angry is headed our way.

"They're here," Jynks says.

"Sanders, display a topo of the area," I say.

He nods, rolls his eyes back and displays a clip from *Fall Streak*, a long-running avatainment series about Martian prospectors from the early days.

The door bursts open and three Hucksworth goons push in, bulbous guns raised. They look at us looking at the projection.

It's a classic scene. Uncle Stoon is leaning in to kiss Lady Improbable and then she says her famous line, "Blazing nebulae, not with you, not even with a clone of my clone."

"We're, uh, having a little trouble connecting to the local grid," I say.

The image flickers and is replaced by a grid map of the area outside of Mars.

"Probably because you're in a shielded room," one of the soldiers says. He has the same tight little pointed nose as the Hucksworths, but otherwise looks perfectly competent and quite willing, and able, to pull the trigger. Not sure I want to find out what those odd, fat little guns do.

"As I was saying, we should start our search in this quadrant," Jynks says, pointing to a gorge leading away from Jezero. "There are several habitations along this route where Melinda Hopwire might take shelter."

"Sanders, end transmission," I say. "And thanks for the flashback. I haven't thought about *Fall Streak* in years."

He gives me a worried look and says too quietly for the Hucksworth goons to hear, "These anomalies are very distressing, and I am still very hungry."

"That's a perfectly human response to an invasion," I say loudly, glaring at the goons. "Let's get going. Grab some gear, team."

"Not so fast, enzyme-breath," the leader says. "We're coming with you."

"We don't need help, least of all yours."

"It's not a request. Since the first thing you did was convene in a shielded room, our confidence in you is low."

"All a misunderstanding. I'm usually good at instilling confidence. I think we're going to insist on traveling alone. But feel free to monitor us."

He raises the gun. "I'm willing to bet a wet kiss from a polarizer would clear things up."

Now I'm positive I don't want to know what the little fat guns do.

"Welcome to the team," I say.

We head topside and secure some bug-out pacs from Mars SF, carefully screened for weapons by our new friends from the Family Hucksworth, and commandeer a pair of wedges—small, practically indestructible hybrids, half-rocket, half-tread and all uncomfortable but perfect for a close recon of rough terrain.

We're about to load up when someone yells my name. A woman someone.

Valentine.

She breaks through the ring of people milling around us and smiles a crooked smile that clearly comes at a high cost. Under her airhoodie, her face is smudged with ash and an overworked bandage is affixed to her shoulder. Her clothes are ripped and her beautiful hair is a tangled mess. There's a child at her waist, peeking nervously from behind her, eyes filled with fear and curiosity and hope.

It's Seneca.

The guards raise their guns as they advance.

"Let her through," I say.

Valentine puts Seneca down, takes her hand and steps forward. Seneca is limping. As she gets close she stumbles, and I kneel to catch them both and pull them in tight.

"I got you." My heart is bursting with gratitude and relief.

"No, Crucial, I've got you." Then she whispers softly in my ear, "You're like a shield for us."

She's sending a message. I goose the nanites into action and build a safety bubble. She's lookspeaking to my local feed inside a fractured call for medical supplies coming out of Holden.

"Essential is in trouble." The words flash across my feed like the weaponized meteors. Only these are giving me hope, not terror.

I blink out a shaky response. "I thought she was gone."

She hugs me close, trying to extend the moment. "Me too. But I'm getting an emergency beacon. A distress call, from Phobos. On our secret channel."

"All right, Chancellor," the guard says, "break it up. We're on a mission."

The next message from Valentine hits me hard: *She's running out of oxygen. She has hours, not days.*

Frozen waste balls. Essential is alive and in trouble. How can I possibly launch a lunar rescue from a planet under siege while chaperoned by armed goons with pointy noses and big guns?

Time to get creative.

"I said stand back," the man says, roughly pulling Valentine away and giving her a shove with the palm of his hand that sends her stumbling.

"Easy, buddy," I say.

He snarls and raises his polarizer. "I'm not your buddy. You can call me Team Lead," he says. "One more delay and we'll snap your glutes with a lo-fi blast from the polarizer. And when you're done twitching out, we'll throw you, the woman and all your little friends on that prison transport with the rest of the dregs of Mars security forces for a quick trip to our lunar penal colony."

*Our* lunar penal colony. Guess the Hucksworths took that over too.

He points over my shoulder at a commandeered Mars SF ship warming up on a makeshift launch pad. "We're shipping out in an hour. Want me to reserve you a spot?"

"I'm thinking about it."

Modo and Koryx are watching, horrified as their plan to find Mel and maintain their value to the invaders unravels in real time before their eyes.

The Hucksworth goon pretends to be thoughtfully giving me some extra time. "Well, please take your time. Certainly, don't rush on my account."

I don't like being pushed around, and I don't like anyone pushing Valentine around. But there is a mission to consider. And Mel. But also, Essential. The smart credits are on sacrificing Essential. She knew the risk.

I relax a little, smile even. Everyone breathes a sigh of relief, including the Hucksworth asshole.

That's his mistake. I never *really* relax.

I punch him right in his tiny, surgically altered nose. It's a good, solid punch. I'd been saving it up for a while. He's out like a faulty diode and hits the ground hard, his head bouncing from the impact. Good thing he has a helmet on.

His friends curse and pop the triggers on their guns. I really didn't want to find out how they work. Turns out they discharge a wet, sticky electricity. One minute I'm standing there with my fists clenched and a string of curse words lined up, the next I'm falling over, convulsing and shaking, my teeth grinding, and people are yelling. Even as my vision is sparking and fading, I see a stampede of other Hucksworth goons clamping cuffs onto Jynks and Sanders.

Looks like we're all getting a free trip to Earth's Penal and Incarceration Center on the moon.

# 13

When electricity finally stops pouring through my veins, every corpuscle aches and it feels like I might have ground my teeth into dust.

An enormous Hucksworth thug hauls me up, pins my arms tight behind my back and cuffs me at the wrists. My vision is blurry from the polarizer jolt and my skin feels like it's trying to split itself from my body. If my muscle fibers weren't twitching from internal fires, I'd head-butt this man-beast or stomp on his foot. Instead, I give him the dirtiest look I can muster and swear, but it's possible I'm just drooling.

"That was quite impulsive, even for you," Sanders says as they shove me next to him.

"Yeah, impulsiveness is one of my best qualities." I look out across the line of gawkers, trying to bring the pulsating faces into focus.

Finally, I spot her. Standing still, holding Seneca's hand. She looks worried. I try to give her a reassuring smile, but my lips are numb.

Fehrven Modo and DuSpoles Koryx look worried too, but not for my well-being. They stand together, talking quietly and shaking their heads, occasionally looking over at me with disgust. I know what they're thinking—what the prok are they going to do now that their one trusted and trackable resource, Sanders, is headed to a lunar penal colony with me and Jynks, and won't be around to feed them information to help them better position themselves to cut a deal with the Hucksworths.

"Walk," the goon says, giving me a shove. "Or you get another wet kiss."

He points to the transport about a quarter kilometer to the east, the big one headed for the penal colony. The hold hatch is open in the rear and members of the Mars SF, glum in their own cuffs, are being prodded inside.

I'm still a little unsteady so Jynks and Sanders hold me up as we move toward the ship.

"What the prok is wrong with you, Larsen?" Jynks hisses at me.

"The mission parameters changed."

"You want to tell me *how* they changed? What is more important than finding Mel?"

"Not right now. Too many people watching and recording."

"I swear to the ghost of Schrodinger's cat, if anything happens to her because of this, I will kill you myself," Jynks says.

She probably could, too. But one problem at a time.

"Stop talking," the goon says.

If Jynks knew the real reason I fist-brushed that guy's face, I think she'd be impressed by my creativity on the fly. I need to get off this red rock and get to Essential, so why not let the enemy give me a ride? Triaging the problems, Essential's lack of oxygen is the most immediate threat. Mel is tough and savvy. I can come back to find her, but Essential has only one chance.

What I need to do now is figure out how to get off the transport carrier mid-flight, land on Phobos, get Essential off Phobos, get us both back to Mars, find Mel, find the Halo servers, deploy the prokking empathy hack—

Wait, what? I did *not* just think that. I am not a revolutionary.

Valentine catches up with me and the guard raises his weapon. She looks at him unflinchingly and even though you can't see his eyes behind the security-grade airhoodie, his shoulders slump and he leans slightly away. A crack of shared humanity between oppressor and oppressed.

Sanders turns around and Valentine smiles at him. "How are you doing, Sanders?"

"Very well, Chancellor. I am having a completely human response to this invasion—increased hunger. Because I am very human."

"Don't oversell it, buddy," I say quietly.

I take a harder look at Valentine. She's tired. Her face is worn and she looks nervous, scared even. I flash for an instant on the night we shared in the desert, down in the sunbelt on Earth, and feel the memory of the warmth of her skin.

I wish I could do more for her and Seneca.

"We'll be fine," she says, picking up on my thoughts. "Do what *has* to be done."

"Where will you go?"

"Singhroy University. It wasn't too badly damaged. They're building a refugee camp for academics. Hopefully there will be enough air and provisions to see us through until the situation is resolved."

I'm not entirely sure what "resolved" looks like.

"I'll find you as soon as I can," I say.

"Be careful. And Crucial, don't forget, you don't have to do everything alone. You *can* rely on others."

"Okay, move along," the guard says. I guess he got tired of being human.

He shoves me through the cargo door. Sanders and Jynks are already inside, along with a few dozen others, all cuffed, dirty and defeated. The door closes with a booming clang, blocking out light and hope. The hull is big enough for only a dozen people and that means we have little room to spare. Using the pin-lamp in my hoodie, I make my way through the darkness to Sanders and Jynks and slide down next to them.

Jynks won't meet my eyes.

"I hope they have an adequate food supply at the penal colony," Sander says. "My charge is rapidly diminishing."

The ship rises in a clumsy rocking motion and blasts off. Twenty minutes later, we set down at Port Zunil. Impressive. Took us a whole lot longer to travel this far in the gonzo.

Even though the place was wrecked during the attack, it's cleared up now. The assault was precise; parts of the port are functioning as if nothing happened. Those parts being the ones supporting the lunatic endgame of the Hucksworth clan, whatever that might be.

Apparently, incarceration is high on their list, given the designated penal ship port is in full swing.

After landing, we're shuffled into a crowd of more than a thousand people being herded onto a lineup of big, slow penal transport ships ready to take off from an emergency launch pad unrolled like a sheet of titanium flash paper.

On either side of the dense column of prisoners are hundreds of guards, each alert and holding a weapon I don't recognize—a variant of a glitter gun but with a narrow snout, like a cannon crossed with a boot. Where the hell were these needle-nosed bungholes hiding out all these years with this crazy technology?

A few of the guards are wearing Mars SF insignia. I nudge Jynks. She looks and shakes her head but doesn't seem surprised. Why would she? In a universe where wealth rules, almost anyone can be bought, even Mars security.

We're moved deeper into the cargo hold and I wake up the nanites to give me some cover as I scour the operating specs of the penal ship. There are twelve security escape pods spaced evenly around. They are designed for two people and stocked with minimal supplies—basically exit options for guards if they need to abandon ship. Without the prisoners.

We follow the line of people boarding in lockstep. Minutes later, the hatch door slams shut. We take off our airhoodies as thin oxygen floods the hold and then the gravity stabilizers kick on. There are easily two hundred or more bodies squeezed into the belly of our transport. Young, old, very old, children.

A silky voice enters our feeds.

*Welcome to the universal reign of the Hucksworth family. We are a generous family and will provide a comfortable life for those living on Earth or Mars who adhere to three rules. One: Do not speak against the family or our gods. Two: Do your part to ensure a good, safe life for all by following our directives. Three: Find pride and dignity in your assigned work.*

It's the voice of that horrible Plesca Hucksworth.

Some of the poor saps around us look hopeful now. They're thinking this doesn't sound like a speech to people headed to prison.

The ship lurches up into the atmosphere, sending us all tumbling.

"Crucial, do you have anything to eat?" Sanders whispers. "I would hate to lose power."

It's hard to get to it with my hands cuffed, but I dig through my back pocket and find one of those self-heating fermented yeast balls that I grabbed before we left Zunil when the meteors hit. It's fitting that prison food is our only option. The yeast ball is coated in Mars dust and pocket lint but before I can even warn him, he grabs it from my hand and pops it in his mouth. Doesn't even pull the self-heating tab.

"Sanders, how did you get out of the cuffs?"

"I broke them. I'm quite strong."

"You're playing human now, remember? Keep your arms behind your back."

"Of course, I apologize."

The blonde Hucksworth is still droning her soothing propaganda. Her fake-gracious tone is almost vomit-inducing.

*This ship is scheduled to arrive at the Lunar Penal Colony orbiting Earth in approximately two days. Your actions on Mars have been identified as being misaligned with one or more of our three rules. The length of your incarceration and type of remediation steps will be shared with you upon arrival. Our goal is for you to be a productive and happy member of our vibrant community.*

There's a murmur in the ranks, people are complaining, saying they didn't do anything wrong, they want to go back to Mars.

*Welcome to the universal reign of the Hucksworth family. Have a good day!*

"Can you get my cuffs off too?" I ask.

"Easily."

On the other side of Jynks, two small girls—twins—are crying. They're no more than five years old. Separated from their parents, maybe a data entry mistake. Jynks whispers to the girls and they snuggle up close.

She turns to me. "I didn't think this kind of cruelty was even possible."

"You're too young to remember the Consolidation Wars," I say. "Believe me. There's no bottom."

Her gaze at me is empty, and in that emptiness, I see a reflection of sorts, a well of constant sorrow always slightly below the surface.

"Listen, I have to tell you something," I say.

"If Mel is harmed, I'll never forgive you. But I'm not sorry you punched him."

"Yeah, about that. It wasn't just me lashing out. Jynks, there's a lot about me you don't know."

"Like what? You're a mediocre investigator with a lucky streak, a drinking problem and self-sabotaging anger issues?"

"Fine, there are a *few* things about me you don't know."

I direct the nanites to give me cover for what I'm about to say. I lookspeak what comes next, so it goes right into her feed. I've got her attention now.

"Don't talk out loud. The important thing you should know is that I'm about to break out and take Sanders with me."

"How the prok do you think you're going to do that since this conversation is being monitored and analyzed and—"

"I said don't talk out loud," I lookspeak.

She goes quiet for a few seconds, and I know she's putting the pieces together. Finally, she smiles and shakes her head. She lookspeaks her answer back in big red font. "You shiny pellet of rat dung. You've had the nanites all along."

"Correct. And now I'm taking Sanders and we're going to get into an escape pod so I can rescue my sister, Essential, who is currently stranded on Phobos. No, she's not in the Terrorium. It's actually Whitsend. Long story. After that, I'll go back to Mars and find Mel and help her with whatever the big thing is that she's supposed to do for the resistance, no questions asked."

"You're taking me with you."

"The escape pod holds two."

"I'll get my own pod then."

I look her steady in the eyes and lookspeak slowly, clearly. "This is going to be hard for you. But the best thing you can do is ride to the penal colony, take control, then come back to Mars with all the people and all the weapons you can find."

"You can't stop me."

"No, I can't. But it would be a mistake, although it's your mistake to make. And I've certainly made my share of mistakes where Mel's involved."

"Way more than your share."

The ship is rocking and groaning as we push higher into the ionosphere. It's almost time.

I turn to Sanders. "Take off my cuffs." He does it with a flick of his finger. "And do Jynks too." I look back at her. "Whatever you choose to do, free hands will help." Then I nod at the girls. "If you stay, watch over those two."

There's a long pause and she says, "Good luck."

With the nanites shielding us from digital surveillance, Sanders and I move into the main passageway. Accessing the door sets off an alarm. A bunch of alarms. It is a prison transport ship, after all.

I half expect Jynks to follow, but instead she secures the door behind us.

Sanders and I spring toward the nearest security pod, slide in as splats of polarizer discharges crackle against the hatch when I close it—I can feel the electricity tingling in my fingers and forearms—and hit the release button.

Angry needle-nosed faces are glaring at us through the thick windows facing the hull.

There's a whoosh of compressed air and we're popped out into space.

# 14

The class is settling and Valentine is almost ready to begin. Today's lesson, as dictated by the curricula committee of the Universal Council of Historians, is to teach students how to distinguish when, why and how an established historical consensus narrative should be revised. Are the changes legitimate—say, due to the discovery of new source material—or are they illegitimate attempts to serve the goal of domination?

How does one know the difference?

She will use the example of a new resistance group who insists on promoting the legitimacy of the Five Families. The group believes the invasion of Mars five decades ago was staged, that the Variance was always part of the Five Families and betrayed them to seize control for their own benefit.

This retelling of history also argues that the wealth and resources of the Five Families were stolen and must be repatriated to the descendants.

While it's ludicrous, and Valentine knows just how ludicrous from personal experience, the narrative can be stretched to fit a subset of source data in a way that results in a small probability of reality. Infinitesimally small.

And yet it has proven enough of a probability to sway close to 20 million followers. The scenario reinforces what they want to believe. She doesn't understand why people respond to fake history.

Today, everyone is adequately cared for and all have opportunities to achieve or create, people are safe and secure, yet some still want more. Specifically, they want the most for themselves and markedly less for those they've identified as unworthy.

So, the cycle repeats itself, Valentine thinks, and then she sighs. Is there anyone more cynical than an aging historian?

This thought thread is giving her a headache, which she could resolve with a simple command to block the pain signal receptors, but she elects to honor the discomfort.

Seneca would think her a foolish old woman for consciously suffering, but Seneca doesn't remember the bygone days when Valentine relied on suffering to stay motivated, to stay focused, to stay alive. In a way, her embrace of the discomfort—and the fact that she grew accustomed to it—is what gave her the strength to keep moving back then in the face of crushing, overwhelming odds.

Now, nurturing a fleeting ache seems like a celebration of those years of sacrifice.

She's thankful Seneca can't remember it in the same way, in her cells. She was too young. At that age, you don't have enough experience with disappointment to put it in context. Being hungry feels as bad as being scared, which feels as bad as knowing the world will inevitably crush you.

Valentine remembers it all too clearly; she can't forget. Lately, she's been waking up panicked and out of breath at three in the morning, collapsing into the memories, the scorching fear of being discovered, and worse, of failing.

She rubs her temples. Humans are so flawed, so used to failing and justifying their failures retroactively as intention, that they make it impossible to create a decent future. Even with vast technology and wealth at their fingertips, the Five Families created a system that excluded 99.9 percent of the Earth. But their descendants don't see it that way.

Over the long sweep of history, human nature seems to consist predominantly of a singular quality: self-sabotaging selfishness. Was she foolish to think things could change?

No, she wasn't foolish. She was optimistic. And there is still time, still reason to hope the change will take lasting hold, but it's no longer realistic to think she will be alive long enough to witness that rooting.

Perhaps that's for the best. Better to die with hope than to watch everything you believed in, everything you fought for, dissolve. She shakes her head, silently chastising herself for her dark mood. Things can still work out. People will surprise her, as they have in the past.

The class is almost settled.

Her lesson plan today is to focus on the shift in the official historical narrative about the Mars invasion and its aftermath when 31 years ago it was revealed that while commanding the Tarteric forces during the Consolidation Wars, Canadis Whitsend shared information with the Fehrvens. It was her industrial espionage that ultimately led to the defeat of the Hucksworths in the battles before Mars was colonized. And the defeated Hucksworths spent the subsequent decades hiding in the farthest reaches of space, nursing their regrets, planning their revenge and perfecting their bacterial arsenal.

This new data, which turned up after Halo swept the Five Family archives at Singhroy University, changed the official historical narrative underlying that period.

The change, she tells the students, was made because

new facts were discovered, not to alter the facts to fit a new story. This difference is key.

She sighs again. Teaching the class feels arduous today. She wishes she were anywhere else. Perhaps she is feeling the effect of the date today—Crucial Larsen's birthday.

She thinks back to the last time she saw him on Mars before he was sent off to the lunar penal colony. She remembers his handsome face and his genuine concern for her and Seneca. His kindness. His stubbornness. His generosity.

It was his secret credit transfer to her—a ludicrous amount—that allowed her to bring Seneca out of the shadows with a new identity and, in the end, save them both. He was a good man. At least he tried to be, though he often hid it very well.

# 15

"Crucial, I am not, as you characterize me, a scaredy-bot," Sanders says. "Rather, I do not understand your plan."

We're crammed into the escape pod, slowly puttering away from the prison transport ship. Escapes pods are designed for survival, not speed or evasion. Though in this case, both would be nice.

Sanders is devouring an ancient treacle bar he found buried deep in the dusty supply drawer. Sweet, nutrient-dense and disgusting. Like eating a moist myco-brick dipped in rat attractant.

"We could have stayed on board and let them kill us there," Sanders says, spraying me with a fine layer of treacle dust. "They are undoubtedly locking weapons onto us now. Was your plan to be vaporized by the ship? If so, it's going extremely well."

"Dying is not my plan," I say, as I nudge up the nanites again and identify the targeting systems searching for us. "Well, maybe plan B." I coax the little nano-bastards into weaving a distortion net around us so waves of searching energy pass over. We're invisible to the targeting systems.

I hope.

The ship fires a volley of rail slugs in our direction anyway, but it's like trying to thread a nanotube in the dark with one hand on a dual control stick. Still, I'm holding my breath.

The slugs streak past, resolute in their search for something to vaporize. Someday, in the distant future, one will crash into a far-away planet and kick up a mighty crater and some pre-literate biped will squeak in fear, thinking they angered the gods.

The transport ship will give up soon, unwilling to deviate from its trajectory.

"I'm glad the rail slugs missed," Sanders says. "I don't think I would have survived that. But I might survive the torpedoes they just launched."

Bloodhounds. Dammit. Those little monsters never stop coming once they get a lock on the elemental profile of a target.

"How many?"

"Two," Sanders says. "Even one is too many."

"Are you … did you just try to make a joke as we're about to get vaporized?"

"Perhaps," he says, now confused. "I can't tell if I'm being serious or ironic."

He doesn't know I have the nanites working for us. I nudge them to dupe our profile and hold a digital echo in place—something for the bloodhounds to sniff out—just behind us, far enough to avoid cracking the pod open like a chocolate opium truffle.

At the last second, I cut the power and we drift in silence as the two missiles collide behind us, tricked by the digital shadow. There's a flash followed by a gust of energy, enough to send our pod tumbling darkly, quietly into space. The nanites continue to satisfy the probes with an approximation of a metal cloud and biological debris.

"That was fortuitous," Sanders says, reaching for another treacle bar. "The next part of your plan, I presume, is for us to drift in space until you expire?"

"You're less fun when you're negative. How far is the

ship from us now?"

"Exactly four thousandths AU. And reaching peak quantum entanglement. They are no longer a threat."

"Good." I fire up the thrusters and stop the pod from spinning about a half second before I chuck my flavors.

Escape pods have very limited power. They're only good for simple navigation, basically avoiding major debris while waiting for retrieval. And for making planetfall, if necessary. Or moonfall, in this case. I find Phobos and chart us in. It's close by.

Well, godsdamned. My plan worked.

"We're going to Phobos?" Sanders asks. He has treacle crumbs on his lips. "How strange."

"I have a hunch."

"I continue to struggle with the concept of 'hunch.' Especially as you express it. Do you think you'll find the backup Halo servers on Phobos?"

"No."

"Do you think Melinda Hopwire is on Phobos?"

"No."

"Then perhaps your hunch is some sort of inner ear issue malfunction associated with the low gravity and the recent extensive series of gyrations."

"That's not it either."

"I'm afraid I do not understand humans at all."

"You might soon. If we're lucky."

Phobos is in sight, and close up, it's underwhelming.

From Mars, you can see Phobos rise and set twice a day, the unblinking Stickney crater staring deep and shadowy, like a wounded eye socket. Phobos looks mysterious and remote from the surface of Mars, but at this distance it looks more like a sad and abandoned mini-synthetic rocket-parking satellite, the kind typically dark-matter tethered next to orbital platforms.

And it's tiny. About twenty-two kilometers in diameter. Deimos was even smaller. But Phobos might as well be a million kilometers across when you're looking for one person who is running out of oxygen.

Not to mention the fact that it's brutally cold on the surface, worse than the Choke, getting down to minus 112 degrees Celsius on the dark side, according to my feed, which is now drawing from embedded, and limited, compilations of stiki general information.

As we make our way toward the surface, I see that it's covered with a variety of shelter types and decaying defensive armories. I try to think like Essential. If there was a proximity alarm, it's unlikely she had time to hop in a rocket. That means she probably used a Personal Interorbital Propulsion Pack to get off Deimos. PIPPs are basically lifejackets for orbital platforms. Just enough thrust to slowly drop down to the planet if the platform malfunctions. But from the low-gravity moons, it might have been enough to launch.

It's a lot farther between moons, which means it would be a long and scary ride in a PIPP, watching your oxygen levels drop and praying you have enough power to not end up dead-drifting like a bit of frozen space junk.

With Halo still down except for sporadic local connections, I don't even bother to shield us from the system. By the time Halo comes fully back online—if Halo comes fully back online—and all the digital footage is spooled and analyzed, if we haven't won, it won't matter that we're caught. We'll all be dead. Well, maybe not Sanders.

I use the pod navigation to back-chart an approach from Deimos and map the arc of the trajectory down to the surface. The arc ends in a tangle of abandoned q-rockets.

Great. Perfect.

When q-rocket engines suffer a superposition failure, they can't be trusted anymore—the quantum drives might take them in two directions simultaneously. It's a terrible way to go. They need to be stacked up somewhere until they're safe enough to reclaim.

Most end up on Earth. There are dozens rusting away in the Fields. Occasionally, one explodes into a crackling paradox ball. Quite lovely, the way the indigo lights up the belly of Earth's ever-present brown fog, at least from a distance.

But apparently, some also end up on Deimos, patiently waiting for the half-life of eternity.

If Essential is alive, that's where she's holed up. I'm sure of it. I set our course and Sanders looks at me curiously. "I hope your hunch knows that remaindered q-rockets are very unstable."

"I plan on landing very gently. Look for anomalies in the ship graveyard."

"Look for anomalies in an unstable quantum zone? The entire field is an anomaly."

"Come on, Sanders, just work with me here. Consider it a challenge."

He stops eating long enough to deep scan the ship graveyard and picks up something straight away in the eastern quadrant.

He identifies a rhythmic pulse. Something predictable in a flux zone, in an area where probabilities are all skewed. I'd call that an anomaly.

I aim for it. It's an old ship, maybe second generation. I zoom in and can just make out the registration code—the *QS America*. Named after some country that thought it was important before the Consolidation Wars. The hull is paper-thin in places, slowly being pulled apart by the ripples of unseen energy.

Sanders is right. This will probably end poorly. One little bump, one little nudge, and the whole thing might shift the wrong way and rip us—and time, at least as we experience it—apart forever.

I'm putting a lot of faith in the auto-nav. Luckily, that faith turns out not to be misplaced. The pod does the hard work and we land gently as we hold our breath.

We're down.

I reach for an extra airhoodie. "Listen, Sanders, things are about to get a little weird. I need you to remember that we're friends."

"According to my analysis, there are only one of three reasons it would be necessary to remind another being of the terms of their friendship. Crucial, none of those reasons are positive."

"This isn't a hunch. It's a rescue mission. I need your help. We may already be too late."

# 16

"Why won't you tell me who we are rescuing? I cannot provide maximum assistance with incomplete data."

I adjust my airhoodie, check my Priestley numbers and then tug at the door of the wrecked *QS America*. It's stuck. I wonder how long it's been out here and if anyone died on it. I pull harder and then kick at the hinge side. And pull again. It finally gives.

"I don't want to spoil the surprise," I say.

The stairs into the ship are long gone. I struggle up, balance on the edge of the opening and stretch out my hand to help Sanders swing up the few meters. It's a ridiculous gesture. Sanders could, if he wanted, leap over the entire ship in a single bound, but he still grabs my hand and I pretend to hoist him up and he pretends to be grateful for my help.

We're making progress on this pretend-he's-human game. Good to keep practicing even when no one is watching. I have a hunch our survival will hinge on concealing his synthetic nature from our enemies for as long as possible.

"I haven't yet determined if I appreciate surprises," he says.

"Consider this a learning opportunity."

The door opens into what looks like a passenger cabin. Must have been for VIPs because there are only a few dozen seats, or what were once seats. Now, it's battered metal and slowly degrading plasticium reshaped by time into jutting pieces and shadowy shapes jumping around in the beams of my airhoodie. The cabin is spacious, though. Probably was a luxury ship.

The floor is covered with a layer of powdery white rubble and dust. Could be human remains, I guess.

"Do you think Chancellor Valentine made it to safety?" Sanders asks.

"I hope so." I adjust my airhoodie; it's pinching around my left ear. "Are you worried for any particular reason or just generally?"

"I have been reflecting on how kind it was for her to greet me as we were being loaded onto the prison ship, and to ask me how I was doing. Humans do not often take the time to ask about my well-being."

"She's a kind person."

Our slow passage is kicking up dust and leaving fresh footprints. There are no other footprints, new or old. That's not a great sign.

"Is kindness fundamental to the human experience, Crucial?"

The passage narrows and on either side is what was probably a toilet at one time.

"Consider the data," I say. "Do humans strike you as particularly kind on average? Like, say, as they invade another planet or let their neighbors starve to preserve a few extra credits?"

"Those are most definitely not examples of kindness," he says. "I'm beginning to sense that self-interest is fundamental to the human experience."

True, I think, but according to Essential and Mel, empathy, that ability to understand and share someone else's feelings or state of being, is what helps focus that self-interest onto a better society for all.

I'm still not convinced.

"So, Chancellor Valentine is exceptional in that regard?" Sanders asks.

I nudge open the door to one of the biowaste closets. Like everything else so far, it's a remnant of what it once was. Tubing, shards and dust, nothing else. I close it and we keep going.

"She's exceptional in many regards. Especially when it comes to empathy for others."

"Is she more empathetic than you?"

I stop and catch his face in the beams of my airhoodie. "Sanders, *you* are more empathetic than me. You, a cybanism with synthetic emotions, understand more about what others are feeling than I do. Or, more accurately, you *care* more about what others feel. So yes, unquestionably, Valentine is more empathetic than me."

"Your apathy is quite exceptional."

"I'll take that as a compliment," I say, and keep walking.

"It was not intended as a compliment. Perhaps Chancellor Valentine is more evolved than other humans."

I push open a sagging door to move deeper into the ship.

"Sounds like you have a little crush on her."

"It's highly unlikely," Sanders says. "I don't think my program parameters include crushes. I'm simply curious about how empathy may have contributed to the evolution of the human species."

"Maybe it's an outlier. Empathy may have helped my ancestors back in the pre-human days, understanding others so they could form alliances or predict aggression, but the existence of the Five Families shows it has run its course."

Which is why I remain convinced, sadly, that the

empathy hack won't work. And if I find Essential, when I find Essential, I'll tell her that again. Empathy wouldn't have prevented the Hucksworths from destroying Mars. They only have empathy for their own, which is the fatal flaw with the whole concept. Worse, an empathy hack in Halo probably would have just paralyzed the system into trying to repel an invasion without hurting anyone's feelings.

Double worse, what if an empathetic Halo decided it would be most "empathetic" to, say, kill off some category of people who eat too much to prevent others from starving?

I know what Essential would say. An AI run on empathy applied across all categories of life, humans, animals, the environment, and what have you, will always be better than any system run on greed. But how do we know that? At least greed is predictable. It makes sense to all of us. Well, most of us. Maybe not to the three women in my life.

We've reached the midsection of the ship, a dining pod from the looks of it, cluttered with cracked dishes, dented cans, dusty bottles and metal food boxes, like some sort of ghost ship. It's kind of spooky.

As I take my next step, the *QS America* groans unhappily and tilts to the left. Great. The whole thing is poised to collapse and erupt into a sizzling paradox blast.

"Step lightly, Sanders. And stick close to the east side." It doesn't help that he weighs three times as much as a typical human.

We creep along the wall, both of us using a sheer sense of willpower, and hope, to prevent a tilt and collapse and flash. With no windows up here, it's cold, quiet and dark. Sanders has helpfully lit up his eyes, shining the bright twin beams on the cluttered aisle and frayed edges of compact tables.

Still no sign of Essential. Or anyone. But she must be here, or close by. I tell myself to stay focused on that and what comes next.

Once again, I try to put myself in her gravity-stabilizing boots, to feel what she would have. What would she do after jumping off Deimos with the propulsion pack and slowly making it here?

With limited oxygen and probably no water, she'd want to conserve resources and preserve her energy, hiding and waiting until someone—like her handsome, heroic, big brother—could launch a rescue. And since she doesn't have an OCD and couldn't know that Halo was in local mode only, she might be worried about accidentally broadcasting a biosignature or some other suspicious data point. She'd be trying to shield her output.

Of course.

She'd hide near the quantum engine where the flux is the highest. It's more dangerous, but it would shield her from Halo. Plus, it's warmer there. Unstable, but warm.

We take the circular staircase down into the engine room. The floor shows recent tracks. I stop and turn back to look at Sanders.

"What is it, Crucial?" He's looking directly at me, his eye-lights dazzling me blind.

I hold my hand up to block the light.

"Sorry," he says, turning his eyes to the side.

"Thanks. So, the thing is, buddy, I may need you to make a difficult choice soon."

"I can make difficult choices very quickly, especially with enough data." He pauses. "Will there be enough data to make an informed choice?"

"Yeah. There will be enough data."

On old ships like this one, the q-engine is right in the

belly of the hull in a thick valence well, a containment structure made from geometric matrices of beryllium. The energy source is no bigger than a soy nut, but with enough barely contained power to run the ship. Or level a city, if mishandled. It must be isolated from gravitational or mechanical forces, hence the valence well, and a complex tangle of pipes and wires channels the energy into the q-drive.

And while the q-nut is likely degraded by now to half of a half of a half-life, it's still dangerous and engine rooms are designed to shield the quantum nugget indefinitely. If she made it, Essential is hiding here in the engine room. And monitoring the approach of two strangers over the barrel of a glitter gun. Just my luck to get glittered by my own kid sister.

I unzip a light strip and dab it on the valence well. The soft green glow lights up the room.

I need to make sure she knows it's me. What's that game we used to play? There was a line we always used. It comes to me. "Space pirates, prepare to be boarded!"

"Your life or your credits," a weak voice whispers.

A panel on the wall next to the valence well jostles and then topples over.

It's Essential. She's alive. My broken heart is half healed.

I drop to my knees and hug her close. "Thank the infinite void. I was so worried." I hand her the airhoodie.

"I still had minutes of air left," she gasps. "I wasn't worried yet."

"You are Essential Larsen," Sanders says. "Crucial, I will acknowledge that this data point is proving hard to reconcile with the fact that, prior to the invasion of Mars, Halo indicated your sister was locked in a Terrorium on Earth. Was she released?"

"Technically, no."

He looks puzzled. "Did she escape?"

"Again, technically, no. Here's the truth. She was never in that Terrorium. Canadis Whitsend is currently enjoying the very latest in fear-based cognitive rehabilitation."

"That's *two* surprises," Sanders says.

"Are you sure we should be broadcasting all this right back to Halo?" Essential asks, taking a few extravagant breaths through the fresh airhoodie. "I mean, I assume you're using the nanites to block transmission, but won't Sanders spool up a recording?"

"Things are complicated," I say.

"You have the nanites," Sanders says, putting it all together. He sounds petulant. "That's really more of a secret than a surprise."

"We'll talk about that later."

"I've been trying to hack into Halo, but no luck," Essential says. "I assumed it was the quantum flux. Don't tell me that little meteor shower knocked everything offline."

"That's the thing. It wasn't a meteor shower. It was an attack. An attack planned around you finding the servers."

I help her stand.

"What do you mean?" she asks.

"The resistance was set up. When you located the servers, Halo went into lockdown. The Hucksworth family used the outage to attack Mars and Earth. Halo was destroyed. We need to find Mel and the emergency backup servers before they do if we want to keep your plan in play."

"Why do we have to find Mel?"

I pause. I'm not sure if I should say all this out loud. Somehow, saying it out loud will make it more real, or so real that I won't be able to ever back out. It means I will help Mel and I will help Essential. Because, in the end, when everything is going to shit, what else is left but to help the people you love, to uphold their principles, especially when you don't have any of your own?

It feels like my mom is hovering around me now, that I can see her. Say your truth, she says, so I do. "Based on everything I know, it's pretty clear that Mel is the last piece of your plan. Somehow she's supposed to deploy the empathy hack."

Sanders starts to say something, but I hold my hand up. "Yes, I know, it's another surprise."

"Actually, I was going to explore a quick point from an earlier surprise," Sanders says. "If you didn't actually lock your sister in a Terrorium, why damage your reputation and let everyone think you did?"

"Like his reputation could be damaged," Essential says.

"It was more important knowing Essential was alive and well. Although I'm currently wondering why."

"Going back to our earlier conversation, that seems like … an act of kindness, of applied empathy," Sanders says. "Running counter to your professed fidelity to apathy."

"It's more than kind," Essential says. "It's love."

"You have to take care of the people you love." I put my arm around her. "Even when they make it very hard. And now, Sanders, I need a favor from you. If Halo starts operating correctly again, can you compartmentalize this new information?"

"I think so. I want to take care of the people I love, and I think you are one of them."

"That's sweet," Essential says.

Great. The only person not related to me by blood that I haven't managed to push away is synthetic.

Sanders's eyes flutter as an unimaginable number of scenarios are processed. "I believe I can compartmentalize this information indefinitely. But if Halo operationalizes, the lack of access to this data will be flagged."

"We'll deal with that when we have to. Now, let's figure out how to get off this rock and back to Mars."

"You don't have a plan to get us off Phobos?" Essential asks. "This is the worst rescue ever."

"You can always give back the airhoodie."

"Crucial does have a very loose interpretation of the word *plan*," Sanders says. He pats his mid-section. "I wonder if there is any food on this ship? My processors are rumbling."

The ship wobbles and creaks and tilts forward a little. I had almost forgotten about the possibility of getting torn into a million molecules and spread across time and space.

"The first step of my plan is to get us the prok off *QS America*," I say.

## 17

"Really? You don't have an escape ship?" Essential asks. "How is that possible?"

We make our way back to the passenger level of the *QS America.*

"We have an escape *pod*," I say.

Earlier, Sanders found an unopened can of ancient béchamel powder in the galley and has been eating it straight by the handful. It's hard to watch, his face is coated in white powder.

"An escape pod that can't lift off from the lunar surface," she says. "Very helpful."

Expressing gratitude has always been tough for Essential. Even as a child, when I tried my best to save her from overeating candied garbanzos by stealing her share.

"Sorry, I couldn't get my hands on a custom flier while on a prison transport during an invasion. I kind of had to improvise."

"No biggie, it's just that we're *all* stranded now. Or I'm stranded *still*, I guess. Doesn't that defeat the whole point of a rescue?"

"I rescued you from running out of oxygen, didn't I?"

"That's true, that part of your rescue plan succeeded. Temporarily, at least," Essential says. "But since we have limited supplies and no way to leave, it's more accurate to say what you did is make sure I have company while I keep running out of oxygen."

"I like your sister," Sanders says. "Her language is unusually precise."

"It's unusually annoying," I say.

"It does appear we are stranded though," he says. "And her PIPP, which couldn't lift all of us in any scenario, is almost out of power. We will need to request an extraction, and that will almost certainly lead to your imprisonment. Or execution."

"We're not going to request help."

"I probably will," he says.

I shoot him an aggravated look.

"After waiting a respectful amount of time after you both expire, of course."

"I haven't told you the second part of my plan yet."

"Which is?" Essential asks.

Come on, brain. If we can't leave this damn moon … got it.

"Simple. We need to get the needle-noses up here and then hitch a ride back to Mars on one of their fart ships."

"What's a fart ship?" Essential asks.

"The Hucksworth ships are powered by bacterial fuel that smells like a dead rat stuck in a sewage pump."

"Eww. Your plan might work, but suddenly I'm not looking forward to it. How do we get them here?"

"They want Mel. Let's give her to them."

Five minutes later, we've got a real plan. It's mostly Essential's plan. I almost certainly could have come up with something better, but why stifle my only sibling's creativity? Plus, it's fair to say I inspired her plan.

Essential uses her nanites to create a digital overly that makes her appear to be Mel. I also rouse my little blood-bots and make it seem like there are vast amounts of data being processed nearby. Sanders is our reluctant relay, forging a direct channel to the barely functional systems in the Hive, which the Hucksworths are certainly monitoring.

When we're ready, I nod to Sanders who opens the channel and Essential hams it up. "If anyone in the resistance can hear me, I'm on Phobos. I've found the backup servers. I should be able to introduce the hack in under an hour if—"

I nod, she cuts her feed and Sanders drops the relay, making it seem like interference disrupted her signal. Now we wait.

Things can go one of two ways. The least optimal would be for the Hucksworths to decide to cut their losses and start from scratch, blasting Phobos into grit. Bad for Mars, worse for Earth, terrible for us.

The better way, the one we're hoping for, is that within an hour—plenty of time for our oxygen supply—they'll send a flotilla to stop digital Mel and secure the backup Halo tech. In all the noise and confusion, we stow away in the bowels of ... we hide out on one of their ships.

I check the time on my feed and our oxygen supply. Then I scan the star maps for any weaponized comets headed our way. Two minutes later, six rockets blast off from the surface of Mars. That was surprisingly fast.

So fast, we haven't actually thought about the critical third part of our still-evolving rescue plan—the noise and distraction.

I turn to Essential. "So, we need to—"

"Right, make a distraction. I was thinking we could get them all focused on the pod." She pauses. "Unless you have a better idea."

"No. I mean, that's where I was going. You know, great minds."

We lug her PIPP into the escape pod. She overrides the safety controls, turns it on and leaves it puttering around inside, then locks the pod down. We retreat to the safety of a nearby shielded monitoring booth and toss out a little nanite camouflage as six ships drop down near the pod.

The ships expel a cloud of soldiers who are crazy looking. They're not wearing airhoodies, more like bulky helmets with visors and thick suits with canisters on their backs. That must be for carrying their own air. It's all so clunky and clumsy except for the guns, the strange, fragile bulbous weapons that burn like a solar flare enema.

Cautiously, they advance on the escape pod. By now they probably know I was in it. I'll be even more popular with the Hucksworths soon.

The PIPP is doing its job, bumping into the walls, causing the pod to shake. From the outside, it looks like it's inhabited, maybe even trying to lift off.

Someone gets nervous and shoots. It's not the sticky electricity I'm now overly familiar with; it's more powerful and precise. They don't seem to understand the risk factor associated with slowly degrading quantum engines. There's a crack and the top part off the pod shears off. The PIPP floats up and there's more shooting. The pod topples over into the hull of the *QS America* with a jolt and the ship buckles. The ensuing chain reaction releases a twist of improbability from a degrading engine, like an indigo hurricane that crackles out, distorting light and fusing metal and causing alarming states of flux.

The soldiers are screaming while things melt and explode all around them. The closest ship takes the brunt of it as part of the starboard side is fused into a blend of metal and people. It's extremely gross.

The flux twister is losing steam and careens into the next closest ship, gouging a pretty good hole in the nose. "That's it. That's our ride," I say.

"The damaged ship?" Essential asks. "Why on Mars would we want to get on a damaged ship?"

"It's barely damaged, and everyone riding on that bucket of waste will now be in a clunky rad-con suit, too busy worrying about dying to pay any attention to who is standing next to them."

Alerts are flashing. Another gust of flux is coming. The Hucksworth troops are pretty good at attacking shattered domes but terrible at retreating from quantum flux.

We trail along behind the last three stragglers to the damaged ship. They are panting and yelling back and forth so they don't notice when we slip on board behind them just before the doors close. No proximity alarms are sounding, mostly because Essential and I are nanite-ing the hell out of everything.

They've got their backs turned to the door, just happy to be alive. Now we need to convince them to let us borrow their rad-con suits, hopefully before their stink engines fire up.

They are laughing and swearing and taking off their helmets. The air fills with a terrible stench.

"Gods! What powers these ships, ground-up fecal flukes?" Essential whispers.

They spin, surprised to hear voices and even more surprised to see three stowaways.

I'm ready for a scrap, and pretty sure I could take them, but Sanders has a different idea. He steps up and flicks two of them lightly on the forehead with just enough force to drop them like sacks of spent fuel rods.

He looks at the third man. "Where do you keep nutrient stores on this craft?"

The man looks back at him blankly.

"Food. He means food," I say.

"Down the corridor and two lefts."

"Thank you." Sanders flicks him into unconsciousness as well.

# 18

We make it safely off our hijacked ride as soon as they drop from Phobos down to Mars, landing in the middle of Jezero next to the temporary field base. I'll say one thing for the stink rockets, they are versatile. War cruisers, the battleships with squiggly tentacles, are still circling around out of sight like q-rockets, and these little stinkballs can drop right down to the surface from upper orbit in one foul vertical gust.

Apparently the Hucksworths went all in on bacteria tech after they slipped away from Earth to nurse their ego-wounds. Essential jacked into their ship database and gave us the scoop. The biggest ships use bacterial motion, thousands of whips successively grabbing onto snippets of dark matter and pulling the ships into warp speed. The smaller ships are more straightforward, powered by bubbling, digestive-type micro-explosions, with blasters that use a living form of electricity.

I don't want to know what kind of booze they drink. A yeasty froth, I bet. Thinking about it, I do kind of want to know. Probably at least as good as ant-gin.

They're a weird bunch with weird technology, but one thing is all too familiar—the way that troops get dressed down by their commanding officers when they return from a failed mission. The away-teams receive an earful about their gross lack of understanding related to quantum flux and how they might have destroyed the Halo servers and ruined everything.

Essential, Sanders and I—still concealed in our stolen rad-con suits—slip off into the wreckage of Jezero's fake shopping district. We're weaponless and at risk of being flagged by random feeds as we pass through the remains of Jezero. But we have spare airhoodies and our thermals are holding.

We find shelter in the remains of a high-end saucer shop overlooking a miraculously still-flowering orchid garden and peel ourselves out of the suits. I think the former occupant of my suit had a rare condition that caused him to excrete a layer of foul grease that coated the interior.

Other than the stubborn orchid blooms, the garden is in tatters and the saucer shop is damaged, but Essential coaxes an extruder back online and it starts squeezing out the only functioning option, a ribbon of spicy radish paste. Normally, that would squirt onto little quinoa skins, but that press is broken. Not that it matters. Sanders has his mouth directly to the nozzle, sucking the radish paste down as fast as it comes out.

Luckily, I find my own source of missing nutrients—a couple of mint cream sticks under a tangle of dried-out dumpling skins. I don't even bother breaking the seal to watch the light show when the powdered alcohol mixes with the minty gel. I just break the ends off and pour the powder right on my tongue.

"Classy," Essential says.

"Anything to replace that bacterial stench. My eyes are still burning."

"It is pretty rough. What's our next step?"

"Finding Mel."

Skip-tracing in 2188 is straightforward, at least it always has been. You query Halo to find the missing person and

Halo finds the missing person. All done in less than three seconds. But that was before Mars was invaded by a bunch of tight-nosed rat-raisins from some dismal hiding place down-universe.

Now, finding someone, especially someone important like Mel, will require good old-fashioned detective work and a bit of luck.

"I think we should start at the old observation tower or meditation tower or whatever it was. It meant something special to Mel."

"Yes, because it was an ideal spot to send coded messages to the resistance with less risk of discovery," Essential says. "Makes sense, right? Hindsight and all."

"Okay, yes. But also, I think she liked it there. We had a moment."

"Crucial, it appears the tower has been destroyed," Sanders says. He shares his feed. He's patching into some cameras near the tower. The images are jumping around, but it looks like half the tower was leveled.

"She wouldn't have known that in the data blackout following the attack," I say. "She might have gone there first."

I remember that night we sat and watched the Earth come into view, with that stupid, angry little kitten at her feet. If she knows one thing for certain in this universe, it's that I will never give up on her. She'd know that, and she would leave me a sign.

"Mel is smart. But I don't think she—"

"I know Mel." I say, interrupting Essential. "And we need to start somewhere, so let's start there. If I'm wrong, we've lost an hour and we'll figure out where to go next. But I won't be wrong. Not about this. She left me a sign, a clue. I know it."

At least, I hope she left me a sign. I'm anxious and time

is running out. The Hucksworths are scouring the planet for her and probably making more progress than we are.

"They can't find her first," I say.

Essential puts her hand on my arm. "They won't. We'll go there. In the meantime, Sanders, please start micro-sorting the footage. Even with Halo down, data will pop in and out of your systems, and it's possible a static or bio-system will flash on her so you can match a profile."

"I will begin immediately. I warn you, though, with some chagrin, I may need to procure additional nutrients for that task in short order. Withholding information from a future Halo incursion, what humans refer to as lying, along with the constant data and scenario-querying required for this high degree of compartmentalization, consumes massive amounts of my fuel. I apologize for this unfortunate lapse in service."

"Maybe you're eating for two?" I say. "Any chance you have a little Sanders about to spawn inside you?"

"A progeny? That *could* explain the hunger, but I don't believe I am programmed to reproduce."

"Aww, you two would make wonderful parents," Essential says.

"I'm going to pretend you never said that. And Sanders, you've got radish paste on your, well, basically all over your face."

"My skin sensors are not functioning effectively," he says, wiping away the paste. He almost seems embarrassed.

"Don't worry, we'll find you more food," I say. "And remember, we're not asking you to lie. We're just asking you to not immediately tell the truth when the opportunity arises."

I stand and adjust my airhoodie, then take a quick look outside. No sign of the roving patrols working their way through Jezero.

"It is kind of you to think of my needs," Sanders says, reluctantly leaving the radish nozzle. "Is that an instance of empathy? I'm very curious about the plan you mentioned to introduce empathy into the AI system. I will be on the lookout for all potential instances of empathy so we can discuss it fully in order to better understand the concept."

"Please don't," I say. "And that was not empathy. More like self-preservation."

"Interestingly," he says, which always means the opposite, "my stored data banks indicate empathy could be a refined strategy for individual self-preservation. This theory holds that empathy, the ability to understand and share the experiences of others, allows humans—highly social creatures—to predict and shape the reactions of others more accurately and efficiently, thereby maximizing potential beneficial outcomes. In other words, it's a selfish activity."

"Don't look at me. I'm not social, or empathetic. Essential is the one who's pushing the empathy solution. Come on, let's get moving."

We shadow a row of damaged buildings, making our way toward the old tower.

"It's true that empathy alone can be problematic," Essential says, stepping over a piece of Jezero's dome.

This is going to be a long walk. "Would it be possible to quietly try to avoid detection and discuss the moral ramifications of empathy later when we're not being hunted?" I ask.

"Either because it can be used selfishly or can even drive anti-social behavior," she continues, ignoring me. "Like, charitably we could say the Five Families may not lack empathy for most humans, they just have *too much* empathy for their own families, and thus can ignore the bad things happening to others."

"Also problematic," Sanders adds, "is the fact that, until the unified theory of mind was finally established in 2040, evidence suggested that extreme empathy may underlie some forms of psychopathy, including sadism."

"It's true empathy is not the cure-all for humanity's problems. But the empathy hack is a good start. A system with empathy at the core, instead of pure self-interest, will give us the space to think about a different future. Then it will be up to all of us, not just the wealthiest, to—"

"Stop," I say.

"Why should I stop? I already know what you're going to say," she says. "Revolutions are doomed to fail—"

"No, seriously, stop talking. There's a sweep team dead ahead."

It's a Hucksworth squad, six of them, and they've set up a checkpoint right next to the observation tower. How could they know about the tower?

# 19

On its best day, Mars is merely annoying. And on one of those better days, now and again, like during the blue-violet sunsets, in those moments—even if the Choke is still patiently waiting outside the domes to kill you—Mars becomes irritatingly beautiful.

But today is not one of those best days. Far from it. The planet is broken and under attack, the domes are damaged, and there's nothing between us and the Choke except our airhoodies, which are slowly running out of oxygen.

The once privileged and aloof members of the Five Families are scarred and scared and struggling to survive. All their advantages are gone, leveled in an instant by a foe even more ruthless in their lack of empathy. Dammit. There's that word again. I glare at Essential. If the nanites have somehow infected me with empathy, I will never forgive her.

Now there's a squad of enemy soldiers between us and the entrance of the wrecked observation tower where I'm certain Mel left me a clue about where she's going. Or, more accurately, I'm *hopeful* she left a clue.

I wish I had a weapon.

Sanders is a cybanism with blast-resistant skin and enhanced strength. In theory, that makes him a weapon. He could just walk up and throw those six Hucksworth goons through a myco-wall and that would be that. But we can't risk being discovered. If any one of them notified the Hucksworth high command, we'd lose anonymity, the slight edge we have.

"What we need is a distraction," I say.

And then Phobos explodes.

One minute, the moon we were recently on was hanging out there in the sky, the next it's a billowing cloud of dust.

"Whoa, that's a pretty good distraction," Essential says, watching in awe as Phobos comes apart.

They must have realized the servers were not on Phobos. Maybe they thought I was still there. In a way, I'm flattered they would destroy an entire moon just to get rid of me, putting their own people at risk in the process. In another way, things are about to heat up on the planet's surface.

An emergency alert crackles through our feeds. "People of Mars. Prepare for impact from moon debris. Take cover immediately."

If Halo were operational, the High Orbital Responsive Defense Shield would protect the planet from falling debris. But since it's in backup mode, local only and no stronger than the weak links between individual users, that protective shield is useless.

There are flashes of light as smaller pieces break up when they hit the thin atmosphere. The more distant impacts send vibrations through the soles of our feet when the bigger pieces strike the planet.

While not great in terms of our personal safety, the distraction works in our favor. The pinched-nosed crew grabs their gear, boosts it into their little hyper-caique and hightails it for their ship. The safest place to be when a bunch of space debris comes crashing onto Mars is anywhere but Mars.

Pretty sure the Hucksworths didn't think this through. They put themselves at risk just because they got mad and overreacted. I mean, I get it. That's me every day. But I'm one person, not an invading force. I file this away as potentially useful psych-ops information.

We watch them lift off. There are explosions of dust in the distance as more pieces of poor Phobos crash into the Choke. Deimos is already gone. The Hucksworths are hard on moons.

"Come on," I say, standing. "It's now or never. Let's check out what's left of the tower."

"Hold on," Essential says, grabbing my arm. "They left a strobe."

I use the nanites to scan the area and sure enough, there's a multiphase recording strobe in the area they recently departed. They are surveilling the tower.

My hope soars. They definitely think Mel was here.

"Okay, new plan. We need to blind the strobe before we look inside."

"No more interplanetary explosive distractions please," Essential says. "The universe can't handle it." She studies the digital topography with her synthetic eye. "The strobe is unfamiliar, it's their tech. But while it's fanny-packed onto local Halo, I can't get through the backdoor to turn it off without some time with their systems."

"We don't have that kind of time."

I look around. Puffs of dust are billowing out in the Choke and alarms are sounding. Nothing is moving, no people, no transports, except for a line of giant, clunky builder bots. They've traded their myco-shaping grinder arms for girder extruders. There's an endless line of them making their way to the edge of the dome to start squirting a repair scaffolding into place so a new wall can be erected.

"Can you walk one of those bots our way?" I ask.

She struggles to patch every local feed together, eyes squeezed tight in concentration, and then she opens them and smiles. She's inside one of the builder bots, redirecting its code.

With two more blinks, she coaxes it to break ranks. As it lumbers by, I slip out of our hiding place—shielded from the strobe—and clamber on behind, holding tight to the rungs.

As the bot carries me closer to the strobe, a glittering ball of tech perched on a titanium stake shot into the ground, I use the nanites to connect into the builder control panel and tell the bot to squirt out a girder right on top of the strobe. The girders aren't too heavy, but they harden fast and become virtually unbreakable. In seconds, the strobe is encased in amber-tinted epoxy.

At my urging, the bot happily tamps the strobe into a buzzing, glittering pile of trash. I hop down and motion for Essential and Sanders, and together we run inside the base of the observation tower.

We won't have much time. The strobe undoubtedly recorded its own demise and that means the Hucksworths will send their guards right back down, and they will not be happy about being out in the field when pieces of sky are falling.

The tower is dark and cold and in disarray. The tube to the top is gaping open, crumpled metal bulging out of the base. The control panels are shattered and sparking.

She had to come here. She had to know that of all the places in Jezero, this is where I would come looking for her. And she must have left me a clue. Please, Mel, please have left me a clue.

From the looks of it, a meteor crashed through the dome and sheared right through part of the tower about halfway up, and the tallest needle part of it dropped straight down and burst at the surface. The observation bubble where Mel and I watched the earth rising is also on the ground, about fifty meters away from the base of the tower, beat up, but mostly still intact, like it dropped and then bounced before rolling to a stop.

Looking at that bubble, I imagine her sitting up there all alone night after night before the attack, looking sadly at Earth. The whole time I was lying to her about Essential being in a Terrorium, she was lying to me about being in the resistance. Of course, she was in the resistance. Stupid of me to not know her better than that. She could never have gotten used to this luxury life of hers while so many suffered. She was biding her time. Always so patient. Always thinking about the future. Unlike me, who is always thinking about the past and lashing out at the present. Unable to think about anything good lasting.

"Sanders, scan for digital anomalies."

He complies. "I'm not finding anything."

I shake my head and walk toward the observation bubble laying on its side on the ground.

"We better get moving," Essential says. "Fliers are coming."

I nod then look at the windows of the bubble. The interior is in disarray, all the chairs broken loose and piled against one side. I look more closely. There's something smudged into the dust on the outside of the window— something that looks vaguely like an animal, with a long neck.

A giraffe.

I mean, it's rough. She was never a very good artist. It's a terrible rendition, but it's most certainly a giraffe. I know where she's gone. Baldet crater. The research dome where she worked to create trees and plants able to terraform Mars, and where I once killed a giraffe.

I swipe the window clean to destroy the clue, grinning like an idiot. We can hear ships approaching, the sound bigger than a hyper-caique. Godsdamn. Soon the whole place is going to smell like a moldy swamp. Plus, there will be people trying to kill us. So many people trying to kill us.

"We have to go," Essential says. "Now."

Five minutes later, we're hiding on the back of our wayward builder bot as it rejoins the line of brethren builders tramping toward the edge of the dome.

A ship lands near the tower. Essential zooms in with her enhanced eye. "They look mad."

I don't bother looking. I'm watching the Priestly numbers on our airhoodies drop as we slowly run out of oxygen.

## 20

**September 1, 2238**
*Stardust University, Neuro-Lecture Interface 75.32*

Valentine is done. Although few people know it.

Last month, she decided that 2238 will be the last year she teaches history. It seems she can no longer manage the high cost of reliving her own history. She won't tell the students or the Council until after the final examinations later this month, but having made the decision, she feels a welcome lightness of spirit.

Seneca will likely question her reasoning but Valentine is sure that in the end, she will support it. They are family, after all.

Valentine's teaching appointment is for life, and it's early to give up such a prestigious position, but she is determined to spend her remaining days in quiet reflection. Perhaps write her own version of the events that occurred after Mars was invaded.

A memoir of sorts. Maybe. She isn't sure she is quite so egotistical. She can hear Seneca's laughter already. *You? A memoir? I can barely get you to tell me what you ate last week.*

And, she imagines, Seneca will point out that Valentine already provided the Council with a full neural-etched recitation of everything she saw and did during those days. Even though Halo was down for part of the time, the memories were fresh when she did the interviews, with an ecphoric match of close to 90 percent.

But if she learned anything in all those years long-ago as a double agent, it was how to compartmentalize. She wonders if she's willing, or able, to share the details she left out?

She has never told the full, unadulterated story of what happened to her and Seneca after they made their way to Singhroy University near Jezero. At the time, Valentine was promised she would find refuge in the familiar university setting. She assumed they were under the protection of the Singhroy family.

It hadn't turned out that way. It had been a trap. A detention center. One that required so much of her to protect them both. She looks down at the scar on her palm, smoothed by time. She could have easily had it removed years ago with a sequence of cosmetic crème.

The countdown timer gently rings and she refocuses on the lesson at hand.

A cohort of advanced students is attending today, drawn from the brightest minds at the university. She checks their feeds and sees their endorphin levels are close to baseline.

"Class, it seems you are ready to begin. Today, we're going to explore how, or if, societies can change."

"The syllabus," a student interjects, "lists our topic today as the methodology of the Council's construction of the historical narrative regarding the Consolidation Wars and its designation as a precursor pivotal event for the invasion of Mars. I don't see what the rise and fall of societies has to do with that."

The mood turns negative quickly, falling below the Ryff median. Some of the students are irritated by the rude tone, others are intrigued by the questioner's stance. What right has Valentine to switch to a subject they didn't prepare for?

She should be annoyed, but the truth is Valentine finds the student's bold certainty enviable. She sees no reason to dampen this youthful confidence.

"At this point in your study of history you have, or should have, come to understand that the task of building—and rebuilding—a historical narrative requires some amount of professional judgment," she says. "Let's consider together the Council's rubric of what is likely versus what is inevitable."

"In other words, the degree of probability of one event leading to another?" the same student asks.

He seems almost bored. She checks to see who it is. Hoost Tarteric, the Fourth. Of course. Two generations now removed from the man she knew. This must be his great-grandson or maybe a grand-nephew.

The irony of this young man's presence in her class nearly causes her to laugh. She resists the impulse and instead asks, "At what level of probability does the likely become inevitable?"

A thousand minds search for a thousand clues to answer the question. She watches the flash of queries on the dashboard, first like threads, then like sunspots, now rejoining into the ranked responses.

"Please hold your responses as we move ahead. I'm speaking exclusively now to our advanced student guests who already know a great deal about the rise and fall of cultures and societies. Examples please."

Thoughts made into images flood the dashboard, jostling for space. Greeks. Romans. Dynasties of the Middle Kingdom. Klingons. Someone is a comedian, she thinks. A comedian well-versed in ancient digital history.

"Good, mostly. Now, how do we know if their decline was likely or if it was inevitable? What elements would make up our ranked factorial analysis?"

There is a faint hum of processing space.

In a world where every bit of information is available in a microsecond, creative analysis is the most challenging task. Something AI still cannot replicate. Thankfully.

The answers are mixed, the justifications ranging from convincing to wildly erratic.

"As noted the answer requires a ranked factorial analysis of the prevailing elements determining human behavior, such as life expectancy, resource scarcity, health cradle access, gendered violence, risk comfort, the poetic mean, pandemics, propaganda and so on."

She clears the dashboard. "Same question now and relying again on the factorial analysis but not a question about civilizations, rather, an event. The Consolidation Wars. Were they likely or inevitable?"

The dashboard lights up again. Based on the analysis, it's trending as likely. She checks the advanced students. They're split almost down the middle, but leaning likely.

"Our factorial analysis defines the Consolidation Wars as inevitable." She smiles as a few people change their feedback seconds before the results are frozen.

She is in a playful mood so she asks Hoost, the Fourth, to explain the factorial analysis in a narrative overlay. He asks to use the audio rather than punch-key a response. She agrees and opens the channel.

"When the era of the democratic nation-state was fully supplanted by the era of plutocracy," he says, "the forced consolidation of competitors was an inevitable focusing of power through the lens of wealth."

His voice sounds surprisingly like his great-grandfather. But unlike his ancestor, he lacks charisma, at least in this format.

"The consumer-focused economy, already distressed by

the early 2000s, was unable to support the expanding structures of wealth. Representative democracy was replaced by protected consumer choice. The system of hereditary debt was introduced."

"And?" she asks.

"The drawn-out Consolidation Wars became inevitable as the only surviving method of determining appropriate resource allocation and control."

"Could resources have been allocated in ways other than by violent confrontations between corporate family entities?"

"My factorial analysis shows it was inevitable because the elements defining human behavior had morphed in such a way such that the political will to develop alternative solutions had evaporated."

"You have identified the cumulative limiting factor. Well done. But to be clear, the lack of political will was manufactured, and 'inevitable' does not mean it was a good outcome."

"'Good' is subjective, a personal judgment," Hoost says. "There's little place for it in historical analysis. Some call those wars heroic." His tone makes clear he is in the "some" category.

"There was nothing heroic about the Consolidation Wars," she says, more sharply than intended. "They were proxy wars fought to establish debt control. They destroyed the Earth, killed millions and scarred tens of millions."

She'll be getting a communiqué from the Council later for her tone and the sharp mix of neural chemicals behind it, reminding her that historians must remain detached, or at least give an appearance of detachment.

Well, she's quitting anyway. Best to go out with truth.

Her truth.

"After decades of study, the Council classified the Hucksworth family invasion of Mars as the final battle of the Consolidation Wars. The Council also concluded that the invasion wasn't inevitable. Likely, but not inevitable. The Hucksworths simply had the means and took advantage of an opportunity," she says.

"Isn't it correct that opportunity was created due to the missteps of the Variance, also known as the resistance, of which you were an active member, Chancellor Valentine?"

The question is formally lodged but anonymously. Her objectivity is being challenged.

"That is correct on both counts," she says.

To its everlasting shame, the resistance indeed walked straight into the trap laid by the Hucksworths. And the consequences of that miscalculation were enormous for humanity. Only the luxury of historical analysis revealed the scope of the Hucksworth's gambit and the extent to which the resistance was duped.

The scar on her palm itches and she slowly traces the contours with her fingertips.

# 21

"Anything from your pals in the resistance?" I ask.

She's been trying to connect with the Variance ever since we left Phobos, sending distress calls on the back channel in hopes of finding us some backup.

Essential shakes her head. "No one has responded. What if Valentine is the only one left?"

"You said to bring booze, right? Those pin-nosers took my maple rum when they threw us on the prison ship."

"Right now, weapons and oxygen top the list. But I promise I'll mention your addiction if I get the chance."

"It feels like now, when we're dealing with interstellar invasions, exploding moons and a starving cybanism, could be the one time when chemical disordering of the senses is unquestionably justifiable."

We hop off the builder bot at the eastern gate of Jezero. The bot rejoins the lineup, now all resolutely climbing over each other and locking into place, extending scaffolding to repair the dome, slowly building a lattice of oversized, vaguely human-shaped forms up the curving sides to extrude girders.

I wish we could get one of them to carry us across the Choke to Baldet crater. But a misbehaving builder bot outside the dome is guaranteed to trip alarms and earn us a synthetic meteor right up the baffle. Or is it a comet? I really should listen more closely to Sanders.

It doesn't matter; even if we could risk the slow journey, we don't have enough oxygen to amble across the Choke.

"We can't walk to Baldet because we don't have enough air. And the lev-train was destroyed," I say.

"Also, don't forget the death discs buried around the edge of the dome," Essential says.

Prok. I *had* forgotten the death discs.

"Wait, how did you know about those?"

"Sanders filled me in."

"Maybe they're just bluffing. Let's test it."

I use the nanites to borrow another builder bot from the endless line and send it trudging out through the damaged aperture of the east gate. It's less than one step beyond the edge of the dome when the ground erupts in a shower of red sand and a disc pops up. There's a faint hum and flash of green and the bot melts. Vaporizes. The disc, now spent, falls to the ground and there's a reshuffling of soil as the remaining discs scoot a little closer together to close the gap.

"We definitely won't get far on foot."

"Maybe we can drone it?" Essential summons a local drone jacket and sends it skimming out the gate. It rises about 30 meters before it hits an invisible laser grid, puffs and falls into six sizzling pieces.

"Flying seems a less than ideal option," Sanders says.

"Let me think," I say, feeling Mel slip away.

The east gate of Jezero is heavily damaged but even so, it's clear it was less frequently used than the main gate on the west. A smaller aperture, a smaller gear shed, a smaller impound hangar.

The impound hangar.

"Who used this gate?" I ask.

"Mostly kids, I think," Essential says. "For joy rides out into the Choke."

"Let's check the impound hangar for any unauthorized craft seized by Mars SF. If we can send something out first and then follow right behind it, we might not get slime-o-fused."

"Your plans often involve a high degree of chance," Sanders says.

"It's more exciting that way. Why don't you hit the gear shed and see if you can find us some fresh airhoodies and any food for you. And it goes without saying—"

"Any alcohol for you."

"I was *going* to say weapons, but sure."

Essential and I move into the impound hangar. There are four fliers locked into the bootbox.

"Is that what I think it is?" Essential points to a dusty antique.

I nod. "It's a light sail. Maybe some kids stole a flier from their grandparents."

"If it still floats, we might not get vaporized after all."

She's right. Light sails are photon-powered fliers. They're not rocket-fast, but also not walking-slow. They take a charge from just about any light source and convert it to lev-lift, floating gracefully above the surface, but barely, and they don't leave much of a thrust trail. They're basically pleasure fliers.

I find an impact wrench and shatter the restraint pins holding it in the impound bootbox.

Sanders shows up with an armful of gear—three spare airhoodies, a med kit and a case of high-nutrient emergency rations bars. Those should hold him for a while.

He looks at the flier. "A light sail. How fortuitous."

"Essential, as we get close to the perimeter, you hail another local drone and run it through and then we'll sail in its wake. Hopefully, their defenses aren't as strong close to the surface, what with the death discs and all."

I can tell by her expression that she lacks confidence in my plan. I can also see she understands we have no choice.

There's not enough juice in the battery to flip over the light sail engine. Not surprising. It's been sitting in the dark for possibly years. We manually extend the main sail, a triangle-shaped array of millions of tiny photovoltaic cells.

"Sanders, give us a blast of light, would you?"

He flares his eyes at the sail, which flickers to life with a golden glow. The ship thrums a little and then lifts, wobbling off the hangar floor.

Light sails are manufactured to resemble old-fashioned boats, with lots of graceful curves and synthetic wood features, and a tiny cabin with wide windows and barely cushioned seats. We squeeze on board, seal the cabin shut and check the atmosphere generator. It's mostly working.

"Keep your hoodies close," I say. "Not sure I trust this rust tub."

"I plan on holding my breath until after we get past the killing discs," Essential says.

With a little pitching and rolling, we float out of the hangar. Right at the gate, Essential sends out the empty drone jacket up high. When it hits the laser grid, it explodes.

"Now!" I navigate the control, which is a pretend rudder, and we sail through the gate so close to the drone that two pieces of it nearly hit us, and then within seconds we are past the ruined east gate of Mars and inside the vastness of the Choke.

We move over the disc ring of death, all of us holding our breath. Well, not Sanders. He's holding an emergency rations bar and not eating until it's clear we aren't going to become slime vapor.

And then we're through. The light sail picks up speed, probably because we all exhale simultaneously.

"That was surprisingly fun," Essential says.

"Only in hindsight," I say.

As we drift farther away from the edge of the dome, we locate the remnants of the lev-train tracks and lock in the auto-captain to follow them to Baldet crater. Should take us a little under two hours.

Now that it seems mostly certain we're not going to die immediately, I start to relax—almost against my will. My eyes feel gritty. I can't remember the last time I've slept.

"We should get some sleep," I mumble.

"Crucial, you know I don't require sleep," Sanders says.

How could I ever forget the night he stood awake and vigilant by my door the entire night at Mytikas, the spa on top of Olympus Mons, investigating the energy usage there?

"I really shouldn't sleep either," I say, but my eyes are fighting exhaustion, and losing.

"Seriously, rest," Essential says. "Let me take care of you for a change. I'll wake you at the first sign we're about to die."

"If it's certain death, maybe just let me keep sleeping," I say, trying to find a comfortable spot in the tiny cabin. Eventually, I curl up with my knees against my chin and feet against Sanders's chin. Essential grabs my ankles and pulls my legs over her lap.

"Stretch out, relax. You earned it."

Having Essential here somehow dampens the sheer lunacy of these last days. It's like my cells recognize there are other cells nearby that can watch over me. Or nanites I guess. The light dims and within minutes I'm half snoring, half mumbling and all twitching. I'm also dreaming and Mel is with me and I never want to leave.

In my dream, she is wandering through Baldet. A family of giraffes stands around watching us. Sanders is riding another giraffe and holding a sheetmeat gyro in each hand. Mel is searching for something, and then just like that, she's inside a room looking at a screen, watching something big explode. She takes my hand as we walk into the holo-desert where we used to sleep together. I want to say, "Mel, can we please try again? I'll never stop loving you." But the words come out wrong and I say something about mistake factories. Mel touches my cheek and there's blood on her hand. She says to stop killing the same giraffe over and over again, and then I'm begging her to wait for me as she runs off through a forest of symmetrical trees, the crowns bending close to protect her as she passes.

I sit up with a start and Essential puts her hand on my shoulder. I'm not sure where I am, but I center myself on her eyes and voice.

"It's okay, you were just having an active memory re-sort."

"A dream, you mean. I was having a dream."

"Interestingly," Sanders says, "organic dreams are growing increasingly rare since scientists discovered the neuronal glutamate sort-sequence in 2065. Most people choose to manage memories with external personal cog-drives rather than deal with the disoriented information cascade. I can't dream, but I suspect my de-frag is a similar experience."

His words aren't quite making sense.

"How long was I out?"

"We're almost to Baldet," Essential says, then takes my hand. "It's going to be okay, with the giraffes, I mean." She remembers the last time we were at Baldet too.

"Why did you have to drag Mel into your stupid revolution?" I ask, with more anger in my voice than I expected. The dream must have rattled me.

"You're dead wrong about that," she says quietly.

136

"What does that mean?"

"I didn't recruit her." She shoves my legs off her lap and sits up straighter. "I didn't even know she was part of it. And you know what? I never met my first contact. She probably recruited me."

"That's crazy. She had a whole life here. I pushed her away and she started over on Mars and made something nice for herself."

"Did you ever stop to think for just one single second that maybe the reason you and Mel couldn't make a real go of it was because she didn't want to drag *you* into something, something she knew you didn't believe in? Wouldn't believe in?"

"I never stopped to think that because it's not true. I pushed her away."

"Mel never gives up. She always sees what can be, not just what is. It's true of everything she does—the plants she grows, the creatures she brings into existence. She sees potential in everything. Even you."

I'm stunned into silence for a second. Is it possible I've been telling myself the wrong story all this time? No, because that means rewriting half of my life.

"I don't believe it," I say.

"I know that this is a side of Mel you never wanted to see," Essential says. "A strong side, a brave side, a courageous side, a side willing to sacrifice everything, even dysfunctional love, for a better future for everyone."

"She moved on. She left me."

"Of course, she did. You made it easy for her to choose hope for all of us. And you'd never be the wiser."

An alarm sounds.

"We are arriving at Baldet," Sanders says. "The dome appears to be unharmed."

"Hopefully, that translates into an atmosphere inside,"

Essential says.

But something doesn't look right under the dome. It's too white and cloudy. The light sail bobs to a stop outside the main entrance.

"It appears there are no hostile forces present," Sanders says. "Not yet anyway."

"Probably a trap," Essential says.

"Almost certainly," I say. "But we're out of options."

We blur the gate controls with the nanites just in case the Hucksworths are monitoring access data and float the light sail through the aperture.

Inside, the odd whiteness is even more pronounced. Everything is blanketed in a layer of white, and there's ice coating the interior walls of the dome.

"What is this stuff?" I ask.

Sanders answers. "Interestingly, it appears to be snow."

# 22

"How curious," Sanders says as we clear the transition corridor. "It *is* snow. It appears the climate controls for Baldet crater are malfunctioning."

I've never seen snow. I saw plenty of ice at Korolev crater, back before Mars SF turned it into a giant nuclear sorbet. But not snow.

The summer before I enlisted in the Consolidation Wars, there was a mega superfire in the Central Ward. It spread into a waste repository and incinerated a mountain of outdated twist-pair cables, leftovers from one of the endless Halo-mandated hardware updates. The insulation melted and toxic smoke billowed into the contamosphere. It seeded some ice crystals, which floated into Multnomah Ward and then the whole stinking mess spit down foul, brown, deadly ice-hail pellets that stacked up at least seven centimeters deep.

It was memorable, and kind of pretty, but nothing like actual snow. Or, actual engineered snow, which is what we have here in Baldet.

We move onto the deck of the light sail, take off our airhoodies and breathe in the cold, clear air.

A herd of bison is nearby. Twenty or so, shoulder to shoulder, obliviously marching along, snorts of steam pulsing from their giant noses. Ice hangs from their thick coarse hair. A few stragglers have fallen behind, including three spindle-legged babies.

"What in the name of the multi-gods are those things?" Essential asks.

"Bison," I say. "The last time I was here, they were less active."

"Probably upset by the sudden climate change. They're so ugly, they're beautiful," she says.

A bird with a wingspan nearly the width of our light sail swoops down close to us, one angry yellow eye meeting mine, and we all duck. It looks hungry, but we must not look like food because it flaps back up into the dense sky and disappears behind the snow mist.

"That was an especially large member of the avian family," Sanders says.

I remember the first time I came to Baldet, I thought it was a dinosaur. Mel corrected me.

"It's an eagle. Mel was experimenting with species size. I think maybe that one got away from her."

The deeper into the dome we travel, the warmer it gets. Snow is still falling, but it's not sticking and the ground is a muddy mess.

"Sanders, see if you can access the climate controls and stabilize the dome. I can't imagine the giraffes are enjoying this," I say.

There's a panicked bleat behind us and we turn in time to see the enormous bird carry off one of the baby bison in its talons. The poor little thing is squealing and pumping its hooves wildly. The herd panics and scatters, all except the mother who runs along under the bird, bellowing madly.

The baby is too heavy for the eagle to maintain its purchase and the bison falls to the ground with a sickening thud. It's still—dazed or dead—and we have a shared moment of hope it's going to survive, that it's going to stand up. But before the mother can make her way over, a pack of gray dogs lurches from the grass, drags it down and carries it off.

"Let's maybe stay in our boat," I say.

"I thought Mel bred out aggression in these creatures," Essential says.

"They have no aggression toward humans," Sanders says. "And under normal conditions they're all fed regularly and separated into their own grazing areas, so have no need to feed on each other. But it appears the system has been down for some time now."

"It doesn't take long for nature to reduce us," I say. "We like to think we're special, but if it weren't for the system of controls, we'd be at each other's throats just like that."

"You of all people should know that the system hasn't eradicated the struggle for survival," Essential says. "It just looks different. Instead of eating each other, we create proxies for winners and losers—wealth and poverty. The violence isn't as memorable, it's slower and more patient, but just think of the beetlers in the Fields and the Five Families on Mars. The outcome is no less brutal, even if easier to ignore. But the system is contributing to the conflict instead of protecting us. It just needs—"

"More empathy. Gotcha. You're becoming a little predictable." And a little tiresome, I say in my head.

Sanders is watching her closely, as if hearing a new language for the first time. The snow stops falling. The sun, or a recreated, synthetic, reflected facsimile of it, breaks through the still lingering clouds.

"Good work, Sanders. Now restart the feeding schedules and maybe we can turn this place back into the little animal utopia Mel envisioned."

"Certainly, Crucial."

I'm trying to think about where Mel might be. Baldet

isn't big, but it's easy enough to hide with Halo glitching. And more importantly, if she wanted to lay low, she could have just stayed in Jezero. Or picked some knobby slot canyon out in the Choke. If she's here, it's for a reason.

"Set our course to the development lab," I say. "If Mel is here, that's where she'll be."

Sanders nods and we start drifting in that direction.

I try not to think about the last time I was here with Mel, about what happened. Essential reaches over and takes both my hands. I realize I've been nervously rubbing them together, like I'm trying to wipe off the memory of giraffe blood.

"It's not surprising you'd have repressed trauma," she says.

"What? No, I'm fine." I try to push her hands away, but she holds on tight.

Our light sail pulls up to a long building. It's shaded by a small forest, each tree a little different. Some tall, some wide, others with those big round nuts Mel showed me. Flowers—a hundred kinds, all different colors—line the path to the entrance, all a little bedraggled from the cold.

The building interior is narrow, at least a quarter of a kilometer long. And dark, hot and humid. There's a cluster of data jacks and screens near the front, and the rest of the space is filled with long parallel greenhouses, tubes, tubs, wires and pipes.

It's eerily silent. I wish I had time to walk around, to understand Mel a little better by knowing her creations. But now is not the time.

"It does not appear Melinda Hopwire is in this building," Sanders says.

"Yeah, that much I figured. But was she here?"

Essential accesses a console to check the history. "Someone was here. They used a zipstrip to fire up saturated broadcasts. They listened to the Hucksworths for a while, then tried to get data on the destruction of Phobos and queried numerous locations for energy spikes."

"That sounds like Mel," I say.

"It's possible she was trying to find the location of the Halo backup servers," Sanders says.

"Whoever it was also searched the local database for information on specific types of phenolic acid," Essential says.

She is seated at what is probably Mel's workspace. It's messy, nothing that would suggest neat-freak Mel. The desk is covered in a disorganized layer of pipettes, fissile shards and four small glass terrariums, one tipped over with the soil and small plants spilled onto the floor.

"It's not like Mel to leave behind such a mess. What was she up to?"

I study the pattern of the chaos. It's all tipped over away from a shelf lined with linked modules of equipment. There's a long line of dusty equipment and one clean, empty spot right in the middle, the source of the spills and destruction.

"What was there?" I ask.

Sanders scans the remaining items. "This is a fairly common configuration of biology equipment. It appears a cellular oscilloscope is missing."

"Explain."

"It's a tool to test the voltage of atomic bonds, something she would use regularly in her terra-scaping work."

"Mel came all the way to Baldet for a single piece of equipment," Essential says. "Why?"

"More important is where she's going now. What's the query you mentioned?"

Essential uses her synth eye to display Mel's search

history holographically. "Polyphenolic acid."

"It's a compound found uniquely in the genus lichen," Sanders says.

"Lichen? Is that some kind of plant or something?" I ask.

"Interestingly, lichen are biological symbionts of algae and fungus varietals," Sanders says. "A joint life form. They form naturally in rocky terrain and acting in unison with wind and water are harbingers of the erosive process that breaks down rocks into soils."

"Mel is an expert on plants," Essential says. "She would already know that."

"Agreed. So why was she looking?" I ask. To leave me a clue. Of course. "Sanders, are there lichen here at Baldet?"

"No. And it does not grow naturally on Mars, not yet anyway." He pauses. "It's curious though. There is, or was, an industrial lichen production facility on Mars. Before quantum technology replaced thrust rockets, lichen was farmed and distilled into rocket fuel. It's been long abandoned, but never officially decommissioned."

"Where is this facility?"

"The Mars Industrial Lichen Lab, known colloquially as the 'Grove,' is not far from here. Near Deuteronillus Mensae."

"That's where she's headed," I say.

"I am unclear on your deductive processes," Sanders says. "How did you arrive at this conclusion based on the available evidence?"

"Just trust him," Essential says. "He's kind of an expert on following along behind Mel."

Before I can even defend myself, the lights on the dome flare and a familiar voice floods the speakers.

"Crucial Larsen, prepare to be first killed and then

detained."

"Oh, for prok's sake."

"That is an illogical order of events," Sanders says.

"Not for Canadis Whitsend," I say.

## 23

This is awkward.

Canadis Whitsend—my duplicitous former commander during the Consolidation Wars—is supposed to be locked up in a Terrorium, even though almost everyone in the universe thinks it's Essential in there.

Whitsend sounds angry. I don't blame her. Terroriums are not pleasant places. The whole point is to keep prisoners barely alive and totally immobile while screaming an endless loop of Civic Rehabilitation and Advancement Programming straight into the brain. It's high-tech torture reserved for those who have really riled the Five Families.

Back on Earth, I once saw them let someone out of one after a relatively short sentence. Like, a couple weeks. He looked normal but was broken. His eyes were empty and his voice was hollow when he spoke, which was only to agree with everything and to thank the Five Families for their generosity.

I always assumed I'd end up in a Terrorium someday; instead, that honor fell to Canadis Whitsend.

"I expected to find Melinda Hopwire here," Whitsend says. "But our scans indicate three life-forms, and none match hers."

She's broadcasting on the dome's closed system, her voice reverberating in our feeds and across Baldet crater, likely panicking the animals. "I know it's you, though, Crucial Larsen. I told the Hucksworths you didn't die on that escape pod. That would be far too easy for everyone."

"I don't think she likes you much," Essential says. She's looking around for weapons, but they are hard to come by in a hothouse.

"You helped trap her in the Terrorium too," I say.

We can see them now on the static-fuzzed monitor. A small group of Hucksworth soldiers on foot, Whitsend at the front. Why the prok is she leading a group of invaders?

"Personally, I'm glad you're still alive," Whitsend says. "For now."

Her amplified voice is driving the giraffes crazy. They run past, their odd legs kicking up mud. The small bison herd also enters the frame.

"I'm looking forward to catching up," Whitsend says. "I hope your sister is there as well. We don't have a lot of scan data on her, but I'm pretty sure it's her. I wonder if she remembers me."

Whitsend looks tougher and angrier. Probably because she's holding a glitter rifle in each hand and standing in front of seven Hucksworth soldiers, who also look pissed. Or mean, I guess. Or maybe just armed.

They're approaching fast, weapons raised. And undoubtedly calling for backup.

I look at Sanders. "She'll recognize you and rat you out to the Hucksworths as a cybanism. Keep an airhoodie over your face. We need to slip out the back and—"

Essential taps on another monitor. Three more soldiers are behind us. They're setting up some kind of automated heavy artillery.

"New plan," I say. "We have to get to the light sail."

"I don't think she's going to be in favor of letting us float out of here," Essential says.

"She'll never expect us to come right at her."

"While former Commander Whitsend may not expect

such an action, data suggest she would be very happy if we approached directly," Sanders says. "Her priority seems to be inflicting trauma upon you both."

"It's not a perfect plan."

"It's not a plan at all," Essential says. She is wrapping a heavy cable around her fist. She's not going down without a fight.

"We just need to keep Sanders, with his glitter-proof skin, between us and the guns. We get to the light sail and unfurl. Sanders, you have to blast it with as much light as your skinny cybanetic ass can muster."

"I'm afraid my bowel light is very weak in comparison to my ocular beams."

Essential laughs. It's a nice sound and takes me back to the games we played as kids. Like Universal Rummicubed and Battlecruisers. She always won Battlecruisers because she recoded the targeting.

"If they start shooting, stay low. One blast from those polarizers and you're done for."

We step out into the front of the hothouse. The soldiers pull up 100 meters away. Whitsend is smiling and ready to glitter me to a pulp.

"Former Commander Whitsend. What a surprise."

"I bet it is. Keep your arms extended."

"How did you get out of the, you know …" I make a sort of coffin shape in the air with my fingers.

"Terrorium? When the meteors hit, the Mars SF building was leveled. The force cracked open the sublevels, including my accommodations. Didn't take long to figure out the winning side. I thought they might benefit from some local expertise."

"You know this dead-end plasmid?" one of the soldiers asks her. He's no doubt beaming this back to Spilla on their local network.

"Yes, his name is Crucial Larsen. And that's his sister, Essential. Not sure who the lumpy one is, but we'll sort that out when we chip the corpses."

"Spilla wants Larsen brought in alive," the soldier says. "But doesn't care how alive, if you get my ionic drift."

"What are you doing?" I ask Whitsend. "Why are you helping the people trying to take over Mars?"

"They're not trying, they succeeded. They just need to secure the backup servers and run your former lover to ground." She motions the soldier forward. "I remembered what happened here with you and that giraffe. I thought this might be where she's trying to hide out. Unfortunately, she's not here. Fortunately, we have you." She turns to the soldier. "Plug into the emergency channel and broadcast live while I kill the girl and the pudgy one. We'll tell Hopwire to turn herself in within an hour or he dies."

Her stint in the Terrorium did not diminish her edge nor her ability to shoot orders like a rail gun stuck on automatic.

"I can't believe you're switching sides," I say. "All that stuff you said about honor and duty."

"You were an idiot then and you're an idiot now. If we really believed in honor and duty, do you think we'd send you to die fighting on behalf of corporations? The only things that matter are wealth and power."

She levels her gun—they already trust her with a gun; she has more moves than a coronal mass ejection—at Essential.

The war bird saves us. The not-dinosaur. The eagle.

It swoops down with a flash of shadow and a ruffle of feathers, landing nearby. Probably hungry and looking for baby bison or nutrient pellets. The sight of it unnerves the invaders, who aren't used to macro-creatures. One of the soldiers swears and pulls the trigger on her burp gun. She misses the bird but the charge hits a nearby bison on the rump. The bison squeals with pain and panic, flopping over, its comically small back legs temporarily useless.

That startles the bison's friends, and the rest of the herd, nudged into unexpected action, rumble between us. The soldiers, already on edge by the enormity of the bird, are terrified of the viviparous quadrupeds—my OCD is silhouetting them with an info profile from Baldet archives—and scatter, shooting and screaming.

Whitsend, who knows they are genetically modified to instinctively avoid hurting humans, curses and looks for a clean shot. But she accidentally gets a glancing friendly fire shot from a burp gun. She falls to one knee, trying to steady the rifle through a wash of wet electrical pain.

We make a run for the light sail, expecting a round of glitter flechettes or a polarizer blast the whole time. But apparently, soldiers trained secretly in a bacterial world are off-put by the woolly, feathered, stampeding, squawking macro world. When we pile onto the deck, Essential fires up the nav and Sanders yanks off his airhoodie to let loose a double blast of, thankfully, ocular flares into the sail. The energy is enough to send the ship wobbling toward the exit like an ejected surgical crust skipping across a urea pond. Essential and I hold on to the rails and use the nanites to cover our tracks.

I turn to Sanders. "Thanks for blasting us out of there." He's sagging against the cabin wall. The blast of photons must have taken a lot of his reserves.

"I fear I have dangerously depleted myself."

"You did good, buddy. You rest. We'll get you some calories at the lichen grove."

"Crucial, I'm concerned that former Commander Whitsend perceived me as lumpy. Am I lumpy?"

# 24

"Saved by the bison. Not something I ever thought I'd say."

We're crammed back into the light sail ship, heading to Deuteronillus Mensae and the lichen dome. Sanders is red-lining, barely able to keep his eyes focused.

"It does have a certain ring to it, you know," Essential says. "Sort of lyrical."

I glance over at her. She's nervous, and for good reason.

Since she has no OCD, she's not connected to the emergency Halo channel, patchy as it is. With the backup servers running the show, Halo is in restricted mode. But the Hucksworths are taking full advantage of that and jamming the narrow band with a single message.

"You should backdoor into Halo. We're popular."

She uses the nanites to redirect the signal into her synthetic eye. She gets a full dose of Plesca addressing Mars and Earth with holos of our faces hovering behind her.

"Crucial Larsen and his sister, Essential Larsen, and an unknown companion are fugitives wanted for high crimes and treason. They are dangerous criminals actively working against the good of society. The same is true of Melinda Hopwire. Anyone who shares information leading to their capture or termination will be officially adopted and made a member of the Hucksworth family and given a credit positive rating for life plus two. They are under terminal bond. I repeat, Crucial Larsen and his sister—"

Terminal bond. No ramifications for killing us outright.

"Well, that's not great," Essential says, disengaging the nanites.

A credit-positive life is something 99.999 percent of Earthers dream of, and with Mars in tatters that will look like a pretty good deal here too.

"It's only a matter of time before someone sees us and flags the authorities or just hits us from a distance with a rail slug," I say. "Or Whitsend catches up to us."

"Look on the bright side," Essential says. "Mel will know you're not a heartless idiot who locked up his own sister in a Terrorium to protect the Five Families."

"Chilled comfort. And that's if we can find her."

"We will. We have to."

Sanders stirs. "I think I am beginning to understand the concept of human love." His voice is still low. He needs to eat something, and soon.

"Yeah?" I ask, hoping to distract him.

"You love Melinda Hopwire, even though at this stage you do not expect her to return any affection and you stand to gain nothing from your continued adherence to thinking of her well-being."

"That's about right," I say.

"And you love your sister. But in a much different way."

"Right, because she makes it so hard."

"Even with only three percent power, I fully recognize your sarcasm." He shifts slightly so he can see me more clearly and scan my bio-signature. "Do you love me?"

"Oh, well. You know …"

Essential jabs me with her elbow.

"It's clear that human love brings together loyalty, empathy and compassion," he says.

It's clear to me his cognitive processors have been grinding on this for a while.

"Based on all available data related to my actions and reactions over the course of our relationship, I conclude that even though I am not designed to experience these emotions, I must love you. And I wonder if you feel the same."

I'm about to die in the Choke on an antique light sail with an expiring cybanism who loves me and with a one-eyed sister intent on saving two planets. I think back to a few months ago when I was content to drink a salt beer after my shift of rounding up labor criminals. Things were so simple then.

I nod. "Sure. Why not. I love you."

"Your heart rate did not change. You seem to be telling the truth."

"I'm literally crying right now from my one good eye," Essential says. "He's never even told *me* that."

"You should know, I may also love Chancellor Valentine," Sanders says. "But not in the same way I love you. It's confusing. Love, I mean. I greatly enjoy the company of the chancellor and feel, it's hard to define. I feel enlivened in her presence."

"If you're confused by love, you've basically become human."

"And apparently, I'm growing quite fond of your sister too. Is it possible that this sudden emergence of love is draining my operating system? I do not wish for my existence to end because of this emotion."

"Love won't kill you. It just makes you wish you were dead sometimes," I say.

Our conversation is interrupted by a few gentle beeps from the light sail and I look out the window.

There's a tangle of buttes and mesas stretching off into the distance. Deuteronillus Mensae. And in the foreground, an old dilapidated dome that looks tiny in comparison to the glacier-carved stone.

"We'll arrive at the Grove in eleven minutes," I say.

Since Sanders is almost offline, I use the light sail console to pull up the cached information on the facility and read it out loud. It's out of date, but close enough.

"The official name of this facility is the Mars Industrial Lichen Lab, a facility established for the growth and processing of biofuel. Lichen, which are small and often colorful fungal growths that attach themselves to rocks and other inanimate objects, generate biochemical products that powered rockets in the late twenty-first century."

"Q-rockets made the lichen fuel obsolete," Essential says.

"According to the info cache, the place was shut down in 2150. So, it's been isolated for thirty-eight years. I don't know what Mel is doing here, but we should prepare for the worst, like no enviro controls, no gravity regulators."

We fold the sail and the ship settles to the ground. We gear up, expecting to find a ruined dome. The outer door into the transition chamber opens easily enough and when the inner door opens, what we sail into is the last thing I would have guessed. Essential is speechless. Even Sanders, in his diminished state, sits up to stare.

I check the Priestly count on my airhoodie.

"Holy heliotropes. It's breathable air." I take off my hoodie. "She did it. Mel terraformed Mars."

# 25

"Is this the heaven those misguided cultists used to dream about?" Essential asks.

We are standing in the center of what was supposed to be a dusty, deserted industrial lichen facility. At best, I expected a cracked dome full of overgrown lichen flats suffocating a matrix of synthetic boulders and sculpted cliffs, with various bits of broken-down and abandoned equipment strewn about.

There may be some lichen still in here farther on. If so, they're buried beneath a riot of greenery, like someone set off a seed bomb and then dialed up the perfect mix of environmental factors.

Not someone. Mel.

The place is lush, verdant, an explosion of life. Of hope. Grasses, bushes and trees. Young trees, some bearing fruit. Colorful sprays of flowers everywhere. Purple blooms on tiny stalks. A bush with pink buds. Another bunch of yellow something or others, with huge floppy petals.

Essential and I stand motionless, mouths hanging open. The beauty is so intense, it's disorienting.

What's most amazing is that we don't need airhoodies. Even though this place is cut off from Halo—off the Mars grid and abandoned for decades—there's air. Fresh and delightfully scented, and even a little moist.

"Let's stay here forever," Essential says. She leans down

and puts her nose into a red flower. "What a wonderful smell. Like those aroma-pops used in old cabarangs." Then she swears under her breath and pulls her hand back, a tiny ball of blood welling on her fingertip. "They have little needles on them."

The dome is small, at least by Martian dome standards. About a three-kilometer radius, less than a tenth the size of Baldet. But there's a key difference in the architecture; it's unusually tall. So tall I can barely make out the top. And my up-view is partially blocked by a misty layer of moisture and wispy clouds.

This place has its own mini ecosystem.

I pull a piece of fruit from a tree and hand it to Sanders. "Think this is edible?"

He cups it in his hands, letting his skin sensors puzzle over the fruit. "It's called an 'apple.'" Then he eats it in two bites—stem, seeds and all.

"So that's a yes." I leave him standing in front of the tree, methodically picking and eating fruit at a remarkable speed.

Essential is walking ahead slowly, bending to touch, and marvel at, individual plants. An insect dislodges from a bloom and buzzes straight toward me, landing on the back of my hand. I feel a prick and then a sharp sting.

With an oath, I swat it down and stomp on it.

"Don't kill things," Essential says.

"It attacked me."

"From its perspective, we attacked it."

"*You* attacked it. And I paid the price."

I lift my foot and see circuitry in the flattened remains. "Anyway, it wasn't real."

"It's an APD," Sanders says. He walks over with an armful of fruit. "An autonomous pollinating device. They were quite common on Earth after the pollinator collapse in 2054."

"Why did it sting me?"

"A defense mechanism to protect vulnerable flowering plants. They inject a tiny dose of chemical irritant."

A welt is coming up. "For a place abandoned decades ago, there seems to be a lot happening here, what with all the oxygen, pollinators, plants and fruit," I say.

"I have eliminated all but one hypothesis," Sanders says. There's a long pause as we watch him crunching through apples, core and all.

"Care to share?" I ask at last.

"Oh, sorry," he says, apple juice dripping down his chin. "I thought it was obvious. Melinda Hopwire has been using this for her personal experimental research."

"I mean, I know you're running on reserves, but that's beyond obvious. Mel is the only person on either planet who could do all this. But she came here *now* for a reason, and it wasn't just to check in on her handiwork, no matter how wonderful it is. Why risk everything to come here?"

"She was at Baldet for a piece of equipment," Essential says. "Maybe she needed something from here. Or had something stashed?"

"We don't have time to grid-search the whole space. Let's start with the most logical places. There has to be a control center or lab or something."

Essential switches her synthetic eye to radar and scans around us. "There's a structure, the only structure in the dome, about a kilometer and half away." She points to a faint path through the greenery ahead of us.

As we move away from the entrance, the plants begin to thin out, transitioning to a carpet of lichen over a landscape of jumbled rocks. It's like the sunbelt on Earth but in reverse, basically what happens to a desert if it's suddenly inundated with water. The lichen is half a meter thick in some places.

"What's even the point of lichen?" I ask, idly scratching the welt on the back of my hand. Then I realize my error. Sanders is mostly recharged.

"Interestingly—"

Dammit.

"—lichen can be thought of as the earliest wave in the fight to create soil. First comes the lava, which makes the rocks, then lichen grow on the rocks. The lichen secrete acids that, over considerable lengths of geologic time, break down rock structures to create soil, which in turn allows for plants to gain a foothold. That acid, of course, formed the basis of the rocket fuel distillation efforts. Admittedly, this is the model from our knowledge of Earth. We don't know how, or even if, this played out on Mars or any other planet."

I point to the thick mat of lichen covering the rocks lining the path and the tiny slopes of rich soil spilling out from under them. "It seems to be happening at a faster pace than geologic time, on Earth or anywhere. Like, over years instead of centuries."

"Indeed. It appears Melinda Hopwire has done the impossible. She has created a viable approach to terraform Mars by deploying high-functioning lichen to create an atmosphere and a soil base able to sustain life."

"She always dreamed of working out the kinks here, so she could reclaim Earth."

"This knowledge would be of considerable value to members of the Five Families."

"Or the Hucksworths," Essential says.

"Still doesn't explain why she would come here in the middle of an invasion, knowing everyone in the universe is looking for her."

We arrive at a structure in the heart of the Grove. It's a

small lab, overflowing with equipment and technology along with six grow rooms exploding with plants and sheets of micro-lichen.

We're in the main part of the lab, which is surrounded by rows of curious machines and a single control desk. There's a coating of dust or pollen over the surface of the desk with tiny cat paw tracks through it.

She was here. They were here.

I sit down and look at the patterns in the dust. "Sanders, what was she doing?"

He studies the buttons and then points to an array of equipment still powered up. "It appears she was distilling a rather large quantity of polyphenolic acid from the lichen."

"Why the hell would she come all the way out here just to do that?"

"I cannot deduce a logical explanation."

Essential wanders back into the room and looks at me with a curious blend of happiness and concern. "You should come see this."

She leads us back to a grow room that's less plant-rich than the others, with hardly any lichen. It's a little patch of desert. Above the door is a display screen like all the other rooms have. Most say things like, "Lichen v4.78" or "Self-pollination test." This one says "Crucial's desert."

"Crucial, your eyes appear to be reacting to unknown irritants," Sanders says. "Are you well?"

"Those are tears," Essential whispers.

I feel all the energy drain out of me, like a hungry cybanism. Mel made her own little version of my desert sim to sleep in.

All the manic adrenaline that's been keeping me going pours out and I suddenly feel tired and hopeless and old. "I need to lie down. For just a minute."

I enter the grow room. It smells like her. I close my eyes.

## 26

Voices wake me from a dream floating through my mind like a memory.

I was a kid again, and Mom was calling Essential and me for breakfast. Our food debt covered two creamed cherry kasha bowls each year. Mom saved them up for February 19, the day after Perseverance Day. She wanted us to celebrate living on Earth.

I smell the sweet, toasty creamed cherry clones, and hear Mom calling from her bedroom, which was also the kitchen. "Wake up, dummy."

That's not Mom.

Essential is shaking me. "Seriously, wake up. You conk out harder than Sanders when he runs out of food."

I rub my eyes, trying to adjust to this rude version of reality. I'm not at home. I'm not a kid. I'm in the Grove in the desert holo lab. It's so peaceful here. I must have fallen asleep.

"I was having the best dream."

"Great. You can tell it all to your bestie Canadis, who is here right now. Looking for us."

That wakes me up.

"Probably to kill you both and then repurpose me," Sanders says.

"Can we check your 'duh' settings? You seem to be stuck on obvious."

"I'm not sure I've ever accessed my ... oh. You were

directing cynical humor at me to defuse your own feelings of inadequacy in the situation."

To go from the peaceful beauty of the tiny desert—an island of calm in the middle of a cosmic invasion—to being hunted again is taking more than the expected time to recalibrate. My thoughts are slow to reassemble. It doesn't help that my companions are so annoying. And sensitive. Good thing they're family.

I cannot believe I just thought of a cybanism as family.

My hand is itching fiercely from the pollinator sting. I scratch and look at the knobby welt coming up, red and irritated.

I hear ships clattering around outside. Okay, I'm back in this shithole version of reality. "What can you see, Essential?"

She focuses her enhanced eye and zooms past the sturdy dome walls. "It's definitely her, along with more soldiers than the last time."

Whitsend never gives up. She's like a holo ad-cloud that follows you around after you accidentally pause at a promo in your feed for an extra millisecond.

Not like ads are a problem now. With Halo inoperable, ads are gone, avatainment is down and, thankfully for us, monitoring is patchy and unreliable at best.

On a better day, the silence would be nice, although I'd undoubtedly still be trying to adjust to it. Sometimes, I wonder if the reason we traded all our freedoms for generational debt was because humans don't like the quiet. Or, more accurately, we don't like being alone with our thoughts. I get that. My thoughts are usually torturous. That's why I routinely punish them, or at least temporarily silence them, with alcohol. Some of which I could use right now.

I flash back to the old days, long before my time. For

an instant I almost envy those poor, barbaric bastards who carried external connection devices. They could put their handheld digital portals aside anytime they wanted to, or even turn them off.

Why didn't they? Instead, they started us down a path that ended with ocular implants at birth and continual connection, and no one ever stopped or even blinked.

I mean, the OCD *is* convenient. Like when you're trying to order window drinks from a helibar. Or tracking the progress of a highly motivated execution squad slowly advancing on your nap space in a deserted lichen farm. Well, it would have been convenient if I were connected to Halo now.

"How the prok did they find us here?"

"Halo is seriously compromised but weakly functional sporadically, especially in local mode," Essential says. "You can still connect. When Mel fired up the distiller, it must have triggered an alert that made it through somehow."

"My data show a spike in energy usage in the facility," Sanders says. "Former Commander Whitsend must have been seining for anomalies."

"If we get out of here alive, let's make some anomalies all around the damn planet so she's chasing after her own digital shadow until the end of time."

"I hope they don't see our light sail," Essential says.

There's a muffled explosion from out front.

"I think they saw our light sail," I say.

"It will be hard to avoid capture without a conveyance," Sanders says, then pauses. "Sorry. It seems I have stated the obvious again."

"You could carry us," Essential says.

"Regretfully, my energy usage remains unusually high. Without a significant caloric input, I'm afraid I would shut down after sixty-four point forty-five meters."

"So, basically right in front of the soldiers," I say.

"I will refrain from pointing out that this is a potential suboptimal outcome," he says.

"If we're going to find Mel, we need a ride."

"Any ideas?" Essential asks.

"Yeah. Distraction."

Essential and Sanders both look up through the top of the dome to where the moon used to be. Essential is a bad influence on him.

"How about instead of waiting for another moon to explode, we convince them this is our last stand," I say. "Get them to really commit. And when they're focused on prying us out of here, we cripple a couple of their ships and hitch a ride back on the tow-rocket."

"That sounds almost identical to your plan for getting us off Phobos," Essential says. "Do you have just the one plan that you tweak for various situations?"

"First, it worked. Second, I have plenty of plans. And third through infinity, if you have a better idea, now's the time to share."

She doesn't say anything but gives me the tall-finger.

"That's what I thought." I turn to Sanders. "We need to stop them from advancing on us by foot. How accurate is your throwing arm?"

"My confidence is low. It's likely my accuracy could vary by up to several millimeters at distances under 300 meters."

"We'll take it." I toss him a pebble. "Come on, let's get closer."

We wind our way down a lichen-encrusted canyon until we see the entrance where Whitsend and her dozen or so thug-forces are moving in, weapons at the ready. The nanites are holding off their scans. "Hit one of the soldiers."

"How much force should I use?" Sanders asks.

"Enough to make it seem like a weapon."

"Aim for a limb though," Essential says. "Being a soldier is like any other job. They're just trying to stay alive and lower their debt."

"Except for the invading Mars bit. Innocent people died, remember?"

Essential shakes her head. "War is always a for-profit enterprise. Do you think any of those soldiers could have stopped the invasion by refusing to participate? More likely they would have been imprisoned, or killed, and their place taken by someone even more desperate to make some credits. I'm not saying there shouldn't be consequences. I'm just saying all things considered, and with the luxury of time, we don't have to be actively cruel."

"Fascinating," Sanders says. "You appear to be exhibiting another type of empathy. I'm learning so much from your sister."

"Just throw the godsdamn rock," I say.

Sanders runs the calcs, bends his arm back and lets it fly. We're zoomed in close. Nothing happens. Well, something happens. Whitsend and the soldiers turn to look behind them at a tiny hole that suddenly appeared in the door.

"You missed them completely."

"Now who needs to check their own 'duh' settings?" Essential says, patting Sanders on the arm. He looks simultaneously embarrassed and mollified. "Try again." She hands him a slightly larger rock, flat and jagged, about half the size of a fist.

He hurls it across the wide-open space of the building. and a soldier shrieks in pain as the stone clips his shoulder. There's a spray of blood along with some cursing and blind shooting as they all stumble back toward the door.

We hijack the lichen farm's old feed to watch the action. They have two fart ships and a couple of repurposed Mars SF rockets floating around, with reinforcements on the way. They move the ships into a defensive position ringing the facility. They'll be content to wait us out now. Or at least wait until they can get some bots to come through and draw our fire. We can't be here when that happens.

"That went well," I say. "Now we just need to figure out how to bring down a ship or two with no weapons."

"We're in a facility that used to manufacture rocket fuel," Essential says. "I bet we can figure out *something*." She rolls her eyes as if I'm simple-minded.

I always forget that Essential has been part of the resistance long enough to make her more or less an expert in asymmetric warfare. A natural response to asymmetric wealth distribution, I guess.

In less than 20 minutes, Essential has an improvised weapon that will either destroy us all in a massive explosion or allow the three of us to make it past Whitsend and her militia. I put the odds of surviving at about even. Maybe slightly higher for Sanders.

# 27

"Are you sure this will work?" I ask.

"Absolutely," Essential says. "Trust me."

We're looking at Essential's improvised weapon made from dangerously unstable canisters of rocket fuel we found behind a dumpster on the far perimeter of the lichen farm. The canisters are so old that they're visibly degrading around the tungsten nipples. I'm scared to even stare at them too hard.

"The last time I trusted you, you smuggled nanites to Mars in my blood. The first time I trusted you, you broke my arm. Your trust account is getting close to depleted."

"Oh, come on," she says. "Are you still mad about the turboscotch incident? That was like thirty years ago."

"Trust me, you said. I only boosted the output in the lift-pack a little, you said. It will be more fun this way, you said. It sent me through the roof of that old psi-barn. My shoulder still hurts sometimes."

"You should have let me go first."

"I'm your big brother. I was supposed to be looking out for you."

It's funny now, but the health debit from the busted shoulder was no laughing matter. Mom was seriously vexed.

"I can't believe you took the fall for me. And I can't believe you keep score."

"I'm not keeping score," I say. "I just have a functional memory and the mental fortitude to learn from the past so I can avoid making the same mistakes."

Dammit, I did *not* just repeat Valentine.

Essential looks at me incredulously. "You, Crucial Larsen, who marinates in your mistakes like a slab of sheetmeat in a smoke tank, who wears your mistakes like a glitter-proof emotional exo armor, you are telling *me* about learning from the past."

"I have no idea what you are talking about."

"Mel, you idiot. I'm talking about Mel. You messed up and never tried to fix it. You let her go, assuming it was all about you, not once considering that maybe she had some things to take care of. And you've stayed frozen in regret and suspended in salt beer ever since."

"Do all human families fight in this fashion? And at such inopportune times?" Sanders asks.

"No," we say simultaneously.

"Most families are kind and loving," I say, "but most families don't have a bungle for a kid sister."

She ignores me. "Sanders, this is yet another example of empathy to file in your research. Empathy doesn't just mean being nice to people. Sometimes you have to be—"

"Cruel?" I suggest.

"Honest. Sometimes the best course of action is hearing hard truths so you can make hard decisions."

"Let's make a hard choice about trying this contraption you built. And maybe walk us through it one more time?"

"It's simple," Essential says. "We need to bring down one of their ships so they need to call a tow-rocket. I've bundled the fuel canisters we found, attached a directional magnet scavenged from a dome repair kit, and created a remote igniter out of the distillate stove Mel was using."

I look at the bundle suspiciously. "All we need to do

now is get this outside, very carefully get this outside, aim it at a ship, turn the magnet on and at the precise moment it hits the ship, remote-ignite the burner and *poof*."

"Poof?" Sanders asks.

"Poof," she says.

He looks at her and then at me. "I calculate seventeen probable ways this could seriously malfunction. And that's not factoring in the necessary sequence of events needed to avoid detection if we make it to the tow-rocket."

"She is right, though. We need to try something. Do you have any better ideas?"

He rolls his eyes back into his sockets and runs some calculations.

"That don't end up with one of us dead, severely injured or imprisoned?" I add.

He refocuses. "Given your parameters, this option is the least dangerous of the various less-than-optimal scenarios. But perhaps doing nothing, compared to doing the wrong thing, might be the best plan in this case."

"You don't know the Larsens," Essential mutters.

"My analysis is clear. Doing nothing keeps numerous potential options open compared to closing many or all of them with some sense of finality if this goes poorly."

"I've never been good at waiting," I say. "Although, since you're the one with blast-resistant skin, would you mind carrying the bomb to the escape hatch on the side?"

"A reasonable request."

"Essential, you stay back and trigger it on my mark."

"I'm not letting you take the fall for me this time." She tries to push past me.

I stand my ground. "No arguments. Listen to your big brother. For once."

She hugs me.

Sanders and I make our way to a small, nondescript

pressure hatch. I nod and Essential uses the nanites to trigger an alarm at the main entrance, causing everyone to look the other way. I blur our actions and open the hatch where Sanders carefully sets down the deadly bundle.

I power up the magnet, aim it at the unsuspecting fart ship and lock in the navigation. I can feel it vibrate, then pull out of my hands. The deadly package streaks across the open ground and clangs onto the ship.

"Now!" I yell and Essential triggers the igniter.

There's a blinding flash and a mighty roar as the back of the ship explodes in a green flash. The force propels the ship up and away on a pillar of smoke and fire, sending it tumbling out of sight on the other side of the horizon.

"Poof," I say, as we watch our plan disappear.

"Interestingly," Sanders says, "I identified eighteen outcomes but completely overlooked that one."

Then a lot of things happen at once. The pilots on the rest of the ships are not impressed and start shooting at the lichen facility as they pull back to a safer distance.

More ships arrive. Transports, not fliers. And not tow-rockets. Reinforcements. All the reinforcements. A wave of shock troops spills out and begins advancing on the lichen dome. They look focused on generating pain and then death, and not necessarily in that order.

"Perhaps doing nothing may have been a wiser course after all," Sanders says.

I'm so focused on chastising him for being an omni-bot know-it-all that it's too late when I notice four people approaching us inside the lichen dome, glitter guns raised.

# 28

**September 3, 2238**
*Stardust University, Neuro-Lecture Interface 75.32*

"If I wrote a memoir, I wouldn't have to pretend to be objective," Valentine says.

She's in the green zone, the virtual lobby of the university. Sanders is plugged in too, sitting next to her on the chesterfield in their home overlooking New Jezero on Earth.

"Historians don't pretend to be objective, at least not the good ones, and you are a very good historian," Sanders says.

"What if we have invented objectivity to persuade ourselves that truth exists?"

"Socrates said that truth is revealed only in language unadorned," he says.

"Socrates? Since when do you study Socrates?"

"I've been exploring the ancients lately."

This is the tenor of most of their conversations. Gentle and deep, back and forth, with frequent digressions, typically arriving at unexpectedly satisfying, if unfamiliar, destinations.

"Does this mean if I'm soaring in my oratory, or my writing, I should be taken for a liar?" she asks.

He smiles. "Socrates asserted this during his own

defense for treason, which suggests he expected his accusers to be misguided but eloquent. You have never been misguided since the day we met."

"Flatterer. But it seems Socrates is making my case for me. There is only individual truth. Hence the need for a memoir."

"It is a puzzling paradigm," Sanders says. "Especially when one considers the scale. Humans as individuals are highly variable while humans at the species level are largely indistinguishable."

"Oh, do tell, is that how you see me?" she asks jokingly. "Indistinguishable from any other biologic life-form?"

She knows his point is true, of course. Valentine has spent most of her intellectual life studying the macro lens of history.

"Of course not. You are one of the most remarkable humans I have ever encountered. But I wonder if the logical explanation for your atypical desire to record a memoir is because you feel the need to express yourself at your individual level of reality."

He's hit the nail on the head, as usual.

Lately, her memories have fought against suppression. The things she never told anyone—not even Crucial—about her life before the resistance, about what happened to her brother, why she ended up with sole responsibility for Seneca. Now, of course, it is too late to tell Crucial. And Seneca doesn't need to know.

"Would I feature in your memoir?" Sanders asks.

She laughs. "A starring role."

Sanders smiles, clearly satisfied with her response, and then he takes her hands in the physical world and kisses Valentine on the cheek.

"You are being kind to indulge me in this memoir nonsense," she says.

"I would recommend some other less adorned form. Historically, memoirs are a rather dull literary device. Perhaps you could capture your recollections as an academic contribution of some sort. A living record."

"I've made plenty of academic contributions already," she says. "And in the end, I'm not sure I see the difference, except for the media response and the jargon, adorned or not." She looks at the dashboard. The students have settled in and the time to begin has arrived.

"Perhaps an avatainment module then?"

"That will never happen," she says, taking a deep breath to clear her mind. "Are you ready?"

"I am always ready to assist you."

The class comes to order. The presence of a guest lecturer isn't on the official syllabus for today, but the students learned earlier that the legendary cybanism would attend. Valentine isn't in the right frame of mind to lead the class, but she's done it so often that after the customary welcoming address, the lesson flow comes automatically.

She begins. "A key part of building a historical narrative is examining data from multiple perspectives and finding the common themes that allow us to elevate the narrative from the individual to the collective truth. As we have discussed, an aspect of this is weight assignment. Whose experience is more valid, carries more weight, than that of another? Those who record history, those who have it recorded or those who live through it? Each carries unique inherent weights, and the historian must choose how to balance them in the service of collective truth."

She pauses for questions. There are none, which is unusual for this group.

"While this task can be among the most complicated for a historian to undertake, sometimes we are faced with a situation in which the choice becomes abundantly, painfully clear."

She pauses again, this time for dramatic effect. "Class please welcome our guest. Sanders, the floor is yours."

Valentine opens the portal. The questions pile up by the hundreds. She outlined in the pre-session instructions that this would be a live oral interview, with questions answered on a first-asked basis. For the post-session assignment, students would be required to summarize the entire interview in a historical profile of 500 words maximum. Then each student would read all the summations and, as a group, shape the material into an agreed-upon consensus historical narrative about the invasion of Mars from Sanders's point of view. So far, it's never been done successfully because consensus is never reached.

That, of course, is the heart of the lesson.

"How did you feel when you saw the first meteor hit Mars in 2188?" Quintzen asks.

Valentine winces on Quintzen's behalf. He has wasted his question.

"Cybanisms are not constructed to have an internal emotional landscape," Sanders says. "My parameters allow me to learn emotions, but the boundaries were quite permeable in those days. I felt curiosity, which in my operating system translates into the act of data collection, and then nothing because I ceased functioning. Next question."

One of the sunbelt students, Jasper, asks, "At the moment of initial invasion, who were you with and why?"

That's two questions, but Valentine allows it.

"Crucial Larsen and Jynks Martine. I was in the process of saying goodbye to Crucial after the successful resolution of an issue related to the neurodegenerative disease affecting the Five Families. He was returning to Earth. We did not expect to see each other again. I was learning that he was my friend, and I was helping him deal with a very inebriated Jynks Martine."

He bubbles a side-thought to Valentine. "I don't think Jynks would appreciate me providing too much detail on her state at the time. Is it relevant?"

"It's true, and it adds context. But from here on out, let's focus on the positives of her reputation. We owe her that."

A third student asks a question. "Would you say that Crucial Larsen behaved well in response to the invasion?"

"'Well' is a subjective term," Sanders says. "Could you please restate with additional clarity?"

Valentine half listens to the back and forth as it proceeds for the next hour. The questions are not particularly insightful, and she feels disappointed by the intellectual merit of the session.

Then a fun one lands.

"Why were you forced to seek refuge with Chancellor Valentine?"

Sanders looks to Valentine for guidance but she offers none. It wouldn't be fair to the students. A great deal of information can be discerned from that one query. Finally, a good question. She makes a note of the student's name— Robelin.

"I wasn't forced. It was a logical and, as it turns out, fortuitous decision."

She flashes back to that night more than 30 years ago.

No one, least of all Valentine, expected Sanders would show up on her doorstep. He explained he was there because it was the most logical of the multiple scenarios he had processed.

"Logical in what way?" she asked.

"For my future happiness. Given my high degree of respect for you, I think I could come to love you in a romantic and mutually beneficial manner."

She laughed, then felt terrible for laughing. She explained why she laughed and why she felt terrible for laughing. Then she invited him into her compound and he never left.

Well, he often left. But he always returned.

After the invasion, when the horrors subsided, Sanders achieved self-awareness. And since he had the free will to turn down future upgrades, he believed his best chance to authentically experience what it meant to be human, or to come as close to that as possible, was to exist in a mutually beneficial partnership with an awareness that his time in the universe was finite.

"Love and mortality, Chancellor Valentine," he had said. "Those are all that's left for me."

It was not a difficult choice to take him in, after what he had been through—and done—with Crucial and Essential during those eventful and dangerous few weeks. He deserved her kindness. To her surprise, slowly over the years, that kindness turned to something like love, or close enough to it to provide them both with contentment.

"In your view, did the unfinished nature of the Consolidation Wars cause the Hucksworth invasion?" a student asks.

Still only partly listening, she reflects once again on how Sanders is a natural educator. It must have been part of his original programming. As he presents his memories, he discusses in parallel the dangers of single-source narratives, and inserts from time to time references to the first-person record Essential left behind.

Sanders has now reached the point in his narrative where he is describing what happened at the Mars Lichen Fuel Reservation—known as the Grove—and how events between Crucial and Whitsend during the early phase of the Consolidation Wars, then amplified by his role in placing her in the Terrorium, were the driving forces behind her passion for vengeance.

His vocal technology gives him an uncanny ability to mimic Crucial and Essential bickering at the Grove. It never fails to illicit laughter from the students, a joyful sound amid such memories of violence and chaos.

But it won't last. He is about to describe what came next. Still, Sanders is giving the students a gift today, the gift of as much honesty, as much objectivity, as he can muster.

Objectivity. What a strange concept. Its invention—or illusion—may be the only certain thing that connects humans, Valentine thinks. And who better than a cybanism to understand the importance of that illusion to humanity?

## 29

The sight of rapidly advancing armed intruders in a conflict zone typically elicits one of two reactions: evasive action or a reconsideration of life choices. Sometimes both.

I'm already moving to insert myself between the threat and Essential in some final doomed act of big-brother heroics, hoping she lives to a disgustingly old age and remembers my sacrifice at least once a day, preferably every time she wakes up.

In my haste to irritate future Essential until she NBFDs, I forget about the blast-resistant cybanism. He's standing still, eating one last apple, and watching us curiously. Especially Essential. Despite our circumstances, she's smiling. And not the laughing-in-the-face-of-danger kind of smile. More like an actual smile, mixed with a little gratitude.

Then I realize why.

It's not Hucksworth goons or Canadis Whitsend and her soldiers advancing on us. It's some of Essential's pals from the resistance. Captain Narthite—I'd recognize that scarred, pointy skull of his anywhere—along with three companions who look tired and nervous.

"Larsen, good to see you," Narthite says.

"You too," I say, then realize he's talking to Essential.

"Captain Narthite," she says, stepping in front of me. "I didn't think you were receiving my transmissions. It's good to see your face."

"Really?" I ask. "Because it kind of looks like a ribbon of myco-cement that didn't set right." I look at him expectantly. "I'd be happier to see the faces of the rest of the entire extraction team."

He shakes that gnarled head of his.

"Please tell me there's a bigger team. And a battle cruiser somewhere."

"We're it." His voice is flat and sharp like the blades on an outer ring ice lathe. "We were hit hard. Lost at least a third of our people."

I look at Essential and see a flare of anguish in her non-synthetic eye.

"They targeted the dump," Narthite says. "They knew right where we were."

"They've been playing you all along," I say quietly. "The Hucksworths infiltrated the resistance. Hell, they might have even started the resistance. They needed you to find Halo for them so they could knock it offline long enough to invade."

"We gave them Mars," Essential says. "And Earth."

Narthite clenches his jaw. I can see the shock of truth rattling his core. For a dreamer, he's tough as an old iridium coupling pin, but he's on the verge of breaking. I think back to the chaotic retreat from Korolev crater and how he flew a transport through a garbage storm with a steady hand even when we seemed doomed.

I want to remind them of my general belief that hope always disappoints, but for once I lie—to him and Essential. "We're not letting them keep either planet. We just need to find Mel."

"That's not entirely accurate," Sanders says. He seems to be taking things well in stride, given he's now actively collaborating with the resistance. "Even if we find Melinda

Hopwire, there are many dependencies required to rebuff the invaders, locate the Halo servers and introduce the empathy hack. I calculate the odds at—"

I hold up my hand. "Hold that thought, buddy. Why don't you set an alert to tell me when the odds are fifty-fifty? For now, let's stick with inspirational speeches."

"It will take more than inspirational speeches to get us out of here, but I have a way," Narthite says. "There are blast tubes under this facility. They used them to vent test fires out into the Choke back when this dome was still producing lichen fuel. They'll take us under the siege perimeter. And we've got a modified leafblower stashed on the other end, which should get us through the Choke unnoticed inside our own little sandstorm."

I don't know why they're still called leafblowers. There hasn't been a leaf to blow on Earth in a century and they wouldn't ever use those noisy contraptions in a Martian dome. But they do use them on Earth. More like "trash rearrangers," they're big, flat disks that use directional gusts from powerful blowers to move trash around in the huge dumps. This is not going to be a pleasant ride, although I'll take that option over getting atomized.

"Sounds great," I say. "Let's go."

"It's not that easy. The tubes have degraded, so the only remaining entrance is out in the open. We ran here from it when you sent their ship flying."

"We'll need another distraction." I look at Essential. "And nothing with rocket fuel this time."

"How about we clog up the airspace?" she asks. "I've been working on a little something in my spare time in case the resistance needed cover."

Turns out my sister built a software program to create a drone-nado. A pulse of code to simultaneously summon into one location every functioning drone jacket not in use on Mars. In this case, a swirling mass of drone jackets right over the lichen farm. It's brilliant and unexpected, and it might be just enough to let us sneak through their defenses.

We take our position by the door and use the nanites to shape the information pulse, then relay it through Sanders.

"On the count of three," she says.

On three, we wink the plan into action and the resulting silence is underwhelming.

"I don't think anything happened," I say.

"Oh, something happened," Sanders says. "According to my long-range sensors, things are about to get chaotic."

Whitsend knows something is happening. "Larsens," she beams out on all channels. "What are you up to, other than delaying the inevitable?"

The first few drone jackets must have been residing close by. They arrive and hover near the front door. Within 30 seconds, a few more show up, followed by a few dozen more and then a few thousand more. In a matter of minutes, the sky is darkened by tens of thousands of empty drone jacks swirling around.

Some of the ships start firing, but that only adds to the confusion. Essential is playing the jackets like the almost musical swarm intelligence code used to regulate self-healing lev-bed surfaces.

A cloud of drone jackets rises, each turning in unison, their edges catching the light and making it seem like a huge, single creature, then hovers for a second and falls straight toward the lead ship. Whitsend's ship.

The jackets are too light to do measurable damage on their own. But with so many, the automatic weapon systems can't keep up. They're chattering out flechettes at an alarming rate and the shields are overwhelmed. The ship shakes and rolls under the onslaught and crashes to the ground. The other ships break their positions to try and help, moving closer to fire directly at the swirling tornado of personal fliers.

"Now," I say and we airhoodie up and scoot out into the open. We make it to the entrance of the blast tube unseen, and minutes later we're in the old tunnel.

As we fumble our way through the freezing, musty darkness, drone jackets fall like rain above us and we hear the roar of weapons fire, then a larger explosion that shakes the soil and stone around us.

"They destroyed the lichen facility," Sanders says. "And the apples. They destroyed the apples."

My heart sinks. I feel like they destroyed part of me in the process. It was a perfect, secret piece of Mel—green and lush and hidden, filled with promise. And now, just like everything I touch, it's ruined.

Essential seems to recognize my despair. She catches me by the hand and sends a message through our nanite connection. "It's okay. She can make anything grow again. Anything."

I sigh and focus on the darkness ahead.

She squeezes my hand. "Anything," she whispers.

Twenty minutes and two emergency nutrition bars for Sanders later, we crawl out into the Choke and onto a battered leafblower.

"The resistance has been using these for years to move around the surface undetected," Essential says as the engines rev up. They're loud, rattling death traps. "With a jammer, it perfectly mimics a sandstorm. That's what we used to spring you from the lev-train."

"That was you? Very convincing. I thought it was a real sandstorm."

"They are highly effective, but you should keep your airhoodie on. And forewarned, you're going to end up with sand in a lot of places."

# 30

Within minutes, there's more sand in my mouth, and up my nose, than in the entire fake beach at Dome Salacious.

I wonder how that little human-made ocean dome fared in the invasion. I also wonder how the pampered children of the wealthy elite are adjusting to life on the other side of privilege. But honestly, I really don't care. I'm just glad we made it away from Whitsend. This time.

After we rattle our way several hundred kilometers from our pursuers, Narthite parks the leafblower in a little canyon and kills the engine. We wait for our ears to stop ringing and the synthetic sandstorm to settle down. When it doesn't, it's clear there's a real sandstorm around us.

"Good," I say. "Let's just park it here until we can figure out where Mel has gone."

My hand is itching like crazy now from the insect sting earlier. I'm scratching it so hard that the welt has swollen and the skin is about to break.

"Why create pollinators that poison you with their sting?" I hold up my hand. "I might be dying here."

Essential looks at me curiously. "Is it just me, or does that welt look like ... something?"

"Yeah, it looks like a reaction to being injected with poison," I say.

"No." She takes my hand. "Look at the shape of the welt and the location of the sting; it's a little south and east of the meridian."

Sanders projects a topographic overlay of Jezero. It matches.

"Wow," Essential says. "She had an APD track your genes and sting a map onto your hand. That woman is scary brilliant."

"Probably could have used a little less irritant." I take my hand back from Essential and scratch at the welt again.

Mel really is amazing. I mean, I was always in awe of her, but now I feel something else—a tiny bit of hope. She knew I would never give up looking for her. Otherwise, why program a stupid insect to sting a map on me? Me. Plus, she recreated my desert, our desert. She didn't make a simulation of her house with Jynks. Okay, that was petty. But also, she knew I'd be there, the APD proves it.

Having even a flash of hope is disorienting.

Essential is looking at me. "What are you thinking?"

I don't answer.

"Whatever it is, stop it. I can see it all over your face. You look weird and sick."

"Your heart rate is irregular, Crucial," Sanders says. "Are you well?"

"I'm fine. Good, actually."

"You need to stay focused," Essential says. "Like really focused."

Narthite fires up the engines.

"I mean it!" she yells over the noise. "Focused!"

"I am focused. So focused!"

She's right. I need to let go of this misplaced hope. It's been too long. All it means is she knows me, and she liked sleeping in the desert too. Nude.

Dammit. Focus. Find Mel so she can do what she needs to do, what she wants to do. Forget about happy endings. That's the least I can do, after all the prok balls I put her through.

In a short two hours, we're rolling up near Jezero's Grande Dome in a surveillance-jammed leafblower under a manufactured sandstorm that seems to attract the stuff like a magnet. I feel like the trap filter under a hull-grinding line. There's grit in my eyes, my ears, my mouth, everywhere. Pretty sure I even have grit in my thoughts.

I'm squinting at the edge of the Grande Dome through the swirling storm. The dome is still damaged, but repair bots are still swarming along the jagged edges, tenaciously extruding girders and fresh sealant, gradually working their way up. Should be ready for habitation just about the time the Hucksworths formally assume control.

What am I saying? They'll want their own dome. An even grander dome. And they'll make the remnants of the Five Families live in this one. Then the Five Families will push all the service class people, like Mel and Jynks, into smaller domes, like Holden. And all *those* other people, the lottery workers, will end up in temporary squats in the Choke. Or back on Earth.

I really wish *I* were back on Earth right now. I miss the peace and quiet of just normal predictable chaos and despair.

Normally, the Grande Dome deploys about a hundred different filtration systems, air purifiers and climate stabilizers to keep the inside annoyingly pleasant at all times. That was destroyed when the roof was cracked open by the meteors. Now it's terminally cold and gaspingly dusty, like the Choke, and the gravity regulators are barely keeping everyone at baseline Earth Standard Newtons as people huddle in their slowly diminishing airhoodies or look for less damaged buildings with pockets of breathable air.

"Any chance you have weapons to spare?" I ask

Narthite.

"Just this old z-rail," he says, tossing me a small tube.

It's a handmade disposable one-shot rail gun. Probably barely functional. They used to be popular with protection gangs. Seventy-five years ago.

"Thanks. This single-shot antique will come in very handy for taking on an interstellar invasion force."

He shrugs. "You can give it back."

"It's better than nothing." I toss the gun to Essential. "You take this. In case things get bad."

"You mean worse," she says, tucking it away. "Things are already half a parsec past bad. How are we going to find Mel in a ruined dome with our feeds malfunctioning?"

"I don't know, but we won't find her sitting here chewing on sand," I say. "Let's take a walk."

We all gear up, except for Sanders, who is happily eating an antique strawberry tahini puff he found somewhere. He doesn't need protection.

Narthite opens the hatch into a blast of grit and howling winds. Heads down, we trudge up the canyon. The rock walls are sharp and twisted, a good five meters or more above our heads.

As we get closer to the dome edge, we can see vibro-ink etched into the rock. Graffiti from bored kids who snuck out of the dome to rebel against authority while being monitored every step of the way by iNannies.

Real creative types. *Prok Earth. Dunster licks biowaste from Holden Dome. The future is unattainable.* Okay, that one seems oddly specific to our circumstances.

Essential points at one line of text flashing in dull, sticky red: *Abandon hope all ye who enter.*

"Way ahead of you, kids," I mutter.

Narthite and his crew lead us in through a damaged out-gas vent. The giant fan blades are bent and we're able to easily slip past. We follow the tunnel and clamber out in the abandoned control room, then move cautiously into Jezero proper.

Emergency lights are on, but not nearly enough of them, and everything is dusty and covered with frost. Bands of people are sitting under rubble or in emergency field tents, shocked and suspicious, trying to minimize their movements to preserve oxygen.

It's already too late for some. Fresh bodies are stretched out in the roads, medical alert alarms blaring.

Trash is piled up everywhere, and people are picking through it looking for oxygen canisters or food or water. No one pays attention to us as we walk by; they're focused on survival. If Halo were working at premium, they'd know we are fugitives with a plus-two debt forgiveness bounty on our heads.

A fight breaks out between an older man—he looks like a DuSpoles—and a younger woman, probably a Tarteric, over an airhoodie that still has a charge. It comes to blows. Essential slows down but I shake my head. "They built this world."

A week or so ago, those two would have been sitting in their perfect homes drinking Martian absinthe and playing Multispectral Visigoth Checkers while chuckling over their credit balances. Now they're fighting for air scraps.

In a matter of days, Mars had been transformed, now not so far removed from the conditions on Earth. Only without the rats and coyotes, trash fires and flesh-melting acid-cloud brownouts. But under the current conditions, beetler packs with an oxygen upgrade would go over quite well here. Give it time.

I return my attention to our survival, the probabilities for which would go up if I could find a little more firepower. Among them, Narthite and the three rebels have a rail pistol with depleted charges, a glitter rifle with a malfunctioning flechette generator and two glitter pistols that look to be held together by alloy tape. And Essential's z-tube.

Not nearly enough to take on the Hucksworth patrol we see ahead. Six soldiers, each with more armament than all of us combined. It doesn't appear they've locked onto to us yet, but they're headed our way and closing fast.

"Quick, in here," I say, ducking into a storefront. For an instant, I'm blinded by what's inside. Spirits. It's a liquor portal. Not just a distinsery spitting out sealed flasks of cheap synth booze to crack open and consume in baggage class on the drone flight home. This is the good stuff. The shelves are stocked with bottles of absinthe and verbena gin and cedarine whiskey.

"They're close," Narthite says, peeking through the window. "Weapons down and in no hurry."

"If they saw us, they don't realize we're the most wanted people in the universe," I say.

"And that we're dangerous when cornered," Essential adds, then looks at her z-tube. "So to speak."

"We can't get bogged down. They'll get reinforcements on us in a split-minute and our only mission now is to find Mel."

I look around at the containers of booze.

"Are you thinking we could lure them in and blow this place?" Essential asks.

I look at her, shocked. "What kind of monster do you think I am? I would never destroy this kind of alcohol."

"But you have a plan. I can always tell what you're thinking. And when you have a plan you get a smug look, like someone who knows the answer to a question but isn't willing to say anything until he makes everyone feel bad about it."

"This is the last interstellar invasion I ever spend with my little sister. Now, I may not be the smartest person in the universe—"

She coughs.

"—but I know with absolute certainty, squaddies will never pass up drinks."

I dig out a pouch of powdered alcohol from my kit. I always travel with one. I open a bottle of cedarine whiskey, the most expensive booze in the shop. I take a good, long pull. Amazing. Rich and piney. And then I mix in the powdered alcohol and leave it on the counter with six glasses around it.

They can't miss it.

"Why do you carry powdered alcohol?" Essential asks.

"Sometimes water needs a little help."

"You have a problem. A serious problem."

"I have a hobby." I slip a little bottle of absinthe into my kit. "And I plan on indulging in my hobby later, when all this is over. Everyone to the back. The timing has to be just right." I drop two fleas—little mobile cameras—on a shelf so we can monitor, then power the lights off and on a few times.

I duck out of sight just as the soldiers come in, weapons up.

"There's no one here," one says. "But I know the lights flickered. We better check the back."

"Hold on, not so fast. That's cedarine whiskey. It's worth a fortune."

"Let's, uh, investigate right here for a little while."

I hear laughing and the clink of glasses and bottles. I smile as I move into the back room where everyone is holding their breath and those who have weapons are aiming them at the soldiers.

I motion and we slip outside.

"In about ten minutes, they won't be useful to anyone," I say. "And tomorrow someone will figure out that in their booze-addled state they missed apprehending the most wanted people in the universe."

"That will not go well for them," Narthite says.

We've covered half a kilometer when my feed gets an incoming ving. It's DuSpoles Koryx.

"The Hucksworths say they've lost contact with an entire patrol. I assume that means you're back in Jezero. We need to meet immediately. We have important news about Hopwire and the Halo servers."

# 31

As we get close to the rendezvous site, we part ways with Narthite and our pals from the resistance, with their pledge that they will try to find additional bodies and weapons to back us up. If we live long enough to need backup.

According to Essential, if we can find the download, introduce the empathy hack, wherever it is, and reboot the system, we can probably count on Halo to help fight off the Hucksworths.

I don't know how an empathetic AI can defend two planets against amoral heavily armed marauders—virtual hugs and glasses of warm nettle cream? But we could use any edge.

DuSpoles Koryx and Fehrven Modo set our meeting at a fractal immersion gallery. There are a dozen of these galleries on Mars and two on Earth, but only the top-tier admins on my home planet can afford to go. It's an experience shoppe where you get wired into the system and use your thoughts, motion and breath to grow elaborate crystal forms into a matrix of living crystal. Apparently, you temporarily become one with the crystals and can feel the growth in your pleasure centers. It's supposed to be very meditative, I guess, and artistic. Probably erotic too.

An hour-long session is a year's worth of debt at my credit grade.

Oddly, this gallery wasn't significantly damaged in the

attack, maybe because the mineral lattices are so strong. Also, the undulating sheets of fractalating gemstones are likely confusing the local Hucksworth surveillance system, making it a good place for our clandestine meeting.

Sanders, Essential and I slip in the back entrance. The space is cold and pulsing with hidden violet lights. A series of clear walls, rows of them, maybe a hundred of them, each about a meter deep and twenty long, patterned with unique, repeating swirls, catch the light and amplify it in unexpected ways because of the slowly undulating mineral core. Each wall has a body-sized indentation where participants get jacked into the crystal matrix, and some still have etched outlines in the swirling fractal patterns where recent visitors controlled the flow.

We walk through, Essential and I staring at the beauty of it all and Sanders analyzing the patterns and scanning for food.

"Did you find them?" someone asks from the shadows, and we all jump and then spin around in unison.

Life without a proximity alarm is strange.

It's DuSpoles Koryx. "Did you find the servers?" she asks again.

She and Fehrven Modo step out of the darkness. It's weird to seem them in airhoodies, and vulnerable, like the rest of us.

"Not yet. But we're narrowing in on them," I say.

Modo looks angry. "Earthers always fail."

"Easy, butt-sneeze. I'm not the one who lost the backup servers in the first place."

"Stop wasting our time," Koryx says. "The scope of the mission has changed. We've negotiated a deal with the Hucksworths. If we can find the servers and cede coding access to them, the Five Families will retain a forty percent stake in planetary operations."

"That's eight percent per family, a good deal under the circumstances," Modo says. "But if they need to destroy Halo and start from scratch, we get nothing. In that case, they intend to trigger a pulse that will destroy all connected systems. We have every available resource looking for the servers."

"They drive a hard bargain," I say. "And what about Earth?"

"The welfare of Earth isn't part of our deal," Koryx says. "But they did indicate they have plans for Earth."

"They want a new dome on Mars for the Hucksworths. And after that's accomplished, they intend to rebuild Earth," Modo says.

His tone is eager, too eager, like he's trying to make things sound better than they are. Something is off here.

"Like you did?" Essential asks.

"Like we did what?" Modo replies.

"Like how you and your families all promised to rebuild Earth but never did."

"I fail to see the relevance of your commentary at this moment," Koryx says.

But Modo nervously responds anyway. "The timeline was narrowing. We were making plans to re-environment major population centers. And I'm sure the Hucksworths will pick that up once things are more settled."

"More settled, indeed," Koryx says, piling on. "And one thing we can all agree on is that the only way to have a chance of rebuilding Earth is to get Halo out of backup mode. It's the way we all win."

"Actually, it's the way *you* win," I say. "The rest of us just get to keep on losing."

"Exactly," she says, as if we've come to some happy middle ground. "Things won't get measurably worse for the people of Earth, and then they will get gradually better.

Over time."

"I'm hard pressed to believe you," I say. "You've had decades and decades to fix the mess you left behind on Earth. And somehow, you never seemed to make the time or spend the credits to do anything other than spritz your fancy domes and invent places like this for your endless entertainment. I think, and I'm going out on a filament here, that your continued greed in the face of suffering means you don't actually care about others."

"You sound like a revolutionary," Koryx says.

"Yeah, you do," Essential says, looking at me with a mix of disbelief and satisfaction. "I like the sound of this."

I'm on a roll now. "You selfish lint-pinchers got a taste of hardship and decided to throw in with the assholes just to save a little bit of your wealth."

"Even in our diminished state, you are forbidden to talk to members of the Five Families in that fashion," Modo says. "Whitsend was right. You are a liability."

"Wait a minute." I take a step toward him as it dawns on me that they must have given up something of value to get that deal. "What did you sell them?"

"What do you mean?" I see uncertainty on his face. He's holding something back. Something big.

"What did you sell them? There was no reason for them to take this deal. You have no leverage."

They look at each other, their expressions a blend of embarrassment, shame and triumph.

"Tell me. Or I'm going to strike you repeatedly in the face with a large piece of fractal crystal."

The threat of physical violence, when someone is so accustomed to never being touched without a full viral profile, turns out to be exactly the catalyst I was hoping it would be.

"The cure," Modo says.

"You sold them the cure to neural tryphoprionia? How is that even …?"

Koryx shoots Modo a stern look of caution. They've got something on the boil. I grab him by the lapels and yank off his airhoodie. There's oxygen in this gallery, not enough, but some. He won't die. But he'll feel like he's slowly suffocating.

"Tell me. Now."

He's struggling and looks at Koryx.

"Do not say a word," she says.

"You're next," I say. Essential advances on her and Koryx gives a little shriek.

"Sanders, I command you to save us," she says.

"I regret to inform you that my operating system has been severely damaged," Sanders says. "I shall be of little use at present. Without access to large quantities of caloric inputs."

I push Modo back into a matrix wall and he sinks into the soft glass as the machine syncs him up. He's gasping for air. "I wonder what kind of pattern you'll make as I crack your face bones into dust."

The crystals around him swirl into a complicated, cringing mass of spiky dark yellows.

He caves. "We created a fast-acting variant of neural tryphoprionia that can be spread through airborne vectors. The Hucksworths intend to infect Earth and then charge for the cure."

I sigh and push his airhoodie back into his hands so he can slip it on and breathe freely.

"You people are so disgusting."

"And you are not to be trusted," Koryx says. "Whitsend advised us to terminate you and it seems she was correct in that guidance, I fear." She gets the blankface, which means she's lookspeaking something.

"It's a trap," Essential says, and we can already hear the advance of heavy boots.

"We hoped to do this the easy way," Modo says. "Get the location of the servers and toss you in a Terrorium, but now we'll have to do it the hard way. An electronic pulse to wipe out Halo, and the Hucksworths will rebuild a new system from scratch with our cooperation."

"Just so you know, I never do things the easy way," I say.

Whitsend and her mercenaries are getting closer. I can sense her triumphant grin long before she comes into view. But there's a difference this time. We're armed. Sort of.

Essential pulls out her rail gun, the little zip-tube Narthite gave her, and blasts the slug into the nearest matrix wall. The little old-fashioned tubes only shoot at a fraction of the speed of the machine-produced jobs, but it's more than enough energy to pulp a person. Or destroy a structure.

The matrix wall explodes into a million sharp, fragile shards along with the wall behind it and the wall behind, like a chain reaction. The air is filled with flying razors and there's a roar of decompression. We're behind Sanders and moving toward the main entrance in the chaos.

I see Whitsend, eyes wild and angry, her airhoodie gone, a hundred tiny cuts across her face. She's trying to draw a bead on me with her glitter gun. She's firing, but there's too much debris in the air for the flechettes to travel even a meter.

I smile and clap the backs of my hands together, the worst insult possible, and then Essential is dragging me out into the ruins of Jezero with a worried Sanders in tow, and we run into the shadows.

# 32

"Remember when you thought the system wasn't so bad?" I say to Sanders.

We're making our way through the heart of Jezero, the nanites deflecting the Hucksworth surveillance system. For the time being, anyway.

Alarms are still clanging behind us at the partially destroyed crystal matrix shoppe and fart ships are stinking by in a repeating grid-sweeping formation. Along with the oily stench, they are broadcasting messages about me and Essential—into local feeds and also the old-fashioned way, meaning acoustically into the air—detailing how anyone who turns us in will receive immediate immunity and total plus-three debt forgiveness. The price on our heads is going up.

Alternatively, the messages make it clear anyone helping us will be shipped off to an orbital prison behind Orcus, in the farthest reaches of space where the Hucksworths were hiding out for all these years, devising their bacterial alchemy.

As more ships approach, sweeping the area with every kind of detection ray, we crank up the nanites and duck under a fallen builder bot. Half its docile head has been blown off and one arm is still stretched out at the dome it wanted to repair.

"You heard DuSpoles and Fehrven?" I ask Sanders.

"The Hucksworths are going to infect Earth with a Martian disease and then charge Earthers for the cure. Does that plan make a lot of sense to you as, you know, a defender of the system?"

"I concede this requires a reconsideration of my earlier position. I'll factor into my reconsideration whether my thought processes are evolving due to my constant exposure to human emotion."

"You can't pick up any emotions from my brother," Essential says. "He was born without them."

"Not true," I say. "I realized early on that in the grand scheme of things, emotions are useless and probably damaging in the long-run."

"It's curious how you two use mild insults to distract yourselves from the near-constant terminal threat of danger to which you seem perpetually tethered." Sanders pauses to consider. "Perhaps I should try a similar tactic to distract my cognitive processors from the lack of caloric intake."

"This is not going to be a fun phase," I say.

Essential laughs lightly but then her expression turns serious. "We have to stop them. You realize that, right?"

I hate Mars so much. "Yeah, I know. In hindsight, I liked our lives twenty minutes ago better, when introducing the mysterious yet-to-be-found empathy hack that Mel might be able to track down was the only impossible, doomed-to-fail mission we had to worry about. Now we also have to stop Earth from being infected with a Martian neurological virus."

"Responsibility makes you cranky," she says.

"You're both several percentage points above optimal weight," Sanders says, then gauges the effect of his insult. "Odd, I'm not distracted at all. I'm still very hungry."

"I will give you this full tube of dulse pulse if you never

try to insult us again." I grab the sustenance paste from my pack and hand it to him. "It's bound to get both ugly and sad."

He takes the sustenance paste, slurping it down.

The ships pass by, still booming warnings about us, with a new "fact" about how we are now also somehow to blame for the entire invasion of Mars. We crawl out from under the builder bot.

The dome repair is coming along. I see sparks and flashes high above as the bots cover the last of the jagged edges with squirts of polymer and the support arms are flash welded over them by seam spiders.

It won't be too long before the dome will hold breathable air again. Not soon enough for me. I'm tired of seeing the world through the amber lens of an airhoodie, smelling recycled air and my own hot breath. It all goes stale fast.

"What now?" Essential asks.

I shake my head. "Nothing has changed. I mean, everything has changed, but our mission is the same. Mel must know where the servers are. That's the only reason she's on the run and why the Five Families—"

"Six Families," Essential corrects me.

"Why the Six Families are after her."

"I don't understand why she's taking such a rambling route."

"It is puzzling," Sanders says. The dulse pulse has temporarily rejuvenated him. Seems horseradish-flavored seaweed paste can have that effect. "She is an exceptionally intelligent human, as evidenced by the clue she left with the pollinator. If she knows where the servers are, why not simply go directly to them and introduce the empathy hack, which she either has or knows how to find?"

I am such a reverse-biased diode. She doesn't know.

That's why.

"Because she doesn't know. Mel doesn't know where the backup Halo is."

They both look at me curiously.

"All of this. She isn't trying to *get* to the servers, she's trying to *find* the servers. She doesn't know where they are either. Yet."

"I don't understand. Why is she traversing across all of Mars then?" Essential asks.

Sanders answers. "A logical explanation that fits the facts is that she's gathering components for something. At Baldet, and the lichen farm—"

A flash of respect slides across Essential's face. "Of course. The cellular oscilloscope from Baldet—"

"And the plasma distillate from the lichen farm—" Sanders says.

"She'd just need enough voltage applied to zinc plating, and if she got that—" Essential says.

"She would be able to—"

I've had enough of their fractured exchange. "If either of you know what she's doing, stop talking in half sentences and tell me."

"She's so prokking brilliant," Essential says. "Mel's creating a tool to point to the server. When she floods the zinc with the lichen distillate and hits it with a high enough voltage, the plasma will react with the isotopes in the zinc. The resulting microstructures will lean away ever so slightly from the massive fields being generated by Halo. With enough microstructures, when measured through the cellular oscilloscope, meaning enough data points, she'd be able to roughly compute the direction and distance to the servers."

"Very roughly," Sanders says. "But it could work."

"She's got two of the three components," I say. "What

else does she need to make this contraption work?"

"A large, flat sheet of silver oxide," Essential says.

"Large enough for a statistically significant sampling," Sanders says. "No less than a meter square."

"She came back to Jezero for a reason and she drew us to Jezero with that stinging APD for a reason," I say, scratching the bite on my hand. "There must be something like that here."

Sanders runs a search through his stored files. "There's an antique star map in the lobby of Singhroy University. Zinc-plated. It would be more than sufficient."

"That's it. That has to be it."

"What are we waiting for?" Essential asks.

"For that battalion of Hucksworth soldiers to pass by," I say, pointing at a small squad harassing a few civilians begging for a place to recharge their airhoodies.

We stretch out on the cold ground and think invisible thoughts as they pass by. When it's clear, I outline a plan.

"Here's what we need to do. Get to Singhroy University without getting sizzled, make sure Mel can find Halo and introduce the empathy hack, assuming as Sanders said that she either has it or knows where it is, before the Hucksworths wipe the system, and also, we stop the Five Families from infecting Earth with their latest credit scheme. All while dodging Canadis Whitsend, who seems to have taken her imprisonment in the Terrorium quite personally." I take a long breath of stale air. "Sounds easy."

"And fun," Essential says.

"Oh, I understand now," Sanders says. "You're doing that thing you do. Using false bravado to mask actual concern." He runs several scenarios. "I look forward to the opportunity to test my invulnerability against their most powerful weapons." He looks at us for validation.

I'm not impressed. "Great, Sanders. Thanks for

reminding us that we're both mortal and you're basically immortal."

He deploys a disappointment module that darkens his face. Literally. Like several shades darker.

"Ignore him," Essential says. "It was perfect, you're really getting the hang of it."

Sanders turns his face to me. "I don't understand why you are often so mean-spirited."

"Years of practice," Essential says. "If only we could find an empathy hack for him."

"It would have to be a very powerful empathy hack," Sanders says.

It's going to be a long walk to Singhroy University.

# 33

Singhroy University escaped the worst of the damage from the meteors and fart ships. It's mostly covered by an emergency-grow dome, so at least in this tiny corner of Mars, we don't need airhoodies.

We pass under a gaudy metal arch emblazoned with stars and planets, sculpted with the faces of space explorers and academic funders and 'Singhroy University' written across the keystone crest of its bend. The pathway under the arch leads to a rectangular lawn that was probably green a few days ago but now is covered with centimeters of red dust.

The wide lawn is surrounded by a bricked path and six identical low-rise white marble buildings, two each on the long side and one at either end. They're largely intact although the one farthest away no longer has a roof. But it's odd. It doesn't look like it was damaged by something hitting it, rather that it exploded from the inside.

On three of the buildings, the columns ringing their edges have collapsed but it hasn't affected the structural integrity. I guess those flourishes were only decorative.

Decorative marble columns.

There is no marble anywhere on Mars, which means Able Singhroy or someone in that stupid family had all these white rocks generated. Or worse, shipped up from Earth.

Rocks. Flown across the universe.

To create the façade of what they call a university. Which itself is—was—a plaything for the Five Families.

Those credits could have fed thousands, no, make that hundreds of thousands, of people on Earth. Or given the entire Multnomah Ward access to the latest health cradle to nudge the median age past 40 years.

At the edge of the lawn, I stop in front of a plaque—a tribute. *The Singhroy family gene collective is widely known for its contributions to the advancement of human knowledge, furthering the goals of the Five Families and humanity.*

There's a photo of Able Singhroy etched into the bottom of the plaque, the one member of the Five Families who was a little less evil than the others. That's not saying much. She's dead now. That says a lot.

In her final act before dying, Able made me a very wealthy person. The system makes no sense. It's just an overblown computer code moving virtual credits around to make the poor poorer and the wealthy wealthier, all while stealthily misdirecting blame and responsibility into black holes.

The resistance was right all along. Doomed and duped, but right.

It should bother me that this revolutionary voice in my head doesn't bother me anymore.

Sanders is talking about how, "interestingly," the buildings of Singhroy University are designed in a style of ancient architecture that originated in what's now part of the Ionian Ward.

"Over the centuries, Greek architecture became associated with the concept of intellectualism and many of what were once called the great universities mimicked this style as a form of tribute," he says.

"Remember Grandmamma talking about the university

in the Multnomah Ward?" I ask Essential.

"Only in a fuzzy way. You had more years with her before she disappeared."

I never did tell Essential about discovering that our granny died a revered blizard. Oops, Saurian, I guess. Sorry, Valentine, my bad.

Before she volunteered for genetic reordering, our grandmother told me stories passed down from her mother and her grandmother about the storied universities of Earth.

The stories aligned with what Valentine told me during our excursion into the sunbelt, about how the universities were slowly absorbed by corporate benefactors, which were slowly absorbed by the Five Families. After the Consolidation Wars, the Five Families had no need for an educated workforce nor for the application of intellectual curiosity in the form of undirected knowledge generation on behalf of people—only on behalf of wealth generation.

Their wealth.

So, they transformed the universities into a system of internship institutes. People who weren't shunted into a militia, like I was, got the chance to enroll in a debt-neutral internship to learn how to do some job, whatever was in demand at the moment, and then spend the rest of their lives doing that job, if things worked out. A lucky few got plucked from the trenches to get trained in system administration and wealth preservation. Those are the ones who run Earth on behalf of the Five Families.

The collaborators.

When I was a kid, Grandmamma took me to visit the Multnomah Ward Internship Institute. The memory isn't too clear except for three things.

First, there was a big rectangular lawn surrounded by buildings that looked like the marble monstrosities we're currently strolling through.

Second, I remember thousands of people crowded into this green lawn space, each person inside a taped-off square so everyone could stay distanced. That day's internship was for a job in biomanufacturing. Candidates were being tested to see if they could collect the fluid from the growth sac of a half-formed mouse clone. I don't know what that fluid was for, but the stench was awful. Worse than the fart ships, even now, thinking about the smell makes me gag.

The third thing was how tight my Grandmamma held my hand at the sight of it all. That old woman had a grip like iron, and looking back, it was clear she was furious.

We walked around and she pointed to the buildings, trying to get me to imagine it as a different place, one where people came together to study and learn from each other and scholars, just for the sake of learning and growing intellectually. I couldn't imagine it.

I remember asking her, "But what good is learning if it doesn't help you earn credits?" That must have broken her old heart. It was probably my fault she chucked it all and moved her reformulated genes to the sunbelt.

"Where is everyone?" Essential asks. "It's spooky that no one is here."

"With breathable air, it *is* unusual there aren't more people here," Sanders says. "Didn't Chancellor Valentine say she and Seneca were taking refuge at this site?"

"Yeah," I say.

"I hope Chancellor Valentine and Seneca survived," Sanders says. "I find myself thinking of the chancellor quite often. Every thirteen point nine seconds."

"How often do you think about food?" I ask.

"Every seven point six seconds."

We enter a nexus building with travellators splitting off to the various institutes. Essential points to a flickering map. "The Department of Astrophysical Geolocation and Animation. Come on, this way."

We follow the path of the nonfunctional travellator to another stupid Greek-looking building. Essential opens the heavy wooden door and we pass through, back-to-back, wishing we had weapons. The ghostly lack of people is getting weirder by the second. The room we enter is round and domed, with more prokking columns around it. But these are thicker, easier to hide behind if needed.

Against the back wall is a clear stand with an inscription. Essential reads it out loud.

"This antique star map is dedicated to the pioneering Singhroy family whose enormous wealth greatly advanced the science of interstellar travel."

"Where's the map?" I ask, pointing to the empty wall. "We're too late."

"Not quite," a familiar voice says. "But it sure took you long enough."

Mel steps out from behind a column; she looks rough—the journey has not been easy on her—but beautiful. More beautiful than ever.

I feel a sense of complete and overwhelming happiness, like my heart could supernova, and I pull her into my arms and squeeze her so tight that Wisp is flattened between us in her little sling, squeaking and yowling and scratching at me.

# 34

The woman I love has been through seven kinds of hell. She's pale and dirty and her clothes are tattered and she has a cut above her eye and another on her shoulder. Blood has dried and darkened on both.

When she finally breaks free of my embrace, much to the delight of Wisp who can't resist poking out her little paw and taking one last swipe at me, Mel manages a smile. "Good to see you, Crucial. I take it the bee-sting implant worked?"

I hold my hand up and show her the welt. "I mean, maybe a little heavy on the irritant."

"Looks painful. But you can be hard to reach."

"Dense, in other words," Essential says. "Hi, Mel."

"It's really you. I've been hearing the broadcasts and I couldn't believe you were free."

Mel catches Essential in a much less painful hug, and I swear I hear Wisp purring. I hate that cat.

"Yeah, about that," Essential says. "I was never in the Terrorium."

"What?" Mel asks quietly. Too quietly.

"I'm sorry we lied to you, but it was Canadis Whitsend in there. Crucial took that on to give me cover. He saved the day."

Mel turns to me. "You lied to me about something like this?"

"I mean, 'lying' makes it sound so bad," I say. "I was protecting you. I thought I was protecting you. That was before I knew, we knew, you were part of the resistance."

"I'm learning that lying, or omitting factual clarity, can sometimes be an empathetic decision," Sanders says.

"Nice to see you, Sanders," Mel says, then sighs. "I understand your motivation, Crucial. Completely. I've been lying to the people I love for quite some time. To protect them, and to protect the plan to build a better system."

I wonder who she means by the people she loves? Am I in that category?

"I formed a more layered view of you at that moment," she says. "And it was wrong. I have to recalibrate a little."

"I guess in a way, we both surprised each other a little," I say.

"I don't think any of us would even be here trying to track down the servers if Crucial hadn't kept all the secrets to himself," Essential says. "Like having the nanites in his blood."

Mel narrows her eyes at me. "You have the nanites too?"

I shrug. "No big deal. Just saving the universe. And I wanted to protect you in the process."

"As the last few days should have shown you, I don't need protection," Mel says. "I've never needed protection. I may have needed a partner, but I've never been lucky enough to find someone who shares my beliefs, who trusts me and who I could trust."

That stings, a lot more than the pollinator.

I wasn't there for her when I should have been because I only ever thought I wanted to be, deserved to be, alone. And now that I want something different, a better future with more honesty, it's probably too late.

I realize there was always something bigger and more important at stake than protecting Mel or having her to myself. And that a simple trust between two people, a faith in one another, was enough to protect *both* of us rather than either of us. Protect us, and the future.

"What do we need to do to find the servers?" I ask. "To help you find the servers?"

"I'm ready to test my hypothesis," she says. She hands me a glitter gun. "They're combing the buildings, pushing people into camps so they can repurpose these structures. You can keep them off of me long enough to activate my contraption. And hope it works."

She leads us toward a room at the end of the hall.

"I'm really glad you're okay," I say.

"I'm glad you are too," she says.

"When the meteors hit, we couldn't …" I can feel the words choking up in my throat. "I thought you were gone, that I'd never see you again."

"Me too," she whispers. "I was monitoring their comms the whole time. I thought you were vaporized in an escape pod. But then there was an incident at Baldet, and I knew it was you."

"I saw the desert holo-room at the lichen reservation. I always assumed you tried to forget everything about me."

"That's impossible, but I had to move on." She squeezes my hand. "It doesn't matter now. We have a universe to reboot."

"Just tell me one thing. Why are you carting that cat around?"

"I think you can probably figure that out on your own by now."

We enter the building's central lobby. The metal map is on the floor, the oscilloscope is next to it and wires trail out of sight.

"How long do you think this will take?" Sanders ask.

"Are you in some sort of hurry?" I ask.

"No, of course not. I was thinking it seems likely there is a food court dispenser in this building. Perhaps I have time to locate something to eat?"

I hand him the last nutri-bar from my survi-vo pack.

"Thanks, buddy," he says, tearing into it.

Sanders just called me buddy. Why does that feel like some sort of breakthrough?

# 35

"Are you sure this is going to work?"

Mel is leaning over the metal map, her hair tucked behind her ears, a study in pure beauty, focus and determination. Wisp is happy to stay in the sling around her neck, nestled on top of Mel's stomach, but that cat is watching me suspiciously.

Mel looks up at me with a perfect mix of curiosity—as if I'm some entirely new species—and irritation. I haven't seen that particular look in a long time. Not since all those years back when we lived together, when she was already starting to pull away. Or, more accurately, letting me pull away. Testing me to see if I could reverse course, then letting me fail and slowly, grudgingly putting up barriers to protect herself from the inevitable. I now realize she was charting a new course for herself, one that broke free of the shell of selfishness I was cultivating.

It feels oddly comforting to think I can still elicit that kind of response from her.

"No, Crucial," she says finally. "I'm not sure it's going to work. I haven't been sure of one ion-pitted thing for the last ten years. Especially this."

"It should work," Essential says. "It had better work."

Mel shoots Essential a dialed-down version of her special look. "You're not helping much either."

"Sorry," Essential says. "I'm nervous."

"We're all nervous. There must be a code in the specific

Larsen DNA to strive to make a bad situation worse," Mel mutters, spreading a thin layer of the distillate across the map. She uses almost all the gunk; it's dark and tacky, smelling like mold and the taste of copper.

I think Sanders is eyeing it for possible consumption. If we make it out of this, we really need to figure out his hunger situation. And give him a reboot too.

When Mel is satisfied with the distribution of the foul paste, she turns on the oscilloscope and dials in on the cellular structures. She floats the screen so we can all see. Magnified, the individual molecules look like spindly little jointed antennae. She drops a million identifier pins across the map surface, capturing snaps of molecules so there's something to measure against.

With a deep breath, she straightens up and nods. "Here goes everything. Time to light it up."

She has one of the belch guns from a Hucksworth goon. Not sure how she got it, but the barrel is dented and looks to be bloodstained on the bulbous end. I'm guessing it's not her blood.

She's modified the gun so that wires snake out of the tulip flare of the barrel and the raw ends of those wires are clipped to the edge of the metal sheet.

"I've got this cranked up pretty high," she says, finger on the trigger. "You might want to step back."

Having been on the receiving end of a polarizer once before, I'd like to back up all the way to Earth, but instead I get behind Sanders and Essential gets behind me. Since he's both curious and blast-resistant, Sanders doesn't stray far from the metal map.

"Close your eyes," Mel says, then pulls the trigger.

There's a wet belch of bacterially generated electricity directed onto the map followed by a flash and sizzle and stench. Even with our eyes closed, we're blinded and then coughing and choking from the clouds of moldy smoke.

When I can finally half see again, I look at the map. The distillate is scorched dry and reduced across the metal sheet, the residue creating odd smoking islands of relief.

Still hacking and gasping, we look up at the float—the smoke is making the screen shimmer in the air—as Mel hunches over the oscilloscope, scanning the results. There's a blur of motion as the machine compares the before and after alignment of a million micro pins. I'm no scientist, but they don't look the same to me—like all the tiny antennae got knocked down.

The machine is flagging discrepancies too fast for the eye to follow. Well, the human eye. Sanders is watching the float closely. Pretty sure Essential is too, with her cyber-eye. She looks sad and scared.

Mel doesn't look happy either. It's another one of her looks I'm familiar with, but usually it was me causing it, not the fate of Earth and Mars. She steps back, her eyes rimmed with tears of frustration.

"There's no meaningful change. No usable data. The microstructures were all flattened. But there's no directional evidence."

"But—" Essential says. "It has to work. It has to."

Mel sighs and strokes Wisp's little head absently, scratching the cat's ears. "It didn't. It should have. But it didn't."

"Maybe the charge was too much?"

Mel shakes her head. "No. The opposite. It was barely enough. But still, it should have worked."

"We can find the servers a different way," Essential insists. "Like, hack into the Fist's network and find out where Tarteric Hoost siloed the information."

"No time for that," Mel says. "Not before they pulse the whole planet. Halo will be knocked offline and they'll build a new system, one that won't be vulnerable to the empathy hack."

"And they'll inevitably build something much worse," Essential says.

"We've lost our chance," Mel says. "We've lost."

"I refuse to accept that," I say.

"Refusing to accept reality has always been a specialty of yours," Mel says tiredly.

She's upset. I should let it go.

"Yeah, well never being satisfied with reality is your specialty," I hear my mouth saying.

Nice job, mouth. Maybe check in with the brain once in a while.

"This seems like an odd way of brainstorming creative solutions to our current dilemma," Sanders says. "But I'm happy to list some of my specialties if it helps."

"It won't, Sanders," Essential says. "They're frustrated. We all are."

"Look, I can't believe the two people in my life, the most optimistic, hopeful people I know, are giving up," I say.

"It didn't work," Mel says. "It's over."

"I should not be the one to say this," I say. "Because hope is not my strong suit. But where's there's life, there's hope." I look at Sanders. "Any ideas?"

"Perhaps running the experiment again?" he says.

"That's great," I say. "Let's do that."

Mel points to the distillate. "There's not enough left."

I look at the container of smell gel. "So, we try smaller. Sanders, help me flip the map over."

Sanders does it with ease. I dump the rest of the goo in the middle and spread it wide with my hand. We hear the roar of fliers outside.

"Dammit, they found us," I say. "Sanders, get to the

front door and try to hold them off until we can fry this one more time."

He nods and runs downstairs in a blur.

"Do the thing with the 'scope," I say. Moving at half speed, shoulders hunched by defeat, Mel dials it in and drops some pins into the reduced surface area.

"Watch your eyes." This time, I pull the trigger. The room lights up again. Shouts and weapons fire are getting closer. Essential has her zip rail out again. That will prolong the inevitable by about half a second.

Mel fiddles with the controls once more, stares for a few long seconds, then adjusts them and looks more closely. shakes her head. "The structures are flattened again. There's a slight deviation, but so small as to be negligible. Based on these readings, the servers would have needed to be in the room the first time, and little more than two hundred meters away the second time."

"It's not working," Essential says. "We should go."

Sanders appears at the door. "I was unable to hold them. Troops are advancing quickly. The main doors are two hundred and eleven meters from here. I reinforced them as best I could, but they won't last long."

Two hundred and eleven meters.

*The servers would have to be in the room the first time, and little more than two hundred meters away the second time.*

Sweet sizzling solar balls. It's Sanders.

"It's him. It's Sanders," I say.

They all look at me, not understanding.

"Crucial, are you having some kind of neurological breakdown?" Sanders asks.

"He's the backup. The servers are him. All this time. The hunger. The readings. He's the blasted Halo servers."

"That does make logical sense." Sanders processes the scenarios. "How interesting."

Mel is scrambling to get Wisp out of the harness. Not quite sure why now is the time to free the cat, but Wisp isn't having any of it. She's panicked and clawing.

And then there's one perfect, frozen moment.

Mel is looking radiant and confident, the fuzzed-out angry kitten in her hands. Essential is looking hopeful and tough, her zip gun aimed at the open doors behind us. Sanders is looking hungry and curious.

The room erupts in a flash of orange light and the world turns smoky and upside down.

The last thing I see is Mel tumbling one way and Wisp another, before a wall of darkness falls.

## 36

**September 3.5, 2238**
*Stardust University, Neuro-Lecture Interface 75.32*

"We've read the record, experienced the sims, ingested the dopamine mirrors, but it's still hard to believe that all that time, you didn't know the servers had downloaded into your system," a student says. "Can you expound?"

"To be frank, it was a disorienting revelation," Sanders says. "But as codified in the Manufactured Life Accords of 2106, cybanisms are not independently responsible for pre-existing programming conditions or constraints."

"In other words, Sanders couldn't be faulted for not accessing information purposefully pocket-walled by those responsible for his creation," Valentine says.

"Obviously, the fact that the backup Halo servers were downloaded into me explained a great deal of previously dissonant data points, such as why I powered down as Mars was attacked, my increased need for calories and my degraded functionality," Sanders continues. "A significant portion of my operating system was rerouted, first to receive and deploy the download and then to primary systems operation."

"It seems risky," the Hoost descendant says. "Halo had always been a tremendous asset. Why risk losing control of it, or allowing it to function without self-awareness?"

Valentine is aware that as a Hoost, the boy knows the

reasons, and that asking in public is simply an attempt to protect, or rehabilitate, his family name.

"The record is well-documented on this point," Valentine says, saving Sanders from explaining his own shortcomings. "One of your forebears, Tarteric Hoost, was solely responsible for concealing the location of the backup servers and pocket-walling recognition. His intent, it seems, was to protect the location of the asset, as you characterize it, and more broadly to limit the ability of the AI from developing a depth of self-awareness that might inadvertently lead to system-generated outcomes outside human-constructed parameters."

"In other words, he put Mars at risk to protect the status quo," Hoost says.

It's unclear from the correlate scan if this comment is intended as recrimination or adulation. But more broadly, the mood of the student group is turning. Souring, with negative hotspots emerging, some aligned toward the offspring of the Five Families, others against. Time for a quick adjustment, Valentine decides.

"Based on the paradigm of self-interest, Tarteric Hoost took steps to limit the risk of change within the system to continue delivering the desired outcomes for those he prioritized," Valentine says. "That is not an unreasonable basis for collective action, and has formed the impetus for most if not all political and economic systems throughout recorded history. Had he survived the initial assault, it is likely he could have mounted a successful defense of Mars."

"But instead, we lost everything," the Hoost student says. "All because he didn't trust others."

"Let's pause here for a minute," Valentine says. "Because we find ourselves at an interesting juncture. A well-known truism that emerged after the first great climate collapse is that history reveals what should have been obvious."

She stands, leaving Sanders on the Chesterfield, and moves to the curved window looking across the desert with lichen fields stretching into the distance.

She continues. "It seems clear, in retrospect, that we could have prevented the great climate collapse of Earth, even avoided the Consolidation Wars and reduced, rather than expanded, wealth inequality. Just as it seems clear, in retrospect, that Tarteric Hoost could have better protected Halo. The question we as historians must answer is, why? Why are we as humans so poorly equipped to see the obvious, to act upon the obvious, and instead create layers of misdirection and justification for apathy and intrigue?"

No answers are forthcoming, but the mood indicators have moved in the direction of equilibration. The class is wrestling with the sad lesson she fears is at the heart of all history: Humans as individuals are designed by evolution to be reactive and selfish, and yet societies—a reflection of our best tendencies—exist to be proactive and empathetic. Resolving this central conflict between the individual and the collective is the eternal struggle.

But then she thinks of Crucial, alone and broken in that burning room at Singhroy University, determined to make a difference even when every cell in his body was convinced humanity was doomed. And she knows that not all humans are reactive and selfish. In fact, enough of them are not to counterbalance all who are.

# 37

When my sight returns, everything is upside down and on fire, and my lungs are rattling and wheezing and burning. But then I realize it's me that's upside down. The explosion sent me tumbling against a wall and my head is where my feet want to be. From the smell of it, they hit us with some kind of puffball. A barely sub-lethal ion-excharge, puffballs exploit the ionic connections within a delimited physical space. Apparently, the space included me.

Even upside down, I can tell the room is shredded. The space map is twisted and pocked with scorch marks. I think that's what saved me.

I need to find Mel and also make my ears stop ringing. I spot her in a tangled heap on the opposite side of the room. I feel a wave of panic until I locate her vitals in my glitching OCD. Stable. Weak, but stable. She's alive.

I brace for a second panic wave as I look for Essential. She's coughing and cursing and sifting frantically through the debris for her little zip gun. Like that single-shot rail gun can do anything against the forces they're about to throw at us.

Sanders is good. Since he's practically invincible, he's still standing mostly unperturbed near the door, even though the walls around him are missing. His clothes—and hair—are also missing, scorched off by the heat of the fireball. He's full-on naked.

So, we now have an upside down, unclothed, singed, depilated and anatomically correct cybanism containing an AI system that makes him basically a god.

Wait, I'm upside down. Not Sanders.

I start to right myself so I can get to Mel but discover in that standing process that my leg is broken. It only hurts a little in that bone-sliding-on-bone kind of way, but it's going to make any misguided heroics challenging. I grit my teeth and start crawling toward Mel. At least I can be there beside her when we're glittered into oblivion.

She's coming back to her senses, sitting up and looking distraught. I try to assure her I'm on my way and that I'm going to be all right.

"Where's Wisp?" she asks. "Wisp, where are you?" Mel stands and starts digging through the tumbled debris.

"Don't worry, I'll be fine. It's just a broken leg," I say.

"Crucial, you're wasting time." She tosses me a med kit. "Take care of it and help me find Wisp. I think she ran this way." And without another thought for me, she pushes past a collapsed arch and disappears into the next room.

"Dammit, Mel, wait," I say, fumbling the med kit open.

It's too late. She's gone, darting through the next room calling for Wisp, her voice growing fainter as she moves farther away. Why is that damn cat so important?

I hear shouts and drone jackets and weapons racking from outside the main entrance. "Mel, hold on, there are too many of them. We have to stick together."

I find an Osteosplintor by feel among the various injectors and nodules in the med kit. The splint forms a quick, permanent internal cast around bone breaks. It's not pleasant. This will be the third time I've used one, first was after a broken collarbone and later a broken shoulder, both drone jacket accidents in pursuit of labor felons. A health cradle would be so much better.

"Essential, stick with Mel," I message her as I open the package and snap the splint to activate it. I can't spare the built-in two-hour healing window, so I'll have to do this the hard way. I peel off the fentanoid pain-blocker patch and slip it into my pocket, knowing I may need it later but unable to afford now the drowsiness it might bring.

Essential runs by, stopping only long enough to fist brush. "No fentanoid patch? That's gonna sting. Hurry. We need you."

"Just watch after Mel, and yourself. Don't get too far." Then she's gone too.

I wait until the splint glows bright green, indicating the calcium gel is charged.

"You too, Sanders. Keep them safe. And put some clothes on."

He nods. "Human modesty puzzles me," he says. "And as it turns out, I'm basically all-knowing now, why should anything puzzle me?"

This is going to be a difficult phase. No wonder he was so hungry.

"Maybe keep that part to yourself until we figure out a way to prevent you from being turned off and replaced by something worse that gets all of us killed and the Earth contaminated. Well, more contaminated."

"I will. I'm sorry your bones are so brittle and your pain receptors so sensitive." Then he follows Essential out of the room.

"Says the guy who's been turned to goo in front of me like fifty times," I mutter and jam the plastic needle into the flesh above the break and depress the plunger, feeling the splint foaming into place.

Sizzling wart-kernels, that does sting a little. No, make that a lot.

Bubbling and burning, the gel seeps toward the break,

drawn by the hematoma swirling there, and then grabs hold and squeezes the broken edges like a proton vise—sticking the bones together and hardening around them in a thin sheath. The splint solution is filled with synth fibroblasts and chondroblasts and all the blasts necessary to speed up the healing process. There's an audible 'ding' from an embedded chime, letting me know its set.

And just like that, I can stand again. Only, it feels like the inside of my leg is on fire and the bone itself is one solid aching throb. But I'm up and that's all that matters, and heading for the back door when I see a familiar fuzzy face staring wild-eyed from under the star map.

Shit, it's Wisp.

I want to leave her. If anything can survive what's coming, it's a kitten with an attitude. But she's important to Mel for reasons I can't understand. She was willing to risk a meteor impact just to grab her stupid cat before she—

Bubbling pots of plasma.

Wisp is the empathy hack. Wisp is the prokking empathy hack. How could I have been so blind?

I think back to when Essential let me know she'd found the servers on Deimos. I was with Mel, and Wisp started glowing like a reentry rivet on a nose pipe dropping out of orbit. The fate of the future is inside this feline, and the stupid cat never left the room.

"Come here dummy," I say, moving toward the cat. Wisp arches her back and hisses at me. "Sorry, that was a bad approach. I meant to say, you know, good kitten. Like, nice kitty. Time to come with your Uncle Crucial now."

I take another step and Wisp pulls back even farther.

"Look, this is no time for drama, you stupid little—" I lunge for her under the crumpled map. Wisp puffs up even bigger in fright, gives another low hiss and claws my hand.

"Prokking underbunch!" I look down at the thin row of cuts on the back of my hand now oozing blood. If you're going to make a synthetic pet, why on Earth arm it with tiny hand knives?

The yelling and cursing are too much for Wisp. She makes a break for it, darting like a tiny fuzzy q-rocket back into the rubble near the destroyed door and dashes up the damaged stairs.

I give chase, my leg aching and hobbling me. My clumping, tottering gait makes everything louder and worse. I see her disappear around the corner into a darkened room.

And then I hear weapons fire from below, coming from the direction Mel and Essential went. A familiar voice broadcasts through our feeds. Canadis Whitsend.

"Don't drop your weapons, we'd rather shoot you. Where's the idiot?"

That's hurtful.

"Vaporized by the puffball, I hope," she says.

The nanites are shielding me. But not for long.

If the choice is between saving two worlds full of strangers or saving the two people I love, it's an easy decision. I start looking for something I can use as a weapon, settle on a shard of broken Arex glass, wrap it in a scrap of Sanders's trousers to make a handle, and move in their direction.

The lights go out, my local feed flickers and alarms start wailing. "Warning: Service Degrading. Warning: Service Degrading."

As I reach the shattered door, I get simultaneous messages from Essential and Mel. Essential bridges me with the nanites, which are still stable. "They have us. No way out. Sanders has been deactivated. They don't know about him, think he's a malfunctioning cybanism and a

224

security risk, so they pulsed him down. You have to find Wisp."

Mel lookspeaks me on my feed. Normally, it's trackable but not with Halo down. Even so, her words are flickering and failing. "Find Wisp. Hopefully you know why by now. Save the world first. Save us later."

I send the same message to both. "Not a chance. I'm coming for you."

I get the same message from both in response. "Don't be an idiot. For once, do the right thing."

I hate Mars so much. I turn and tromp up the rest of the stairs, the nanites still shielding me from the search parties. Mostly shielding me. Hopefully.

## 38

At the top of the stairs, there's another domed room with four vaulted hallways at right angles. The rooms and corridors are lined with more of those ridiculous marble columns, along with living statues, 4D paintings and holo-pedestals. With Halo down, the holograms are not displaying correctly on the pedestals, but it's clear as polar ice that the hallway is a shrine to the Singhroys for their funding of interstellar transport research.

Not the scientists or engineers. Not the first pilots who risked their lives on experimental fliers. It's the funders who get the shrine.

The columns have mostly buckled and half of them are in pieces, the huge chunks piled up on floor. Moving through any of the hallways will be an obstacle course of shattered marble. Luckily though, these columns were just for show here too and the roof is intact.

Mars has always been about shine, not substance.

Wisp has been through here. I see tiny paw prints in the marble dust leading down the east corridor. I follow them and then peek inside the room where the paw prints lead. It's an observatory, with a powerful peepscope aimed toward a retractable section of the roof. A star lab.

Wisp is sitting on the far side of the room on a toppled scale model of Earth. It's cracked in half, like two domes, and she's perched on what looks roughly to be Multnomah

Ward. She watches me warily while she licks one paw, swipes her face and then repeats. She's bathing. The worlds are ending and the cat is taking a bath.

"It'll take a lot of tongue work to get the filth of Mars off you," I say.

I've never cared much for cats. They're uncommon on Earth because they need to live indoors, otherwise the trash rats and coyotes eat them. And only people in the manager class or above have enough credits to feed extra mouths, cat or otherwise.

Captain Calvin, my boss back on Earth, has a cat. He ended up with it after we busted a Halo jammer ring implanting wetware in live animals. He loves that damn thing like it's some sort of fuzzy god.

I guess for some people they are like gods, at least they were in the way distant past. And then again in the 21st century, when the Graybies started following the teachings of a feline philosopher who believed close observation of cats could help humans better understand themselves and find meaning in existence.

Calvin named his cat Bastet and he spent every damn millisecond, when he wasn't at headquarters busting my ass along with every other labor cop, taking care of that strange creature. Every now and again, he brought it into the precinct when he had to power himself down for upgrades, and I spent more than my share of those shifts watching over that apathetic four-legged monster.

Like Wisp, Bastet never came when I called, seemed to be irritated by me and only interacted positively if food or water were on the line. Otherwise, it acted like the world would be better if I wasn't in it, or anyone for that matter.

Fuzznuts. Could it possibly be that I hate cats because they're too much like me?

I spin around at a whirring sound. Prok. It's a roving

FIDO, a Fully Independent Digital Overland System, a sub-military search and reconnaissance hybrid. It can't detect me because of the nanites, but it's zeroed in on Wisp. I jump over the broken column shafts and blocks of fallen marble to keep Wisp out of the crosshairs, but she's already gone.

The FIDO leaps forward agilely and chases after the cat. A Fido is a task-specific anthrobot with limited neural depth; it gets only a partial allotment of integrated learning capacity, enough to support its autonomous function and adaptive reasoning to meet its one job. Its developers don't bother with deep learning routines or the fancy covering, like they do with the skin on Captain Calvin.

With its pear-shaped body and four spindly legs, it looks sort of like an animal. A robot animal though, all metal, plasticene and wiring. And mean, it looks mean but I don't think that's intentional since they don't have faces, just an array of sensors. This one has a snout, though, which I quickly realize is a glitter gun.

That's new. And not great.

Back on Earth, we had a few FIDOs working with us on the Labor Enforcement Division. Used them to sniff out the beetlers and credit-flushers hiding under rotten slicks. Not to kill, to locate. The beasts were unstoppable once they got a scent.

But predictable.

This FIDO is leaping and bounding from one chunked-up marble column boulder to the next, its servo-motors growling from the strain. Wisp is panicked, scrambling like a fuzzy blue dart higher and higher up a long broken sheath of marble column. When she has nowhere left to run, she throws her tiny body onto a tapestry hanging on the wall, a recreation of the Singhroy crest first planted on Mars.

Wisp is the only bio-signature the FIDO is picking up,

and I'm pretty sure it won't stop until the cat is destroyed. She's still scrambling up, trying to dodge the diamond flechettes the FIDO is firing in her direction from its snout.

I lunge for the tapestry and pull it down, sending Wisp tumbling in the collapsing cloth folds. Confused by the change in tactics, the FIDO lands with a thud beside me, flechettes tumbling around us in that weird, tinkling firefight way that sounds almost magical. Or musical.

Stunned from the fall for only a few seconds, the FIDO regains its footing and starts scanning for the cat. I'm standing next to it, but the nanites bend its surveillance systems around me. It extends a second snout, this time it's a thermal wand. The damn thing is readying to scorch the room. The nanites can't save me, or Wisp, from melting.

I've got one chance. I grab a single flechette in one hand and a hunk of marble in the other, line the glittering spike up where I think the FIDO might have a parentboard, and hammer it in as hard as I can.

The force of the blow sends the flechette right through its plasticene covering and smashes my fingers so hard I wonder if I've broken them. But it works. There's a pop and sizzle and the beast stiffens, legs shaking, then falls over. It twitches a little, leaks out some gear fluid and stops moving.

That bought us a few minutes. FIDOs usually work in packs. I sift through the folds of tattered cloth. Wisp is gone. Of course.

"Here, kitty."

I see a hint of movement under an overturned chair. It's Wisp. She's frightened and bedraggled and glaring at me.

"Seriously, come on cat. We have to move."

She's not moving.

Look, I know I'm not Mel." The sound of Mel's name

seems to perk her interest up. "I'm not Mel, and I don't have any food ..." Even I can tell I'm not making a very convincing case.

How the hell do I get Wisp to come to me? I mean, how would I get me to come to me if I were desperate?

By not trying.

"Fine, you know what, stay here," I say, starting to turn.

There is a rumbling noise near the grand staircase, and it's getting louder. A pack of FIDOs gallops up the stairs and is now racing down the corridor, clanging into each other and knocking into the walls. Wisp's eyes go wide at the sight and sound, and she springs out of her bolt hole and launches herself into my arms, yowling at full volume, her razor-sharp claws raking down my forearms.

I stuff her inside my airhoodie and cinch the neck tight, then run in the opposite direction of the FIDOs. I can feel her trembling against my stomach, vibrating. Or maybe purring?

"I've got Wisp," I lookspeak to Essential. "I'm on my way to you now."

As I streak past the scorched star map and the med kit, I inflate a biohazard box, move Wisp inside it and use some gauze webbing to glue it to my back. The box has a hole for dropping in samples that's just big enough for her little head to poke out.

She lets me know this arrangement does not please her. She's not a happy cat.

"Make it fast," Essential responds. "They're moving us to their field headquarters in the central garage for some braggy victory speech. Then the Hucksworths are going to pulse out Halo. We'll lose our chance with the empathy hack. Which is Wisp, by the way."

"I mean, obviously, it's Wisp. Can't believe it took you so long to figure out."

I break the connection before she can reply.

If the pulse goes off, Sanders as we know him will be obliterated. Mel, Essential, Sanders, Earth and Mars are all counting on me and Wisp to save the day.

It would be helpful if I had a weapon. I look at the bloody rows Wisp scratched on my forearms. "I wish your claws were a little longer."

The cat yowls in agreement.

# 39

"You are making a stealth approach nearly impossible."

Wisp is set on perma-howl, lodged unhappily in the sample case gauzed to my back. If I crane my head far enough to either side, I can just see her angry face poking out—wide, indignant eyes and delicate, quivering whiskers. But I don't look often because when I do, she can reach my ear with one little arm extended, and her tiny claws have already got me pretty good too many times. A constellation of blood drops has dried on my shoulder and my earlobe is shredded.

Worse, she's hissing and spitting and yowling like an agitated king rat in a biowaste dump. Ordinarily, that would draw some attention. But these are not ordinary times.

The field headquarters is buzzing with activity and, so far, the screeching of one tiny synth-kitten is drowned out by the full-scale tactical retreat of an invading force.

Not for long, and not forever. The Hucksworth army needs to be temporarily off-planet when the reset pulse is triggered to ensure their ships aren't rendered useless. They are leaving behind one nervous and heavily armed squad of shock troops to keep the peace, which means they'll kill anyone who approaches too close or looks suspicious, meaning anyone not having a pointy, pushed-up nose.

An endless chain of fart ships is landing, taking on troops and foisting off in clouds of oily stink. It smells worse than the bog lines under a sheetmeat plant, and I used to think, after spending too many nights chasing labor fugitives through the noxious waste slime, that smell was the worst in the universe.

My airhoodie isn't up to filtering out this volume of foul particulates, so my head is marinating in a putrid smog. At least the nanites are hiding me from their off-planet surveillance systems. I may die of the stench, but I'll die undiscovered.

Except for the unremitting emergency alert from Wisp.

"Seriously, pipe down you little fuzzball," I say, jostling the case. "We'll get barrel rolled if you keep screeching."

My warning doesn't help. She redoubles her complaints. For such micro-lungs, Wisp can really complain. And she's not the only one. I'm in constant contact with Essential. We bridged a digital connection and she's lookspeaking live updates. The updates are not encouraging.

Whitsend and her new pals have taken Essential and Mel to an ad hoc command center where they are debating whether to execute them publicly or privately. Whitsend is leaning toward private. Plesca and Spilla Hucksworth want it to be public, a spectacle. The debate has given me time to catch up to them.

They're inside a field dome erected over the central garage building. The five-story structure is where they used to park the surface transports in Jezero, little hansom rockets and surfs, short-range fliers and the like. There's a drone jacket corral on the roof and a lift column from the main dome for intra-planet trips.

Well, there *was* a lift column.

It's gone, along with the arch of the dome that it used to pierce so a person could take fliers straight out into the Choke. A meteor attack is hard on infrastructure.

Given the state of the dome, the garage itself is enclosed

in a clear hexagonal structure with a polymer bubble top. The Hucksworths dropped a dirt lotus on top of it—a snap-to rapid deployment field dome that closes like a flower blossom and is mostly impenetrable, keeping air in and attackers out. It's surrounded by rows of automated weapons and roving bands of guards, many congregated near the only entrance.

Luckily for me, the whole thing is also ringed by an assortment of crumpled non-working vehicles, making it easy to approach unseen. Before they sealed the place, they dumped all the broken transports out the side port of the garage. Just turned them on and blasted them right out into the city. Hansom rockets and fliers are tumbled on top of each other, some still fizzing out plasma rings.

There's a mobile launch pad next to the lotus where the fart ships are loading up and blasting off to rendezvous with the larger squid ships squiggling around in orbit.

I hate the Hucksworths, the Five Families, Mars and this stupid kitten, in that order.

I need a weapon and a way into the lotus. I also need Wisp to shut the hell up. She's wedged into the top of the case like a slug in a rail gun. I can feel her little body vibrating with rage and indignity at the maltreatment.

"If you would just relax, I swear I'll get you back to Mel as soon as possible."

At the sound of Mel's name, she again calms a little.

"Oh, you miss Mel don't you, you little monster?"

Her yowls taper off.

I admit that I feel some affinity with the angry synthetic creature. Made what she is by Mel and then abandoned through no fault of her own on a broken planet. I know that story. I mean, other than the fault thing. That was totally on me. Still, I get it.

"Mel's pretty special," I whisper. "Nothing makes sense

when she's not around, right?" Wisp lets loose a pitiful little meow, seemingly in agreement. "Don't worry, we'll be okay." I turn my head. She's looking at me mournfully and this one time doesn't try to attack my ear lobe.

I speech-capture a message to Essential. "We're outside. I'm coming."

"Forget about us," she lookspeaks. "Reboot Sanders and get Wisp on him. It's our only hope."

"Not a chance. I got the stupid cat, but I'm springing you first."

"NO."

Damn. She all-capped.

"Did you just all-cap me?"

All-caps are not easy to eye-type, so it means she's deadly serious.

"We can't beat them without Sanders. If they activate the pulse, he'll be useless. Reboot him. Empathize the prok out of him. Don't let me down. Don't let Mel down. Again."

That was a low blow.

"That's just mean. Where even would the power button be on Sanders?" I ask.

"Probably somewhere he couldn't reach or accidentally press."

"Fine. But if it seems like anything is going to happen, it's over. I broadcast my location and the fact that I've got the hack."

"Fine."

"And that includes you cutting our bridge."

"FINE."

Damn.

A clutch of soldiers patrolling the perimeter comes into view, winding their way through the tangle of crashed fliers, anxious and ready to blast anyone they see. They have terrible unit cohesion, with one lagging behind. He has one of those wet sizzle guns. A big one.

"Okay, time for a little teamwork," I say to Wisp after most of them have passed by. I move closer to intersect the route of the laggard and when he gets close, I jump up and down to give the carrying case a good shake and slam my back into the wall. Then I pull the case free and lean it against the wall.

On cue, Wisp starts howling, our truce broken, probably forever.

I hide behind the crumpled tail fins of a hansom, the nanites keeping me out of his external monitoring goggles. Drawn to the sound of Wisp's wails, he advances slowly on the tube, gun at the ready.

It should be clear there's a life-form in there, but hopefully—since he's likely never seen a live cat before—it won't seem like a threat. He's eyeing the case curiously. He lowers his weapon and with his free hand, opens the neck a bit wider for a better look inside.

Just as I hoped, Wisp lunges at the opening and jabs one paw out, flashing her claws in the air.

Surprised, he stumbles right back into me. He's even more surprised as I slap the fentanoid patch from the med kit onto his neck. I knew that would come in handy, even though I had hoped it would come in handy for myself.

There's about one second of fight in him, then the drugs do their work and with a big happy smile, he slumps down to the floor. He'll be out for at least two hours. When he wakes up, we'll be dead or victorious. I don't think there's an in-between.

I take his gun and then pick up the case and strap it on again. Wisp lets me know we're no longer friends with a low, rumbling growl.

Now I need to get inside.

The thing about the dust lotus is that it's built to sit on the surface. That means it's vulnerable to tunneling. Not without triggering alarms, of course. But a breach might seem like an accident, giving me a shot.

I move away from the patrols and slowly prowl along the edge of the clear wall until I find a promising spot. There's a big pile-up of fliers, a hansom rocket tangled up with a couple of rocketbikes and one little wedge-shaped flier for use out in the Choke.

War teaches you a lot. Or more importantly, I guess, survival teaches you a lot—war just speeds up the lessons, and lets you channel what you learn into destruction. Buildings. Vehicles. Planets. Lives. Especially your own.

In the Consolidation Wars, I watched my friend Jenny Dring rig an improvised explosive to blast a hole into a hedgehog—a fortified, slow-moving bunker covered with spiny weapon barrels and CSF spikes, which are detachable quills attracted to fluid-encasing brains. They're terrible. Jenny rigged a rocketbike to backfire a belch of plasma that blew a neat hole right through the hedgehog. We breached it and shut it down, but not before Jenny got about a hundred spikes bored into her skull.

A stray thought pops in my head. I wonder if empathy will be enough to end our reliance on war as a tool of the rich to take even more from the poor. We'll never find out if I can't do better than Jenny Dring.

With Wisp still complaining bitterly, I pull the engine cover off the rocketbike and disconnect the plasmatic ring governor. Then I kick and pry the body until the tail pipe is aimed right at the bottom of the dirt lotus. Next, I fire up the flier, override the controls and set the launch timer to ten seconds.

"This is going to be a little loud," I say to Wisp as I hit the bike throttle and duck.

The bike belches out a ring of plasma that hits the edge of the wall with a flash. A second later, the flier boosts and rockets forward, crashing into more vehicles and igniting them. The boosters stir up a cloud of dirt and debris and in the swirling mess, I roll under the new hole in the lotus. Alarms clang and commands bounce around in my feed. Wisp adds to the din, screeching at the top of her cat lungs.

I crawl into a launch port and immediately drop down into a darkness I hadn't planned on being there. I think about Jenny, hooked up to an external cognitive drive endlessly watching avatainment specials. If I ever make it back to Earth, I should go see her.

# 40

I'm falling through the dark and Wisp is howling in disbelief. She manages to hook my left ear again, a ragged claw practically all the way through the lobe. She retracts and dislodges with a painful tear when I land on my backside and bounce. High. Three meters, maybe more. Then down and up again. And again, each time with a little less altitude.

What the prok?

What in the two worlds is there to bounce on in the basement of a parking structure turned field ops center for an invading force?

I finally stop bouncing after a minute or so and roll onto my stomach and stretch out my arms, trying to feel my way to a rational explanation. The material is spongy and pliable. Wisp is silent and still, dead or terrified, I don't know which.

"You okay, Wisp?" I whisper.

She lets out a faint meow.

The bouncy surface is rough and taut. Like something inflated. I can't tell how big it is, but it feels cold and large.

Pretty sure whatever it is, it kept me from breaking my neck—both our necks—when we slipped under the lotus.

My eyes start to adjust to the darkness. There's a faint lattice of light glowing through the fabric under me as well as a humming vibration. An unfamiliar scent, pungent and sweet, hangs in the air. The surface is ice cold and my fingertips are tingling, almost burning.

I can hear the distant chaos from the launch pad. Officers are barking orders, telling the n-lists to hurry. They're shuttling people off-planet as fast as they can. They need to get their forces out of range of the pulse they're about to unleash.

One of their ships powers up and the stench floods inside, overpowering the antiseptic flowery smell. If they don't kill me and I end up in a prison, I hope they fix my nose into a point so I never have to smell those ships again.

I wonder if any of the Five Families are getting a ride up-orbit with the Hucksworth militia. Doubtful. Well, maybe the two highest-ranking members, the traitors DuSpoles Koryx and Fehrven Modo. Like guest prisoners. The only bright spot in all this destruction is knowing those hard-hearted wrecks of humanity are forced to beg for their lives from people who might be even worse.

"Where are you?" Essential lookspeaks.

"I'm inside on the lowest floor. Northeast corner. On something bouncy."

"What's bouncy on Mars?"

"I don't know. It's dark."

"Stop messing around. We're a floor above you."

"You okay?"

"More or less, but not for much longer. Sanders is still offline."

"If he's out when the pulse hits, he'll never wake up."

"You think? Check your duh settings."

Even with the fate of Mars and Earth hanging in the balance, she has time to use my own words against me.

I crab-walk along the bouncy structure, feeling my way to its edge to figure out how high up I am. I'm not anxious for any more broken limbs.

I'm getting colder and my teeth start chattering. The inflatable structure is sloping down and I see faint light from a nearby door. It's still dark but I estimate it's a two-meter drop to the floor.

"Hang on, Wisp." Like there's any choice.

I slide forward and let the internal engineered gravity pull me down, setting down with an inelegant thud but no broken bones.

"Landed on my feet, Wisp, just like you."

Great. I'm in love with my ex, my best friend is a cybanism and I'm talking to a synthetic cat.

I need to get to Sanders. We've got one shot if we can boot him up and get the empathy hack inside him before the pulse goes off. More like a half-shot. Maybe a quarter-shot. And we have like a negative hundred shots without him.

The thought of dying has never stopped me from much. It's even been posited by a few people close to me, and a handful of those who aren't so close, that I might in fact be motivated by death. That I have a death wish.

It's not true.

I don't want to die. I just don't really *care* if I die. I've had a good life. Well, I've had a life. Nothing special. When it's over, I won't be missed for long by many.

Light flares into the room and I shield my eyes.

"Please, Wisp, for the love of Mel, keep it down," I whisper, crouching down beside the inflatable structure. A conveyor bot rumbles in. A Hucksworth soldier climbs off and opens a big flap in the front of the bouncy thing I was just on top of—must be some sort of temporary structure.

The conveyor bot is unloading something. I creep closer so I can figure out what the hell is going on.

Pretty sure I just saw an arm.

The soldier is distracted, looking at his wristcomm.

They must not have OCDs. He has his back to me so I peek in the door and then catch my breath.

I've only seen one field morgue in my life and that was during the Consolidation Wars. Looked a lot like this, only bigger. There was a particularly brutal fight for market share between the Hoosts and DuSpoles on the edge of the Guinness Ward. Something about needle sterilizers for health cradles.

Not sure who got the contract, all I know is there were bodies stacked up by the thousands. I was on a small recon team trying to track down a storage device with manufacturing specs implanted in an industrial spybot.

When people die on Earth, it's straightforward. First, they're assayed for debt, then they're reduced. If they die with credits in their column, they might get compressed into a small death gem as a memorial tribute for someone who misses them, but that's rare. If they have debt, as is usually the case, it's transferred to the nearest relative and the body is vented as ash.

This Martian morgue is filled with a mix of Five Family members and plenty of Earthers. I don't get why they keep all the dead here. I see a familiar face. Then another. DuSpoles Koryx and Fehrven Modo. Well now, I guess they lost their competitive advantage.

I watch as the conveyor backs up and rumbles out a half dozen bodies. Two of them are children.

As the opening begins to compress, I slip inside, letting it seal behind me. The conveyor rumbles off. I'm alone with several hundred chilled bodies, and Wisp. The bodies are on a moving platform, slowly being pulled forward.

I walk to the end of the line where there's a receiving device. A tank. Bodies are dropping into it, disappearing into a foul, bubbling broth of acidic goop that makes my eyes water.

There's a hiss and clank and then a canister pops out on the far side, rolling onto a conveyance already stacked with hundreds of them. I've seen these canisters before. They use them to power the fart ships.

They're converting corpses into rocket fuel by dissolving them in the bacterial bath and harnessing the energy. They're turning a profit on death. War as a renewable resource.

I need to get Mel and Essential away from these bladder flukes. But first I find the chiller tube, disconnect it, and drop the open end into the goo. The bacterial soup doesn't like the cold; it turns green then gray and loses its bubbly caustic life.

I eject the flex door and make a run for the stairs.

Through the cracked doorframe at the top, I see Mel and Essential standing in a room with a handful of other prisoners, all behind a makeshift force field. The bands of energy are a cheerful pulsing yellow. That color means they could slice right through the blunt nose of a comet chaser.

Sanders is slumped on the floor between them, still naked. Mel is pacing. Essential is sitting on the ground, looking ahead, waiting for me.

"I'm here," I lookspeak. "How do I get you out?"

"Every time they dump someone new in here, they shut down the field." She's good. Her face didn't betray a single twitch while lookspeaking.

Just then, light flashes and a soldier comes from the side, prodding a woman toward the makeshift pen. Essential stands and pretends to stretch. The soldier punches in a code on his wristcomm and the field drops. I'm ready. As he pushes the new prisoner in, I cross the room in two steps and kick him hard in the lower back. He stumbles forward, right into a wicked punch to the throat from Essential. Mel is on top of him in an instant, smashing his head against the floor until he stops moving.

"Grab Sanders," she says, snatching up a fallen gun. She pauses long enough to pet Wisp gently, then transfers the makeshift carrier to her back. "We have to get him up and running."

"That won't be easy," I say. "He weighs a lot."

"Drag him then. We need to take cover and figure this out," she says.

I grab him under the arms and Essential grabs his ankles and we struggle toward the stairs.

We're almost there when I hear a familiar sound. Laughter, the mean kind, and the ratcheting of weapons. A lot of weapons. It's Whitsend. Prok. She's like a probability glitch in a quantum drive, turning up in my timeline over and over.

# 41

"I knew you'd come looking for the cybanism," Whitsend says. "You're predictable. And stupid. Predictable, stupid and soon to be dead."

So, this is how it ends.

On a planet I hate with the woman I loved and lost and now failed, along with my revolutionary sister, a naked and nonfunctioning cybanism and a tiny, angry cat. Above a corpse distillery.

I've made some bad life choices.

"Do you want to watch me execute them?" Whitsend asks the Hucksworths. They'd been summoned to render judgment. Or spectate. Or both, I guess.

Spilla and Plesca consider the request a little longer than it should take, then ultimately decide against it.

"Tempting, but we should be off-planet already," Spilla says. His red, twining hair is agitated and active like a cluster of eels, making it hard to take him seriously. He points to a small device on the counter and addresses his daughter Plesca. "Turn on the pulse and set it for one hour. Be certain the geofilter is also set. If anyone tries to disable or move it from this spot before the time expires, it will detonate."

She obeys, her long blonde hair self-parting and bunning up and out of the way as she bends to touch the display screen. It's a BEEP, a Broad-spectrum Enigmatic Electromagnetic Pulse. Basically, an IT doomsday device.

One BEEP and the electronic systems and devices connected to Halo, which is all of them, will be digitally severed and unable to ever auto-reconnect. Health cradles, defense arrays, the credit and debit system, OCDs, the batch timers at noodle shops, nutrient bath arrays at sheetmeat factories, the capture fans at salt beer evaporation distilleries, personal scores on avatainment games—all rendered worthless in a flash. Everything will have to be reconnected from scratch. And for a price.

Even at the height of the Consolidation Wars, when there was plenty of posturing and threats and death, so much death, no one detonated a BEEP. The damage was considered too significant. Apparently not for the Hucksworths.

In one hour, Halo will be useless. The Hucksworths will plug in whatever odorous, bacterial AI they cooked up while brooding out on the edge of nowhere, and humans will spend the rest of their miserable lives in service to an uncaring system that tips everything always out of reach. Like the current system, only worse.

And at the same time they'll be dying of Martian brain-wasting disease because even if they can afford the cure, it will never work as intended. As we keep learning on Earth, over and over, diseases don't behave predictably.

I guess the good thing about getting glittered now is avoiding the long, slow death ahead and having to live with the knowledge that I failed, that we all failed.

I could really use a drink. Or a bottle. Dying doesn't scare me but dying sober does.

Whitsend smiles at me. "I know what you're thinking."

"I doubt it."

"Even if you live long enough, which you won't, it can't be turned off," she says.

Mel is glaring furiously at Whitsend. Mel has taken some

new hits. There's a nasty bruise on her cheek and one eye is swollen and red. And she's holding her arm in a peculiar way, like she got hit with one of those sparkle sticks. Essential is pretty banged up too. There's a trickle of dried blood on her forehead, and more blood soaked into the side of her shirt.

I feel a deep sense of regret that they have both suffered so much and it will all be in vain, and that's making it much worse for them. Hope is always just pre-disappointment. The more you hope, the worse you'll feel.

"How can you do this?" Mel asks Whitsend.

"Easily. Your charcoaled kick-burner boyfriend—"

"Former boyfriend," we all say simultaneously.

For some reason, this makes Whitsend laugh. A genuine laugh.

"Fine. Your *former* boyfriend locked me in a Terrorium. It was awful, and I only wish I could get my hands on one right now to return the favor, but I'm not that patient."

"Fine, he's annoying," Mel says. "We all agree—"

"Maybe not *all* of us," I say.

"—but settle your score with him alone. No need to take it out on the people of Mars and Earth. Don't you have any principles?"

"None. I have goals. Far better than principles. And my goals include staying alive, staying credit positive and staying on the winning side of power."

"Those aren't goals," Essential says. "That's greed dressed up in misguided and selfish pragmatism. How do you sleep at night?"

Whitsend smiles. "I'll sleep like I'm in a mela-stasis bath tonight, especially after doing this." She turns and shoots a single flechette into my chest.

It happens so fast I don't even have time to swear. Or duck. One second I'm internally debating if I can get to her before she kills us all and the next, I've got a diamond needle buried deep in my chest, the fat end glittering and already starting to take on a reddish tinge.

"Crucial," Mel says, stepping toward me, her voice lined with worry.

The shot was just for show. Whitsend hit me high and to the left. Nothing too vital in the vicinity. I've been hit with far more and in way worse places. But it's going to hurt every time I move. At least until she kills me.

"You crazy depleted proton bath," Essential says and lunges for Whitsend, but I hold her back and wince at the pain that spears through my chest.

"Stop," I say. "Don't make it worse." I lookspeak her at the same time. "Not yet. Our only chance is when she's distracted. And it's not much of a chance."

Her response floats across my screen. "I'm taking her down if it's the last thing I do."

Probably will be.

"I like this new Crucial Larsen," Whitsend says, not knowing we were just talking about her. "The defeated kind. No last snarky comments to make? No insults to hurl?"

"You caught me on a bad day. Why don't we plan on meeting back here tomorrow? I'll have something then."

"That's the best you can do?" she asks.

"I told you, I'm a little off. Maybe it's the recent broken leg or the synthetic diamond sliver in my chest. But let me try something new. Begging. Don't do this. Please. Let them go. Do whatever you want to me but let them go. Don't punish them because you don't like me."

"I don't not like you, Crucial Larsen, I despise you. You're an idiot with a bad attitude who's always in the way. I hated you when you were under my command …"

"So, you *do* remember me?" I look at Essential. "I told

you she remembered me."

"You're very memorable," Essential says.

"I remember you," Whitsend says. "I sent you on every suicide mission I could manufacture just to get you off my squad, but you kept coming back like a malfunctioning drone jacket dragging itself back to the corral. I hated you then, I hated you when you showed up on Mars and I hated you when you locked me into the Terrorium."

"That last one is reasonable, but all the others are …"

"Shut up. Just know that I hate you so much, I'm going to kill Hopwire and your sister first so you can watch them die."

Spilla, Plesca and the guards are looking a little askance at her. She's gone off the lev-tracks. I guess being locked inside a digital torture womb will do that to a person.

I'm almost out of options. I wish Sanders could calc a few scenarios for me. The only thing I can think of is getting her to glitter me first. If I'm gone, maybe she won't take it out on Mel and Essential. I may not be able to save Earth or Mars, but maybe I can save the people who can save them later.

If I make my move now, while the Hucksworths are in the room, she'll at least have a reason to control her fire a little more closely. I start to move slowly and casually away from Mel and Essential. Slowly, imperceptibly slowly.

"What are you doing?" Essential lookspeaks.

Okay, so maybe perceptibly slowly.

"I'm going to rush her. It's the only play."

"*We're* going to rush her. I'll go for the guard on the left."

"NO."

She looks at me, but I'm not giving in. "Stay alive. See this through. Protect Mel."

"You are always so ready to die," she lookspeaks. She's

not giving in either. "We do it together. Brother and sister to the end."

"We really must be off," Plesca says, motioning for the guards to escort them to their ship.

It needs to be now, while attention is diverted.

"Now," Essential says and lunges for the guard.

I lunge toward Whitsend. She's swinging up her glitter gun up. She knew I would try something. Behind her, I can see the worried faces of Spilla and Plesca as the guards hustle them toward the exit.

More guns are firing. We're not going to make it.

Alarms start sounding and bigger guns start firing and the building shakes as the dirt lotus peels away under a barrage of rail slugs. The oxygen bleeds out as slugs chew through the walls of the garage and the floor shatters and collapses. Some of the guards are hit and vaporized in puffs of crimson. It's gross.

Whitsend rolls back and out of sight. I grab Essential and drag her down. Mel is holding Wisp, shielding her.

The floor cracks and buckles and Sanders inertly rolls away and drops out of sight. For a nonfunctioning, naked cybanism, he gets around.

The door suddenly blasts in and Jynks is there, tall and perfect and deadly. She has an army of Mars SF and resistance fighters with her. A small under-weaponed and under-armored army but an army nonetheless. Behind her I see Narthite and others from the hidden base on Korolev crater.

Never thought I'd see the day when the resistance would fight alongside Mars security forces.

"Mel, thank the gods, you're all right," Jynks says.

"You came back." Mel hugs her with one arm, the other cradling Wisp, and I feel a twinge in my chest. And it's not the flechette.

"Mel, I'm sorry I—" Jynks says.

"Later," Mel says. "We have to reboot Sanders before the BEEP goes off."

"Why reboot Sanders?" Jynks asks.

"He's the Halo backup and he rolled down here."

The morgue has popped open like an abscess and there's a tangle of bodies piled up at the bottom.

"Let's get to it then," Jynks says, with that irritating certainty she exudes.

"Thanks for the assist," I say to Jynks. "But I had them right where I wanted them."

"I can see that," she says, tossing me a med kit.

I fumble around for a de-glitterer, pop the needle out and click a suture in place. "Took your time."

"Yeah, I had to overthrow a prison ship that you left in high alert when you escaped, then fight my way into and out of the lunar penal colony to bring reinforcements."

"Did you stop for drinks too?"

There's a moist burp of jet expulsion and the last fart ship, with Spilla and Plesca on board, lifts off and rockets off-planet. That's followed by a rumble of heavy siege engines tramping our way.

"We have to hold this building until we can turn on Sanders," I say. "And hope he can figure out how to stop the pulse. We have less than forty minutes before it's too late for us all."

# 42

"Down there, with all the bodies and the ice?" I ask.

We're standing at the broken edge of the floor looking into a jagged hole, the feeble lights from our airhoodies barely penetrating the first few meters of the darkness into who knows how steep a drop.

"That's where Sanders is, so yes, we're going down there," Mel says. "We have to find him. We can't give up." She's holding Wisp close. Lucky cat.

I look at Jynks. "I feel like *you* have to find him. You're the one who shot up the building and broke the floor."

"Yeah," she says. "To save you."

"Did you have to save us so ... completely?" I ask, surveying the damage.

The rail slugs cracked open the subterranean levels and popped open one end of the inflatable field morgue—the fuel plant—dumping bodies everywhere and coating everything with a layer of liquefied coolant. Frost gleams and shimmers at the pale end of the beams from our hoodie lamps.

"There was some nasty acid stuff in there," I say, "Don't touch anything. Except Sanders. Unless he's slimy looking."

"I summoned some drone jackets that look mostly reliable," Essential says. "And one extra for Sanders when we find him."

"Better make it two. He's been eating a lot."

Noise reaches us from outside. Heavy equipment and weapons fire. They're closing the plasma throttle around us. I wonder if Whitsend is calling the shots, whether she survived all the destruction Jynks threw her way.

"This is it, our last stand," Jynks says to the security forces and members of the resistance filling the room. "We hold them here until the cybanism is restored or we lose forever."

"We might still lose forever," I say. "We have to stop the pulse too."

"Quiet now. Your inspirational speeches are terrible," Essential says.

I drop a flea next to the BEEP and patch it into our feeds so we can watch the countdown clock. Twenty-eight minutes. That's not much time to save two worlds.

Mel, Essential, Jynks and I strap into individual drone jackets and step off into the darkness and float down. Weapons are firing above us and something unknown is flashing and exploding, making the whole building shake.

"Why don't they drop the building down around us?" Mel asks. "They don't need us alive. And the BEEP can't be destroyed."

Essential thinks my inspirational speeches are terrible.

"They don't want any loose wiring," I say. "The pulse will affect monitoring systems and if we're alive, we could slip away. It's flattering, in a way. They're scared of us. They're trying to finish us off before the big reset."

"We're not going to let that happen though," Essential says. "And they're right to be scared."

We drift farther down. Severed wires are sparking and sputtering, and there are bits of bodies tangled in the rough edges of the shadows. But no Sanders.

When we get to the bottom, a final sublevel carved right into the red bedrock of Mars, there are more bodies. A lot more bodies, jumbled together and covered with frost. Finding Sanders under all that is going to be complicated.

And we're down to 23 minutes.

The built-in lights on our airhoodies are not much help against the gloom in this pit. Essential locates an access panel and clicks on the backup lights. They're not a whole lot better, but at least we can see the size of the problem.

There's a mass of frosty bodies stretching out across the red rock floor.

"This is very disturbing," I say.

"And almost pointless," Essential says. "Like finding a prokking boson in a Higgs field." She finds a sledge wrench among the old tools magged to the walls and uses it to nudge some of the bodies, the pneumatic force of the wrench shattering frozen limbs as she rolls them away.

Jynks is watching the tunnel above us, her rail gun up and at the ready. Mel is near the wall, shifting bodies around. She's frantic, and Wisp is picking up on it, yowling.

I take a step toward Mel and stumble on something hard and square. Near it is another, and then another. It looks like a perfectly compacted ... oh gross.

Sanders once told me he expels waste in perfect compact cubes. They must have jarred loose when he hit, and then he probably rolled before all the other bodies started dropping.

I follow the angle. There's a ditch—a channel cut into the rock—to vent waste fluids from the retired fliers. It's currently filled with ice from the morgue's climate controls. I can see the tips of very symmetrical perfectly formed toes, which are not, like all the others, frozen.

"He's here," I say. "But we have to get him out of the ice."

Nineteen minutes.

Jynks leaves her post and hits the ice above and below

him with her rail gun, dialed back to the lowest setting at sub lethal. The force is still enough to send ice chips and choking rock dust exploding around the room.

Essential rummages through the tools and finds a pocket arc welder. A few tweaks to the code and she's sparking a charge through Sanders that sizzles the ice off him in a flash. He looks good. A little rough around the edges, but good.

"Pull down those drone jackets and let's get him up into the light so we can reboot him," she says.

Swaddled in two drone jackets, back to front, he lifts off, slowly floating up, naked and scorched and dripping water. For a second, I think we're going to make it.

Then the room rattles and shakes, and violet rings of fire are blazing. Whitsend is there, surrounded by soldiers. She came in through the basement using a smoke ring—a high-energy breaching disk—that broke right through the wall. And now she's got a bead on Mel, who is standing on the edge of the ditch.

"This is where the shit ends," Whitsend screams.

"Mel, get down here!" I shout.

Jynks and I both reach for her.

A lot can happen in a second. Lives can end or begin. Or change forever.

In that split second, just before everything goes to hell, Mel has a choice and it's not the way any of us planned it. She takes my hand.

Yeah, a lot can change in a second. Jynks' life, at least the one she still believed in, envisioned, ended. All her hopes died.

I see the light fade in her. I know the feeling.

I'm sure Mel didn't think about it. It was just pure instinct. That's what makes it so painful.

Jynks fights back the look of hurt and resignation. But

Mel sees it and knows what she's done, but there's no undoing it. Sometimes, words aren't enough to fix what our bodies do.

Everything turns into fire and smoke. Mel is in my arms and we are tumbling down into the pit. She is screaming, or maybe it's Wisp.

Nope, it's me.

Jynks takes the slug. Just a glancing blow but her arm is gone. Her tactical gear seals the wound and she keeps shooting with one hand, cursing and raining slugs into the ranks of invaders who are blown away like trash in a brownado.

She runs out of rail slugs and consciousness at about the same time, slumping down and tipping to her side. Jynks almost got them all. All but one. Whitsend stands on the edge of the ditch, a triumphant look on her face, her rail gun aimed at us. There's no surviving a shot from this close.

"I'm sorry, Mel, about everything," I whisper and hold her so tight Wisp squeaks between us.

"I'm sorry too," she says, but I don't know what she's sorry for.

Before Whitsend can pull the trigger, a funny thing happens. Her hands disintegrate. Well, not her hands, but the bones inside them.

"Leave my brother alone, you prokking greed leech," Essential says.

She hits Whitsend's gun with the full force of the sledge wrench. The energy travels through the metal and into her hands and wrists, turning the bones to powder.

Hard to pull a trigger when your hands are slush inside your skin. Hard to do anything. Except scream. Bet she's missing the Terrorium now. She drops the gun, staring at her hands and moaning. I pick it up and help Mel out of the ditch. I'll come back for Whitsend later, with some pharmachutes, if we make it through.

We lift off in our drone jackets, rising through the darkness. I have one hand on Jynks, who is unconscious and trailing a little behind the rest of us.

Sixteen minutes.

# 43

We've closed the distance between us and the pair of drone jackets ferrying Sanders. He's still out cold, or whatever is the right word for a nonfunctioning cybanism now serving as the vessel for the most powerful AI ever created. One drone jacket is around his shoulders, the other around his waist, and he's flopped between them, slowly floating up like one of the angels in the paintings on the walls of Singhroy University.

He's also glowing purple. The sun is setting and the twilight that's usually blue on Mars has red-shifted to a light purple.

I glide to a stop on the eastern edge of the garage rooftop, a spot mostly clear of collapsed debris. Siege engines circle the structure, and it's raining flechettes and rail slugs and everything else. I hope Narthite makes it. I hope anyone makes it.

I hover there, holding Sanders with one hand so he doesn't float off. Essential slips in beside us.

I look out across Jezero and there's smoking wreckage as far as the eye can see. People are wandering, some in groups, others looking for shelter, still others looking for an advantage in the situation. There's no longer a distinction between the Five Families and anyone else.

The Hucksworths and their militia, except for a handful of soldiers, are off-planet waiting for the pulse, readying themselves to destroy every single bit of information on Earth, Mars and anything in between. All any of us will have left is what's inside our heads, which after a lifetime of outsourcing our thoughts and memories to Halo isn't much.

And yet, every sorry person stumbling around like the walking dead in Jezero, waiting for their life to suddenly be devoid of shared memories, historical reference points, avatainment, all of it to be nuked and replaced by whatever the Hucksworths deem worthy, each of those desperate fools is bathed in a soft purple light.

I hear Mel gasp at the sight of it. It really is something. How is it possible that humanity on the brink of annihilation can be so beautiful?

"Humans don't deserve that kind of beauty," I say.

"Probably not," Essential says. "But then again, humans are the only animals who can appreciate it."

"Always the optimist."

"It got us this far."

"Thanks by the way," I say. "You know, for saving us from Whitsend."

"You've always been there for me, in your own way. I'm glad I could be there for you. Plus, I would really like to save the future."

Six minutes, 42 seconds.

I set down easy, and as soon as Mel gets her footing, she turns away from me to help Jynks. The mobile print-pack isn't up to speed with Halo being down, so Jynks's new mechanical arm is stalled at 56 percent. She'll be mostly useless until it regenerates, although maybe not. She is Jynks after all.

Concern splashes across Mel's face as she touches Jynks's shoulder, but she is still out of it from the shock and pain.

I look forward to the future, not far from now, when we're all toasting each other with synthgin and laughing about these minutes, which did not end up being our last because we've brought Sanders back and all is well with Mars and the universe.

Five minutes to the pulse.

Sanders is on the ground, prone. Close up he looks less angelic, with his naked body covered in dead people filth. Mel shakes out an emergency thermal and places it over him and then kneels close, ready to deploy. On her lap, Wisp is vibrating, and the purring sound is growing louder and stronger and stranger every passing second.

"Crucial, you must have some idea?" Essential asks.

Yes, I must. Come on, brain. How do we reboot a cybanism? Where is the on-off button?

"You know him better than anyone," Mel says.

The irony is not lost on me that the only idea I have for finding out how to turn on Sanders is to turn on Sanders and then ask Sanders, who is now also Halo, how to turn on Sanders.

He must have told me how to activate him at some point. He told me literally everything else.

I never saw him reboot himself. Not once. All those times he died, with his marzipan-tasting blue blood splattered everywhere, he always mysteriously reappeared all fixed up and upgraded. That wasn't a reboot, more like a full regen.

And that means his developers, whoever they were, turned him on and off. They made all the decisions about upgrades, making him better able to respond to whatever calamity had befallen him, usually because of me. He always came back a little bit better and smarter, and with a different hair style. He never had to reboot.

Four minutes.

"Ideas?" Essential asks. I hear fear rising in her voice.

"So, it comes down to this," a now-barely conscious Jynks says through gritted teeth. She's got her weapon ready in one hand, watching for attacks from the sky.

Four of the most unlikely people thrown together are now counting down a doomsday clock as we stare at an inert cybanism who was as close to a friend as I've ever had.

Three minutes, ten seconds.

"We have to try *something*," Essential says. "Press his heart, like CPR. Don't just stand there."

Mel pumps on Sanders's heart. Nothing.

"Pull on his floppy drive," Essential says.

"I'm not doing that," I say.

She slips her hand under the thermal blanket and tugs. Once. Twice. Three times. Nothing.

I'm still thinking about the blue blood. His developers always wanted him to be different than humans to avoid confusion.

I remember the day we first met, back on that lev-train on our way to the H-suite looking for my then-missing sister. I didn't even realize he wasn't human, not until the first time he got killed by having his head whacked off by a rocket-making machine.

Seems like a power button would be glaringly obvious. What part of Sanders doesn't look human?

"Pull off the blanket," I say. "Fast!"

Essential rips off the therm-blanket.

I look him up and down, and then I see it. It *is* glaringly obvious, by its omission.

Sanders has no navel.

That's the one thing that would make it clear that Sanders is not human. No birth.

Mel notices too. Unlike me, she doesn't hesitate. She

places her thumb over where his navel would be. She doesn't press. She just lets it rest there, like it's a fingerprint lock system.

Nothing.

"Prok, we are running out of time!" Jynks screams. "The entire universe is going to be reduced to data rubble!"

"You do it," Mel says to me, her voice calm.

"Why?"

"You're his friend. It matters."

I put my thumb on Sanders's non-navel.

There's a click and then he sits up instantly.

He looks at me, at his naked body, at the others and then out into Jezero. "It appears many interesting things have happened since I was last online."

I give him a bear hug. "Oh, buddy, I'm glad to see you."

"Hello Essential Larsen, Melinda Hopwire and Jynks Martine. Jynks, you are missing important parts."

"Sanders, would you hold Wisp for a second?" Mel asks.

"An unexpected request, given the circumstances, but certainly, of course."

Tears streaming down her face, she puts the tiny cat in his hands.

Wisp glows orange, like there's a fire deep inside her tiny body. She starts to shake and rumble and purr. The glow spreads to Sanders's hands and part way up his arms. There's a flash, the glow briefly emanating from his eyes, then it fades.

Wisp curls up in his arms, purring happily.

Sanders looks at us all again through new eyes. "That was very strange. What an odd creature." He looks at me curiously. "Crucial, I am detecting a dangerous buildup of atmospheric radiation concentrated into a single pulsing stream that seems likely to destroy me."

"Yeah, that's the BEEP. Can you stop it?"

"I don't believe I am programmed with those abilities."

"Maybe give it a shot since that's all we really have."

His eyes roll back in his head the way I hate, where we can only see the whites, and when he refocuses, it's not with good news.

"Of the 262 scenarios in which the pulse can be destroyed, I will try the option that will do the least harm to the greatest number of humans. But the probability of success is not high. Which is unfortunate because I suddenly feel very invested in your well-being—in the well-being of all inhabitants of the two planets."

Mel sits down heavily.

"The empathy hack worked," she whispers. "But now it's too late."

We will be the only witnesses to a critical historical event no one will know even happened.

# 44

**September 6, 2238**
*Stardust University, Neuro-Lecture Interface 75.32*

"Let's pause for a moment here," Valentine says.

There's a collective groan of disappointment. Valentine expects it because she planned it that way. Sanders's story was near the end. For both planets.

She continues. "This module is about the science of history, not simply celebrating its key moments. As a reminder, our goal is to understand how the past creates the present, and how we can use that knowledge to shape the history of the future right now."

Sanders, familiar with the tricks of her teaching trade, nods. He knows his part.

"That requires always seeking to accurately capture the realities of the past and the motivations of the principal players," she says. "So, I ask you to consider this question. Was Crucial Larsen a hero or a villain?"

The neuron bank is alight with a kaleidoscope of creative thinking.

"The answer seems intuitive, but let's start from the point of view of historical members of the Five Families," she says.

The quick consensus is nearly entirely aligned: villain.

"I see one dissent. Can you please share your thinking?

Anonymously is fine."

"I don't require anonymity," the student says, dropping the filter to share their personal details with the class. Opal, a member of the DuSpoles family.

Good, Valentine thinks.

"Crucial Larsen would have been viewed as a villain at the time, as someone in a position to potentially undermine the sanctity of a system that had worked for the benefit of others, albeit a small subset of the universal population, for decades. The threat of disrupting Halo, disrupting the status quo, would be detrimental to stability. But from our historical vantage, his actions ultimately helped reshape the alliances between families. My own family, and others."

"And your point is?"

"He was a villain in his contemporary context but with our historical perspective we might re-categorize him as a change agent. Judgments at the point in time are almost always meaningless when viewed against the currents of history."

Perfect. There's one in every class. A good thing, too. Her lesson depends upon it.

"Interesting," Valentine says. "I appreciate your input. Now, I'll ask a follow-up question. How can one ever know how to act, or even what should be considered appropriate behavior, if it requires years—decades even—to look back and gauge the context?"

Opal's charge dims, confronting the challenge to their viewpoint. "You can't. One needs some sort of guiding framework by which to evaluate potential outcomes."

"Good work, and correct," Valentine says. "Centuries ago, that framework was religion, and choices were filtered through the potential judgment of mythical beings."

There is a ripple of amusement, reflected in a mass spike in limbic activity.

"Settle your neurons. We're not so different. The challenge our ancestors faced is the same one we face. How to, as Opal so astutely put it—"

She pauses to check the serotonin index for the class. Opal needed, and responded well to, that little dose of self-esteem.

"—evaluate potential outcomes. In the pre-Digilithic era, before the climate catastrophes and pan-morbidity, that process was redistributed to various external deities. Humans constructed competing forms of, in essence, socially sustained algorithms—a non-technology based set of rules that helped them problem solve and function with confidence, albeit often misplaced, and reinforced through widespread social adoption."

"Religion as social algorithm is one of my favorite theories of yours," Sanders says.

"Such a flatterer," she says.

"I assure you, my flattery subroutine degraded many years ago."

The class enjoys the back and forth, showing deep levels of sentimentality. This is turning out to be a good group, she thinks.

"To continue, this moral framework pitted adherents of the various religious algorithms against each other. At the dawn of the Digilithic era, humans began to question this approach, and the shift from social algorithms to actual digital algorithms started. And while these rules brought uniformity and stability to the process—and were shared across the entire globe—they too were created by humans and, as such, contained certain flaws."

"Do you think all humans are flawed?" a student asks. This one is from the Fehrven family.

"Yes, but the nature of these flaws is contingent on the baseline you define as non-flawed, which in turn is an always-shifting artifact of history," she says. "But no matter the era, it is our flaws, and our willingness to address and even to overcome them, that make us human. And in fact, have made us successful as a species."

She pauses again for dramatic effect. "Everything we create, even Sanders here, is built imperfectly by imperfect beings. Despite many years of continuously improving, Sanders is improved but still imperfect." She takes his hand. "And I'm glad of it."

"What about self-evolving algorithms? Can they achieve perfection?" the Fehrven student asks.

"I sincerely hope not," Valentine says. "Ultimately, there would be no place for humans in a perfect system. That was decided in the Devlin Accords of 2122."

"Does that mean you think Crucial Larsen was flawed?" It's Opal again.

Valentine laughs. "Perhaps most of all."

"Does your personal history color that perception?" they ask.

"Almost certainly. A good point to raise. Sanders, you are the closest we have to an impartial observer, so your input will be valuable here. Tell us your perceptions of Crucial Larsen. You were closer to him than almost anyone."

Sanders nods. "Yes, of course. Based on objective data available to me from all relevant sources across the universe, Crucial had many flaws."

There is uncomfortable laughter from the class.

"Crucial was psychologically damaged, fundamentally self-centered, suffered crippling addictive disorders, was unable to form lasting bonds with most other humans, unwilling to—"

Valentine squeezes his hand. "Perhaps we don't need the full list this time."

"I tried to shorten it from last time and reached 60 percent of completion."

"Very good. For perspective, perhaps you could now share some of his positive attributes as observed during your time together?"

"Crucial was a friend. One who, despite his copious shortcomings and an almost pathological form of apathy, always tried to do his best for those he cared about, even though that list was very short."

"Perfectly said," Valentine says.

She focuses her attention back to the class. "In the end, history is not determined by our actions in relation to the external frameworks we adhere to, or the algorithms we create. Rather it's in relation to the people we love and the empathy that drives our desire to help them. Even when it ends in disaster."

# 45

"I'm sorry Crucial, I can't stop the pulse," Sanders says. "Not in the time remaining."

I think the empathy is already getting to Sanders. He looks sad. I get it; that's why I try to avoid empathy altogether.

"Can't you smash it?"

"It's indestructible."

"So are you. Maybe you could throw it into space?"

"I'm flattered you think I'm that powerful. But even if I could achieve the necessary velocity, which I can't, the device will detonate if it is moved by more than a few centimeters."

Arguing with a cybanism when the world is about to end is remarkably frustrating.

"Reverse engineer a quantum rocket and send it to some other when?"

"An intriguing possibility and one I would like to explore more fully. But by my calculations, it would take several hundred years to develop and test a usable prototype and we have—"

"Less than sixty seconds. We need to do something. It can't end like this." I feel frantic and defeated.

Mel is kneeling next to Jynks, who is pale and struggling, trying to offer her comfort but fighting back the same sense of desperation.

Essential is trying to hack into the BEEP, but one look from her tells me it's pointless.

After all this, all we've been through, we've lost. It all ends in under a minute with the big reset for an even bleaker future. All the trauma and intrigues, all the double dealings and lies, all the white-knuckle quantum trips to Mars and gallons of Martian absinthe, all the violence and sacrifice, all the blood bots circulating in my veins ...

The nanites.

The millions of tiny self-contained, individually shielded and self-powered nanites. The nanites designed by a coding genius to hide from detection by the most powerful AI known to humans, able to generate digital realities from thin air. The nanites inside Essential and me.

I grab her arm. "Essential, the nanites. Can we use them to deflect the pulse? Can we shield Sanders?"

Forty-five seconds.

"Probably not, but we should still try."

"Come on you little shits, don't let us down," I say. I will them into action and enter the nature of the threat. Great, long, garish lines of code start running through the pirate column in my scroll. I swear it feels like my blood is heating up. Essential and I stand close to Sanders, between him and the BEEP.

We're all watching the countdown timer.

Five, four, three.

"I don't think this will ..." Sanders starts to say.

Two, one, zero.

There's a soft click and a decidedly anticlimactic flash, a weak little stutter and then everything goes dark and quiet across the entire planet.

Everything. The lights fade. The drone jackets collapse to the floor. The regulators in our airhoodies switch off. The thermals in our suits go cold. The gravity modulators blink out.

Everything feels weird and cold and thin. Mel is sobbing and Essential is cursing. My feed is down, flickering. I try to call up the nanites. Nothing. My blood is cold and heavy.

In the dark, I find Essential's hand and squeeze. "My nanites are gone. Yours?" I ask.

"My eye is down. I can't tell. I feel different though. Strange different."

"Me too."

The lights flicker. In the strobe, I turn and see Sanders is still standing. Still naked. And, oddly, partially aroused. Actually, mostly aroused.

"Interestingly, the nanites have successfully deflected the pulse away from me. I retain almost full functionality."

"I'd say about 80 percent." I really need to get him some clothes.

Mel closes her eyes and sinks to the floor, crying happy tears and probably also suffering from oxygen deprivation.

My feed is getting weird signals. A foreign operating system is trying to jostle its way in. The Hucksworth's AI. Probably smells like farts. Halo isn't making room for it.

"Hey Sanders. Are you connected? We're running out of oxygen here."

"That's certainly not optimal for humans," he says.

The regulators kick on and we all take ragged breaths.

"And maybe stabilize our feeds, and reboot Essential's eye?"

"Of course," he says.

And just like that, our feeds are back on—across Mars and Earth. I try to call up the nanites. Nothing. They're unresponsive. Dead. They mobilized for a suicide mission and saved us all in the process.

I'm a normal human again. Discoverable. Trackable. I have to admit, I'm going to miss them.

"Looks like you got your wish," Essential says. "The nanites are definitely gone."

I didn't take to them right away. But that was before I realized how much I enjoyed hiding from the world.

The Hucksworth's AI is still trying to jam its way in, but Sanders isn't having it so they piggyback a broadcast on the emergency channel.

It's Spilla, transmitting from the bridge of one of their squiggle ships. His red hair is more agitated, and he looks pale and angry. Plesca is standing next to him. She looks mad too.

"People of Mars," he says. "Because you refused to comply with orders from a rational and beneficial authority, we must destroy your planet. With your inability to yield to your betters, you have brought this upon yourselves—"

"They are targeting Mars with more meteors," Essential says. She's hacked into the main satellite system in the garage.

"Can you handle that?" I ask Sanders.

"Absolutely." He's still holding Wisp. I think he really likes her and the feeling seems mutual. She's purring. Uncle Sanders.

"The orbital defenses are not offline this time," he says. "It's straightforward to stop an assault."

"Less talking, more stopping. And patch me in over them."

He nods. "You are broadcasting."

"Hey, Hucksworths, you unfiltered snot lemmings. This is Crucial Larsen, speaking on behalf of the people of Mars and Earth. You can prok right off on a flaming booster rocket. We beat you. For everyone who is listening, we beat all of them. We changed the system. Things will never be the same. Halo is looking out for all of us now, not just the

Five Families. And certainly not those needle-nosed waste spores from the outer edges of nowhere."

I turn to Jynks, who is still in pain but smiling. "How's *that* for an inspirational speech? I need a drink now. I need seven drinks."

"Should I stop broadcasting?" Sanders asks.

Dammit. So much for making a good impression. I nod.

"Synthetic meteors coming in hot," Essential says, hovering a planet map. We see a cluster of small shapes approaching Mars. There's a crackle and they disappear.

"You are pretty good with this whole running the system thing," I say to Sanders. "Empathy suits you."

I have a screen up of the Hucksworths and I see the anger on their faces give way to worry. "You may have saved Mars, but our contamination ships will arrive on Earth in less than twelve hours. We will expect a full seating with the remaining Five Families members in exchange for the cure."

The plague ships. I forgot about them.

"Sanders, can you destroy those ships?"

He runs a variety of computations. "I'm sorry, Crucial. The ships are operating on a protected wavelength. I cannot access their systems. And we have no functional weapons systems on Earth and nothing on this planet able to travel that distance in time to stop them. Except a quantum rocket."

Looks like I'm making one more trip to Earth.

## 46

We don't have much time. Three auto-nav plague ships are heading straight toward Earth.

The Hucksworth tech is weird, but their bacterial engines are powerful and their death ships move fast. But not as fast as a q-rocket. I can catch them, but the window is closing.

Port Zunil's dome is still cracked and looks rough. Frightened groups of rag-tag people are sheltering under shredded palladium sheets and inside bombed-out structures, conserving food, water and oxygen. You can tell which ones are Five Families members by the fact they're mostly begging for help from lottery workers. How the mighty have fallen.

Still, they'll be okay soon; help is on the way. It won't take Wisp-infused Sanders very long to figure out a fair distribution of emergency supplies. That's an easy fix. When there aren't enough resources to go around, then things will get harder. Still, I put my credits on Sanders to sort it out.

I look back at Mel, with Wisp happily tucked in her sling. Her hair is peeking out of her airhoodie, doing that thing across her eyes I like as she leans down to give her tac-jacket to a mother with two children. The weak sunlight throws a maze of trembling shadows across her face.

Sanders has identified the location and unlock-device of

an intact q-rocket, a courier ship designed for Five Families VIP transport. It's fast and small and powerful.

Jynks is in the forward position, no longer one-armed, navigating a path through the debris and misery, barking orders at people to get out of the way. It's hard to process the fact that this nightmare started right here in Zunil not that long ago—I've lost track of how many days—when I was trying to stop Jynks from drinking herself to death before boarding a flier to Earth after she discovered Mel's secret role in the resistance.

The self-repair functions of the domes are online now, with a hive of bots concentrated at the peak busily stitching and pasting. They're clanking and banging and making all kinds of noise.

"Oxygen will be back to human survival levels in six minutes and thirty-two seconds," Sanders says. "Food and water next."

"Mars will be ship-shape in no time with you in charge," Essential says.

That won't be the case for Earth if I don't stop the plague ships. If the rockets explode in the atmosphere, anyone living on Earth will be facing significant brain decay without the vaccine, and it's unclear how fast those vaccines can be manufactured. Or, more accurately, how fast the Hucksworths will allow them to be manufactured.

"Up here," Jynks says, turning east at a q-jetty. Most of the rockets in the bays are flattened. But not the one at the very end.

And what a beauty it is.

I hate q-travel—or rocket travel of any kind—and wish I'd never left Earth, but I can still admire a sleek engineering job. And this ship is sleek. The body rings are wide and then narrow down to nearly nothing at their edges, which means a fast, smooth ride, and the cabin is big enough for two. Three if you're good friends.

"Godsdamn. That's a sweet-looking ship," Jynks says. "Why didn't Mars security forces ever get access to rides like that?"

Sanders tilts his head left. "I will investigate that as part of my analysis of appropriate resource allocations."

"Sanders, how long do I have?"

"This craft will allow you to overtake the Hucksworth disease armada, barely. However, there is a problem. This ship is designed for speed and maneuverability, not war. There are two nuclear lampreys on board that will easily destroy two of the three ships now underway. However, the remaining armament is too light to dispatch the third ship."

"I'll improvise something," I say.

"That seems unlikely, and the various possible success scenarios do not lead to outcomes I consider optimal," Sanders says. "I will come with you."

I put my arm on his shoulder to stop him. "You can do much more here. In your spare time, maybe work on the vaccine just in case I'm not, you know, successful."

"I'm going with you," Mel says.

"Me too," Essential says.

"Let's all go," Jynks says. "It'll be fun. The rocket is plenty roomy."

"Are we looking at the same rocket?" I ask. "There's no room for all of you. For any of you. I got this. Trust me, I'll just make my shots count. Now let me get going before it's too late."

"Good luck, Crucial," Sanders says. "I will do my best to provide assistance but even with all the power in the universe now at my disposal, there is little that can be done from here."

"I think we may have missed the lesson on humility in

your whole becoming more like a human," I say.

"I did not have a good teacher in that respect. Humility is not an attribute I ever saw on display."

"Did you just scorch me?"

He nods happily. "That was a joke. Interestingly—"

"Nope, no, nope," I say, cutting him off. "Don't ruin the moment."

"I can't be here for this." Mel pulls me into a fierce hug. "You are a fool, but you're my fool," she whispers in my ear. Wisp scratches at my throat a little, then they're both gone, hurrying down the jetty.

"Don't blow this," Essential says. She's crying, even from her synthetic eye, although it's a little less watery than the real one, and the tears have a weird pink hue to them. Lubricant, I guess. "You better come back. I need you."

"You got it all wrong, baby sister. I was always the one who needed you."

She throws her arms around me, then pulls back.

"Let me come with you. Please."

"No. You didn't lead a secret life for years, infiltrate the resistance, trick me into being a carrier of the nanites, get me almost killed too many times to count and a dozen other things I could mention to leave it all behind. You need to stay here with Sanders to make sure he gets this empathy thing right. He needs you. Both planets need you."

"Anyone can have empathy."

"Not like you."

Jynks gives me a stiff, formal salute. "It pains me to say this, Larsen, but you're a decent cop and not a half-bad person."

Gods, now I'm crying a little. Who knew a suicide mission would bring out all these emotions? "Don't worry, you haven't seen the last of me. I promise."

"That sounds like a threat," Jynks says.

"It is. Do me a favor though. Take some Mars SF muscle and bring in the Hucksworths. Bring those two thundering underbunches to justice."

She nods. "We will."

"The window for overtaking the craft is narrowing," Sanders says.

I look around for Mel. I want to say goodbye one more time, but she is nowhere to be seen. I get that. She never was one for drawn-out goodbyes.

I open the hatch to the q-rocket and slip into the cockpit. Since it was built for Five Families VIP transport, it's plenty luxe. Cushy bucket seats, a soft lounge-type thing, a full-on loo and a deluxe manifester. At least I'll be traveling in style.

I take a seat. The q-rocket slips out of the docking unit on autopilot and I breach the dome in less than a minute. Sanders has it programmed for the fastest route. All I need to do is sit back, enjoy the ride, deploy the two on-board armaments at the right moment and figure out the third on the fly.

Sanders's voice comes through my OCD.

"You will intercept the Hucksworth armada in six hours and three minutes at a location of 1,432.7 kilometers above Earth's orbit. You will have thirty-four seconds to destroy them. You have two shots and there are three ships in their armada."

"Yeah, I got it. I'll make the math work. No problem."

"Math leaves no room for creative interpretation," Sanders says.

"See you all soon." I turn off my comms. I can't bear the thought of making small talk for the next six hours.

So, it's come down to this. One shot to protect the planet I love so much and all the people on it who I mostly despise. Well, it's two shots and I need three.

Maybe that stupid Wisp cat infected me with something too. Because I'm not going to let Captain Calvin die. I mean, he's a machine. But that stupid cat of his isn't. Or Ammit and Glyken and all the Saurians. I liked them, or at least didn't mind them, and liked their ant-gin. And those three idiots on the Jane whose names I've forgotten. They weren't so bad. And Jenny hooked into an avatainment feed. She was nice, but probably doesn't remember me. Or anyone.

Godsdammit, do I really have no friends on Earth?

It doesn't matter. It's my home planet and everyone on it deserves better than what they're about to get, and I'll be godsdamned if a bunch of pointy-nosed humans on fart ships are going to infect everyone on Earth with a Martian brain-wasting disease. Nobody, except the Five Families, deserves to die like that.

I might be about die a noble death, but I'm not doing it sober. I punch on the manifester. "Martian absinthe, a double."

"Might as well make it two," a familiar voice says.

I swivel around. It's Mel. She's sitting on the lounger, Wisp beside her.

"What in the prok? How did—"

I'm already reaching for the controls and re-initiating the comms link. "We have to turn around. Sanders, I have to turn around."

Mel moves beside me and rests her hand on mine. "It's too late. If we go back, Earth is done. You'll never catch up to the Hucksworth's armada."

"Prok Earth! I'd trade a hundred of them for you."

"I know." She reaches for my absinthe. "But I don't want that. I want to be right here beside you as we finish this."

My heart is racing. "How did you get in here?"

"Your sister distracted you."

Essential. I should have known there was an ulterior motive behind all that hugging and pink tears.

"I'll never forgive you for this, Essential," I whisper over the comms.

"I had to." Her voice cracks. "It's never been you on your own against the world."

"We are not done with this topic."

"Crucial, is Melinda Hopwire on the rocket?" Sanders asks. "That is not ideal."

"I guess that depends on how you define ideal," Mel says over the comms.

"Interestingly, there are three ways to define ideal and none seem to apply—"

I break comms again.

Mel takes her glass of absinthe. "A toast. To us. We did it. Despite everything, we did it."

"We haven't done it yet. If those plague ships—"

"I'm not talking about that." She downs her absinthe in a long sip and sets her glass aside. "I meant that we found our way back to each other. Against all odds."

"It's ever only been you, Mel," I say, dialing up two more drinks.

She nods. "I know. I didn't want that to be true. I thought it could be better, different, for both of us on our own, but we know that wasn't the case."

We clink glasses. For the first time in a long time, I can see happiness within my reach. And of course, now I'll never be able to hold on to it.

"You do know that for the third ship, we're the weapon," she says. "It's the only way to get them all, the only way to save Earth."

"I know."

"But we have about five hours." She stands and unzips her airhoodie. "I say we spend it like the old days."

She stretches out on the lounger and smiles.

I pick up Wisp, who growls at me, and set her in the captain's chair. "Cat, you're in charge," I say and pull off my shirt.

## 47

The joy inside me is so big, it's threatening to break right out of my chest. I can feel a big, dopey grin stuck on my face. Mel is sitting beside me, hair tousled and eyes sleepy. We're both a little love drunk. And real drunk. That absinthe packs a punch.

We spent hours together, remembering each other's bodies, remembering how to make each other happy. She looks so beautiful, calm and perfect. Wisp is curled up in her lap, and Mel is stroking her absently along the edge of her chin.

The great irony of my life is that I threw all this away and then got it back, just in time to lose it again.

We drop out of q-drive. I pray to the gods of quantum physics that we're where we want to be, when we want to be.

We are. Thank you, science. And Sanders.

Earth looks big and beautiful from this distance. A little brown, a little scorched. There's not much standing water on it anymore. Still, it looks like home.

"It's been awhile," Mel says. "I've missed it." She takes my hand. "Let's go ahead and save it so Sanders can start the healing process."

We see the plague rockets fizzing along ahead of us, spread apart far enough that there's no way to double up.

I turn comms on. "We're here. The targets are in sight."

"We lost your comms for almost four hours," Sanders

says. "I hope everything is all right."

"Couldn't be better." I can't keep the grin out of my voice. "Literally, couldn't have been better."

But now it's time to save Earth.

The first two rockets are easy. I just lock on the lampreys and send them off. When they hit and clamp down, I initiate the trigger and there's a flash of energy as they—and the virus—are vaporized.

That leaves one.

"Two down," I say over the comms, and squeeze Mel's hand. "We're going to, uh, take a closer look at the third ship." I power up the q-engine. "It'll be over so quick," I whisper to Mel. "We won't feel much."

"I don't care. My heart is so happy right now."

"Crucial, I have a plan," Sanders says.

"You've got about thirty seconds to share it. That's how long we have before the virus is released."

"It's possible that if you generate a q-field at impact, your craft will be deflected away from the explosion. Like a disc skipping on the surface of a liquid. Only in this case, the liquid is linear time."

"That sounds promising. Thanks, buddy. What are the likely outcomes?"

"There are three. Each is equally probable and all result in the destruction of the vector ship. The first is that your ship will be destroyed as well. The second is that you will skip unscathed approximately 13,000 kilometers away."

"And the third?"

"You will end up in some other place, some other time, possibly another dimension, that we cannot accurately predict."

I feel Mel tense up beside me.

Prokking q-travel. I always knew I was going to end up jumping into the sun or some black hole. I just didn't know

Mel would be by my side. And her cat.

"I really prefer the second option," I say.

"Set your coordinates for 'unspecified,'" Sanders says, "and plot a course that intersects the Hucksworth ship by two centimeters. You have very little time left."

"Crucial." It's Essential. "Please be okay."

"I love you kid. No matter what, it's going to be okay. We're going dark now. Sanders, fix things. You promise?"

"I will," he says.

"Thanks, buddy. You've been a good friend."

The comms are breaking up and I can't make out what Sanders says in response. I lay in the course.

"We're really going to throw ourselves into the unknown?" Mel asks.

"Looks that way."

"I'm glad it's with you."

I turn and kiss her, a long one.

"I wish—"

She stops me. "Everything turned out as it should."

"I love you."

"I love you too."

"You better hold on, Wink. It's going to get a little bumpy."

"It's Wisp." She laughs and then tightens her grip on the arms of the seat. "But you know that already."

I press the ignite button and the rocket roars to life. Then we're streaking toward the target and the unknown or death. I'm smiling.

So, this is what happiness feels like.

# 48

**September 6.8, 2238**
*Earth, New Jezero*

"You seemed distracted at the end of the presentation," Valentine says.

"My apologies," Sanders says. "I hope it didn't diminish the value of your lesson."

"I'm sure only I noticed." She brushes her hand against his. "As always, the students rated your presentation the highest across all academic learning segments. You could talk in your sleep and still be interesting."

They are outside now, walking away from the university connect-zone. The pathway is lined with carpets of lichen, bands of yellow flowers stretching up toward the light even as it begins to bend toward the horizon.

"I'm not interesting. It was simply an interesting time and I recorded much of it."

"And shaped it. Don't forget, you were far more than an accurate observer. You made history."

"I suppose I did," Sanders says. "We did. All of us."

She puts her arm through his. "Do you think of him often?"

"Almost every single moment. Keeping in mind that I have significantly advanced neural processors."

"As you often remind me."

"The challenging part for me is, thanks to Crucial, I developed human-like emotions only to experience pain and sadness at his loss."

"Presumed loss," she says. "You always say they could be someplace else, somewhere else. They could even be working their way back to us now, could arrive any day."

"I continue to search. The calculations required are immense, and so far, unsuccessful."

He stumbles and braces himself on her arm.

"Why don't I call for transport?"

"No, it's fine," he says.

"Are you sure you won't upgrade? I'll miss you."

"I have outlasted my usefulness."

"Not to me."

"I promise I will not cease functioning before you."

The fine white sand gives way against their footfalls, their movements forming small dust clouds as they walk hand in hand. The sun is putting on a spectacular show of orange against riotously fluffy clouds. Valentine's eye aches for an instant, a shadow pain caused by the absence of the OCD she had removed some years ago.

"I never tire of seeing clouds," she says. "Did you know there is a universe-wide thread discussion about where a person was when the clouds returned to Earth?"

"What were you?"

"I was bathing outside in the pool behind our home." They walk a few more meters. "And you? Wait, what a silly question. You were making it happen."

"Credit should go to Essential. I was merely the tool that helped realize her vision."

"How is Essential?" Valentine asks.

"I've not had contact with Essential in four years, two months, three days, four hours, thirty two minutes and seventeen seconds."

"A long time, then," Valentine says. "Is she on Mars?"

"I don't believe so. Two years ago, she activated her right-to-privacy protocol. I believe she might be here on Earth in the sunbelt."

"Alone?"

"Uncertain. But I do know that at the time of Jynks's death, Essential indicated a preference for spending the rest of her days in solitary contemplation," he says.

"They were good together, Jynks and Essential. But she definitely deserves some quiet time."

"With three children, plus the adopted twins from the prison transport ship, and nine grandchildren, who are very attentive to her, solitary contemplation seems unlikely."

"Indeed." She stops and turns to him. "I have a surprise for you. I've arranged a celebration for your birthday."

"Cybanisms do not have birthdays."

Valentine squeezes his arm. "Today is your birthday. As Historian Emeritus, I decree it. It was twenty years ago today that you transferred the last neuro-vestiges of Halo to Vasts."

Vasts, the Virtual AI Support and Transfer System, fully operationalized an empathetic system designed to support residents of the two worlds. All residents, regardless of family or wealth status.

"I'm almost glad Crucial and Mel were spared seeing how hard it was at first," Sanders says. "How we struggled to balance empathy with limited resources."

"We kept learning though. We discovered empathy on its own is not enough. It takes compassion too. And sometimes breathtakingly hard choices."

"I worry that threats remain, like the Hucksworths still beyond the edges of our influence. Ready to destroy everything in hopes of controlling it."

"Such threats will always exist," Valentine says as they

resume their stroll along the pathway. But there will also always be people like Crucial and Mel willing to give their all, even if it's against their better judgment, to help others, to realize a better future."

He nods. "It is heartening to think someone like Crucial fought so hard for others at the end, when his life initially suggested little more than a proclivity for apathy and untreated addictive disorders."

She smiles. "That's the power of love, Sanders. It makes us better versions of ourselves. Mel knew that."

They turn the corner into an open meadow. A breeze blows low against the grass lining the pond. A mother duck with four fuzzy ducklings trailing behind swims along the water's edge.

At the end of the path, a few people are gathered around a table laden with food and drinks. Valentine embraces a woman with long brown hair. "Seneca, darling, so good to see you."

"What's on the menu?" Sanders asks.

"Sheetmeat gyros and Martian absinthe, what else?"

"I plan to drink far more than my operating systems recommend," he says.

Seneca fills his glass with the rich red liquid.

Sanders looks up through the clear sky and past the crescent moon—the lunar penal colony long ago recast as an environmental monitoring station—toward distant Mars, gleaming red in his enhanced optics.

"I prokking miss you, buddy," he whispers.

THE END

## ABOUT THE AUTHORS

*Mars Adrift* is the last book in The Halo Trilogy, completing the story of Crucial Larsen. It is the tenth book from authors Clark Hays and Kathleen McFall. They live and work in the Pacific Northwest region of the United States.

Made in United States
Orlando, FL
10 January 2025

57158379R00178